PRAISE FOR *THE FINAL OPUS OF LEON SOLOMON*

"Unforgettable and moving ... What a powerful vision to find in a first opus; all Mr. Badanes has to do is to go on writing like this and he will haunt us forever."—Paul West

"The Final Opus of Leon Solomon will anger some people and make others cry ... This is a sensational book."—Susan Slocum Hinerfeld, *Los Angeles Times Book Review*

"Daring and disturbing—daring because its large ambitions drive toward the very center of the Holocaust universe; disturbing because the visions of 'survivorhood' one encounters along the way are so relentlessly shocking ... He is a marvelous writer." —Sanford Pinsker, *The Forward*

"Studded as it is with lyrical passages and unforgettable descriptions, Badanes' novel exudes a very European flavor and is both a perceptive meditation on the past and one man's attempt to explain himself to himself."—Douglas M. Greenwood, *The Washington Post*

"Nothing less than the end of Jewish history is contemplated in Badanes' beautifully constructed novel ... His 'last opus' is so vital, so stunning in its exploration of 'Jewishness' that its legacy may yet salvage a future for others."—Patricia Holt, *San Francisco Chronicle*

"In this striking representation of the past in the present, Jerome Badanes has drawn a haunting portrait of loss; loss of power, identity and love. If the historian's art is the realization of detail, this sensual and honest story is unforgettable."—*Book Preview*

"This is a moving book. Wrestling with Leon's complex personality helps heighten a reader's consciousness. He is a man at war with death even as he seeks it. Badanes has written a contemporary novel of stature."—Molly Abramowitz, *Hadassah Magazine*

"Jerome Badanes' extraordinary first novel explores the dilemma of memory—memory as moral imperative and as destructive force."—Eils Lotozo, *The Philadelphia Inquirer*

The Final Opus
of Leon Solomon

JEROME BADANES

A FIRESIDE BOOK
PUBLISHED BY SIMON & SCHUSTER INC.
NEW YORK   LONDON   TORONTO
SYDNEY   TOKYO   SINGAPORE

F

Fireside
Simon & Schuster Building
Rockefeller Center
1230 Avenue of the Americas
New York, New York 10020

First Fireside Edition, 1990
Published by arrangement with Alfred A. Knopf

FIRESIDE and colophon are registered trademarks
of Simon & Schuster Inc.

Designed by Peter A. Anderson
Manufactured in the United States of America

10 9 8 7 6 5 4 3 2 1 Pbk.

Library of Congress Cataloging in Publication Data
Badanes, Jerome.
  The final opus of Leon Solomon/Jerome Badanes.
    p. cm.
  Reprint. Originally published: New York: Knopf,
1989.
  "A Fireside book."
    I. Title.
PS3552.A29F56   1990
813'.54—dc20   90-37511
                                                    CIP

ISBN 0-671-70303-X Pbk.

For my mother, Rose Badanes,
whose songs of Vilna enlarged my childhood,
for my friend Marianne Burke,
whose poet's ear helps keep my own attuned,
and in memory of my father, Leon Badanes,
whose kind sense of humor taught me
that life is not a joke

The Final Opus of Leon Solomon

Late Evening the Second Day

I

There is a metaphysical law, and you can depend on metaphysical laws, that unity is a figment of the imagination. As soon as a unity is slowly, bloodily forged it has already started breaking down—and right in the bitter heart of the breaking down a new unity is already being dreamed up in the darkness.

You could say that this law describes my life.

Take this hotel. The sour smell that sits here like a trapped creature slowly dying is the smell of disintegration. Yet the terrible air I am breathing now is the same air, exactly, that has remained imprisoned here unmoving behind unopenable windows since before the war. (Maybe the last time these windows were opened all the way up was in the weeks after the day they call "Black Tuesday," when the market came crashing down and men who looked like penguins flew from the windowsills of the best hotels and plummeted down onto the population milling like carp in the midtown streets below.) This air of disintegration unifies us: decades of men, of remnants, not exactly living but certainly dying in this room—my final universe. Once this hotel was a palace.

Yesterday, my first evening here, I lay quietly in bed and began to become acquainted with my new surroundings.

Early, in the twilight, the sluggish dread in my heart became, without any cooperation on my part, became suddenly, like a summer lightning shower, a passionate and not-to-be-ignored ache. The second pillow became the woman I embraced. Who was she? Well, she wasn't my wife. Afterwards, in the stillness, I thought of what they would make of discovering dried semen on the corpse. Should I remember to do it again when the time comes? Will I be able to? Then I noticed across the room, on each side of the medicine chest above the sink, the thin brass pipes with little spigots sticking out from the wall maybe eight inches each. For gas, I knew right away. The spigots had been painted over years ago, but not so long as the windows, my historical sixth sense told me (I am after all an historian; and I am not unfamiliar with the techniques of the archeologist). You could still, if you have a very sensitive and discerning nose, sniff out the faint odor of gas in this mélange of sweat and decay, these smells of disappointment and final desires. How many men died to the tranquilizing hiss of the gas? Now we no longer require the open window or the airtight welcoming of the gas. Now we have pills, and when they find you the next day or the next month they can always declare a massive heart attack.

It is not yet time for me.

II

Why not my wife? She is a handsome woman, an elegant dresser. The perfume she uses, when I sniff it elsewhere, in the reading room of the Forty-second Street Library, for example—where just four days ago, the final visit, I encountered the scent—it envelops me with dread. It was all I could do that day not to fall to the floor and begin to whimper like

an old dog abandoned by his mistress on Broadway. Was that
why I was caught? Was that why I fell apart when the detective put his Catholic hand on my shoulder? Afterwards it was
all like a blitzkrieg. I was not prepared. Question after question they fired at me at the precinct house. I've dealt with
worse inquisitors, more dangerous men, smarter. Why then
did I talk so much? Why did I spill the beans, as they say, a
silent man like me who knows how to make others uncomfortable, avert their eyes from me? It was all the fault of the
Joie de Patou. Twenty-seven years the same pungency. It
made my mouth water when they introduced us in the Luncharsky apartment in Paris. Now it shrivels me up. Even my
son, the few times he comes to see me at the Institute, smells
faintly like her. After he leaves, for weeks it lingers on the
fourth floor. Even the heat from the radiator smells like her.
And all he does is snarl and scream at me. "Fuck you, bastard-bitch," this he screamed at me, his father, just two weeks
ago. The whole Institute listened in. Solomon, they thought
to themselves, even his son despises him. Small wonder he
lives alone in two rooms.

Every year on her birthday I would buy my wife a bottle.
The last time I bought her one, now more than eleven years
already, it cost sixty-five dollars. The worst time is when I
smell it from a young woman, the sweet odor that is also at
the same time not sweet. If the young woman is also beautiful, I can no longer work that day. How many articles will I
leave unwritten because of that phenomenon?

So I think of Oscar's daughter. A college education he gave
her, a janitor's daughter with an African name. When she
would visit him at the Institute and I'd see them whispering
together in his small room in the basement I would dream of
her coming up to my fourth floor office. I knew the smell of
her black perfume—Patchouli—would obliterate the smell

of my wife. For my antidote, when I felt the heart beating in my empty chest, I would ride down in the elevator to the basement stacks and breathe the aroma of Fulani.

Was it that outrageous for me to dream so of her? Wasn't this new generation of black females, I innocently asked myself, interested in exploring other territories, so to speak? After all, I remain an attractive man. I still have a head of black, curly hair, merely streaked with white, as they say. My green eyes, and I have been told they are bedroom eyes, are not yet bloodshot. The dark circles, particularly when I have not been able to sleep, give them a more penetrating—a soulful—gaze, one might say. I need glasses only for reading. Though in America I am not a tall man, at five foot eight I am not short either, particularly among my émigré compatriots. Fulani is not one whit taller, and her father is a good inch or two shorter. Hours of walking every day have kept me from becoming bent and arthritic, as so many of my colleagues are. I have never cared enough for food to develop a large stomach. Though my rheumatic heart has started to fail a little, no one could know that by looking at me. Since 1947, when I regained my normal muscle tone, I have kept the same weight. Oscar breathes heavily, without shame, when he performs even the simple task of mopping the halls. He walks with a shuffle and pulls up his pants which slide under his bulging stomach. I have estimated that he is at least three years younger than I am, but he looks older. Wouldn't the conviction that pulled her to the exotic name "Fulani," I asked myself with no irony, draw her also to the numbers on my wrist? Loneliness and lust can overcome reason and even a man's sense of historical dignity.

Oscar told me her name was Ruth but she would walk out of the building if he called her that.

III

I have the urge to write this all down, to write it down shamelessly and leave it for another. For whom? Later I will decide. I use the word "later" so matter-of-factly. Perhaps I should mail it to that ex-student of mine, the Ph.D., the university professor from Arizona, the specialist on the shtetl with the foolish face who came to my office to visit last Monday—just a day before the end began, though I can hardly remember even one moment from before all this started. Ten years he waited to thank me for all I did for him, with a beautiful sweater, dark gray, one hundred percent lamb's wool from England. It fits me just like a glove on my hand, as they say. What I immediately remembered when I looked at him was that he still had the same foolish expression on his face—a mouth that remained a little opened when he listened. If I could have spit understanding into his face, I would have made him an historical genius.

"Mr. Solomon," he said with his gentile accent, "now I too know and it is for them to find out."

He was referring to the one time I closed his mouth. He had asked me if I knew—me he asked if I knew—where he could locate certain documents indispensable to his research. Research! I can hear even now how he said "research," as though he were holding the word between two fingers. I looked into his eyes, or maybe I should say into his mouth, and told him, "Mister, that is for me to know and for you to find out." And in that I taught him an invaluable lesson: to work with rigor and with silence, and to play his hand close to his chest, as they say, because the world is filled with cheaters.

I didn't let on that I recognized his allusion. "Professor," I said, "do you want to see my collection of photographs of

Jewish prostitutes in Warsaw from 1935 and 1936?" His eyes
bulged with no understanding, but still his mouth remained
opened slightly. Did he not know what a treasure I was offering him to look at?

"Mr. Solomon"—he ignored me as I had ignored him—
"your prose style is the most lucid in Yiddish scholarship. I
await your monographs with hunger." Does he understand
them? That I did not ask him. After all, he did stop by to give
me an expensive sweater of pure lamb's wool from England
with a wonderful smell.

"Are you married?"

"Yes," he replied without surprise.

"Is she Jewish?"

"Of course," he answered, again with no edge in his voice.

"Do you carry a photograph?"

He showed me a color picture of a plain girl, pale, her lips
tight together, looking right at the camera, between smiles,
just like a passport picture.

"She looks smarter than you," I said. "Her mouth is
closed."

Some people are as impossible to insult as they are to
teach. But a man who cannot learn very much is probably
lucky, and if on top of that he cannot be insulted, he is destined to go far with his scholarship. Such a man will have a
cautious mind, a methodical mind, combined with a soul
that is unfamiliar with shame. Such a man could even become president of the American Jewish Historical Society.
Since I never learned his name, I cannot mail him these
pages even if I desired to—a desire I would never have,
though he was but the second person in many years to bring
me a gift, and also the last person, ever. The softness of the
sweater gives my fingers pleasure and if I turn my nose to the
arms I can inhale still the luxurious fresh smell of the wool,
even in this evil room.

Maybe I will bequeath these sheets to the Institute with instructions to display them in the glass case in the lobby by the front door. Welcome To The Jewish History Institute. These Original Handwritten Pages Are From The Final Opus Of Our Late Archivist and Great Yiddish Stylist Leon Solomon, 1919–1985. Better yet, I'll bequeath them through Hirsch himself to the Harvard Judaica Collection. Let the busy man get the credit. Maybe he can offer them as reparations to the Forty-second Street Library.

IV

The students today are worse than even the one from ten years ago. Take the little pest with such pretty black hair and eyes so luminous she should keep her lips zippered. Shocked she said she was when she complained to our Madame Director because she spied me trimming a few documents with scissors so I could fit them in the display case. They think that there is a door between now and then—a cellar door—and they descend, these captains of scholarship, to bring back artifacts to examine closely, but from a safe distance, as they say, and in order to write illuminating articles about our rich Diaspora heritage. Where do they think we are living now? They are like foolish rabbis declaring the Talmud ended. The commentary goes on as long as history goes on. When I cut out pages of commentary from a sixteenth-century manuscript in the Forty-second Street Library and sell them for sixty-five dollars a page to Harvard, or when I take one to my apartment to look at it by a single light at 3 a.m., and touch it carefully but with firmness, mingling my fingertips with the prints of scribes and rabbis, scholars and poets, a man who paused, perhaps, from his labor four hundred years ago to caress the white thighs, the moist nether lips, the resilient buttocks of a woman—these removals are in their way a commentary. If a colleague of mine discovered such a shifting of documents from one great library to another one, in the medieval period for example, he would attach historical significance to it. He would think and think about it and if he were smart he would learn something— and then he would write an article that would be stored in a library. What could he possibly learn beyond the facts? He could learn that to be kept from death, documents must be handled by living hands.

Why, you should ask me, did I charge sixty-five dollars a page? Why not? Even that I charged, and how much I charged, is a commentary, an insight into our times for future scholars. If the Library remained open all night or at least until midnight, as it once did, I might never have begun cutting pages.

V

I can hear a radio now from the next room, or maybe from two rooms over. A woman is singing. It is not Marlene Dietrich. My wife and I first became acquainted in Paris, after I was released from D.P. camp. I was working for the Centre de Documentation Juive Contemporaine, attempting to reconstitute the numerous collections. She would come to my rooms and we would listen to a record of Marlene Dietrich that I had discovered in a box of German record albums in a used bookstore. More than the main song, "Naughty Lola," we listened to the second side, "I Am Ready for Love from Head to Foot." She sat on the edge of my bed; I sat on my desk chair which I pulled close. We drank Beaujolais and listened to Dietrich singing on the Victrola. We even danced, and our first kisses were accompanied by the mesmerizing rhythms of the German tongue and Inge's lingering fragrance.

The name of Fulani's fragrance I discovered by stealth.

"Do all black women smell as pungent as Oscar's daughter?" I remarked to Perl, the Institute's cow-eyed Lubavitcher switchboard girl who always wears dresses with long sleeves and scarves around her neck and smells faintly of lavender talcum powder.

"Mr. Solomon," she said, giggling, "the woman wears a strong perfume."

"No, that is no perfume."

"Yes, Mr. Solomon—Patchouli."

"Patchouli?"

"Patchouli."

I took the bus right away to the fancy department store Lord & Taylor's, and located a bottle of Patchouli at what is referred to as the Fragrance Bar. It was their last bottle. The salesgirl tried to put a drop on the back of my hand, but I held my hands away from her. A whole drop would be too much and the location too public. I was already dizzy and out of place standing there among such tall slender women.

"The perfect gift for your daughter or for your niece in college," she crooned at me with her red lips. "It may well become a popular fragrance again next year."

I bought the tiny bottle, for five dollars—it was much cheaper than I expected—and I made her gift-wrap it for me. Then I walked through the store, slowly, like Mr. Lord. I let the escalator lift me to the second floor, where I strolled among the matching brassieres and panties, and then I ascended to the third floor where finally I discovered the men's toilet. I locked myself in a stall, tore open the package, unscrewed the cap, and sniffed. It made me dizzy, worse than my wife's perfume. Without first being on Fulani, it wouldn't help me. I shook the perfume into the toilet and flushed. The

next customer would wonder what went on in there. I threw
the bottle into the garbage and washed my hands in the sink.
I can see still the stainless steel soap machine where you
pushed in a plunger for drops that smelled like the pink satisfied hands of doctors. If I had had my revolver with me, I
would have shot myself right there and then through the
heart—always the heart, remember, because if through the
brain there will be a moment of unendurable insanity before
you expire.

With the vacuum cleaner noise from the hot-air machine
roaring suddenly inside my ears I knew that even making an
end of it wouldn't help me. I stood there watching each hand
of mine rub the other one dry under the hot blower. Nothing
would help without Fulani.

VI

Late one afternoon, it was on a Thursday, like today, I noticed Fulani's long black coat hanging alone from a hook in
Oscar's room. Father and daughter must have left the Institute for a coffee and Fulani, it was clear, had left the coat
behind because the afternoon sun was warming the city.
Could she have left it hanging there for me to find? With a
sudden and unusual abandon and with quicker steps I
walked into the small basement room. I discovered I could
not face the black coat beckoning me.

The room was filled with brooms and mops and pails, neat
piles of plastic bags on a shelf. But it was Oscar's swivel chair,
with its torn and taped-over upholstery, standing there alone
in the middle of the floor, bereft, that impelled me to surrender to my urge to wrap the coat around my face. I pressed my
mouth against the black silken lining at the place where it
meets the hood and I breathed the inscrutable aroma of Fu-

lani. As if it were ether, I breathed in and felt transported
back before the war to Warsaw. Why Warsaw? That was
a mystery I would not solve for a number of weeks. Then,
pressing them tightly against the coat, I moved my hands
slowly down my body and, surrounded by a basement filled
from floor to ceiling with precious volumes that seemed to be
watching me, their archivist and savior, I rubbed the lining
against my genitals. Not since the end of the war when I
scoured the used-book shops of Paris, and the books called
out to me, "Solomon," they would sing, and I knew which
ones to bargain for, which ones to pretend indifference
toward—I am a master of the poker face; not since then had
I felt so on the edge of something, a discovery, a punishment.
What if Fulani and her father returned and discovered me?
That possibility, I must admit, thrilled me. Still, I had exer-
cised caution in my abandon. A Jew who can go about his
business among the Gestapo in occupied Warsaw can smell,
even lick, the inside of a woman's coat without being seen.
Such a Jew could even excite himself to a climax and spill
his semen into her black pocket and no one would be the
wiser.

I thought of doing that, but with what would I be left? It
was I who needed, I needed something from Fulani—a memento, an artifact, a vapor, to carry up to the fourth floor
with me, to keep cleverly disguised in my small room, and
maybe then the papers on my shelves would wake up from
their long sleep: they would open their eyes again and look
at me as intelligently as they once did.

I made a plan, a simple plan but difficult to carry out. I
would buy a pair of the fanciest lace panties and rub them
through Fulani's coat. The fragrance of the Patchouli, I now
knew, was no help by itself in the bottle. But mingled as it
was inside the coat, especially in that frayed silken part
under the hood where the nape of her brown neck nestled,

mingled as it was with the natural aromas of her body, it was nearly unendurable. The next time she left her coat I would be prepared. Not nylon, not Dacron, not polyester, but pure silk panties, with lace, a touch peek-a-boo, as they say—the kind you can see in the windows of certain stores in midtown or in Greenwich Village, or described in the last pages of certain magazines, to send away for, to Frederick's Of Hollywood. Though her behind is prominent and round, Fulani is slender and high-waisted—her firm globes need no uplifting. I knew the size would be small, a five or maybe even a three. I would have to search these stores until I found a salesgirl with a body like Fulani's—she would help me. They would be the color of cream, to give a contrast and to pay obeisance to her slender bronze thighs, her flat belly, the curving small of her back. The darkness of her mound would show through only slightly.

VII

Do I debase myself? Very well, I debase myself. But keep in mind that our main work now, and I've known this since 1944, much earlier than the others, is to find—to touch up William James a drop—the spiritual equivalent of vengeance. Remember that vengeance gives us a purpose, a sense of mission, a thing worth dying for—and a concentration on another, on every smallest detail of his person, each mole as it were; and a passion to research, to spy out his most private history. The pictures we paint in our brains of his excruciating torture are liberating and in that way spiritually uplifting. You might say that this devotion to vengeance brings us closer to God. Certainly it is one of the few available techniques for living through hell. I knew as early as 1944, when we began to perpetrate acts of resistance in

Auschwitz, and the taste became quickly insatiable, that this thirst for vengeance might well turn us into Christians.

On the other hand, a concentration on the other Jews in Auschwitz nearly unhinged me. Only the task of retrieving the archives from all the corners of the world immediately after the war ended—before they fell into the hands of collectors, professionals who knew the value of their possessions—only this saved me, because it forced the beings who gnawed ceaselessly at my soul, as they say, to slow their carnage, temporarily, and to become my conspirators in this common work. Sometimes dangerous work, undercover work.

In the midst of the night, half a lunatic from hunger, from the cold, the bright bulb on the ceiling always burning, casting dim yellow light over the barracks, I would begin to study the others. I developed the power to bring them into sharp focus. The almost uniform shapes of the bodies, one man next to the other, most on their backs on the hard wooden shelves arranged like a warehouse or an oversized archive. The moans, the groans, the breathing, the in, the out, at differing tempos, the various styles of snoring—some snores were sudden short gasps, others were punctuated with a popping noise, still others ended with a click, and behind them always was the long, steady snoring keeping time, as it were. Take these together with the almost inaudible but never-ending whimpers and I was listening to an orchestra of drunken musicians tuning up for a midnight concert.

But mainly my eyes would prowl like a searchlight over the faces of the men. Some smiled in their sleep. What could they be dreaming? Some ground their teeth like adolescent boys. On some I could see the lips tremble as they exhaled. A number of times men stopped breathing just as I looked at them. What united the dozens of faces, even the ones that smiled, was a look of excruciating worry. They began to de-

range me. Yet I clung to my nightly activity. I thirsted for my
nightly activity. It was my work. I was sitting shiva. To this
day I have trouble sleeping at night. The sound of every siren
enters me like a knife. I record each laugh, each scream,
every moan on 110th Street. You see, I knew that memoriz-
ing the faces of the others was keeping me alive. They were
like a map through time. I could see again scenes from my
childhood—my father tiptoeing into the darkened room to
kiss me good night; my mother, her belly large and incom-
prehensible, bathing me in the kitchen; my younger sister
learning to read with her finger on the page; the small lending library where I read all the books of Charles Dickens and
Leo Tolstoy available in Yiddish; climbing in the mountains
on an outing with my companions in the youth group; and
even from later, the faces of my so-called comrades in Warsaw. Where were they all now? But during those moments
they were as focused as the faces before me—those luminous
moments when what is is, right there before you, jumping
into your soul. The memory, I learned, not only squeezed me
so I sweated unfathomable sorrow, and nudged me like a
used-up horse toward the edge of a cliff; it kept me alive because—if only for a few timeless moments every night—I
lived in a time before (and maybe, therefore, after) this universe of excrement we all inhabited.

Many didn't understand that. They could not bear to remember or even hope, so they scraped out the eyes of their
minds—but most of those perished. Also, it gave me a mission—to keep alive in me the beings of the others. Every day
more would be gone, but I had the knowledge that they once
were—no, more than the knowledge, I had in me their very
beings. Of course, I too was disappearing. We were all the
keepers of each other's beings—and I knew that the others
knew that—yet we were all disappearing. Or becoming
blind. Who then, I would ask myself, would be left to rescue

all these beings, each one of which was filled with many other beings from his earlier life, from his parents' and grandparents' lives, which he was carrying inside himself? My strength derived from my obligation as an historian and, I must add ironically, as a student of the ontologist Heidegger, to remember not merely the biographical facts concerning each man (though those are of vital importance) but their very beings, which lived already like glowing worms inside my head. I would write a commentary, I daydreamed, a memorial, longer than Dubnow's *History of the Jews of Russia and Poland*. Now, as it was impossible to steal or even to bribe for a pencil and paper, or to keep them safely hidden if I had them, all I could do was memorize and live.

VIII

After I was liberated, even after the director of the reborn Jewish History Institute fished me out of the D.P. camp, when I was already in Paris chasing after our scattered archives, buying here, selling there, bribing bankrupt collaborators, even blackmailing a few rich ones, even then the beings continued to dance before my eyes, pleading, demanding, punishing, consuming. They were interfering with my ability to function logically and decisively. In order to rescue the papers I had to defeat these lions, tame them, make them my secret colleagues. Then I met my wife in the Luncharsky apartment.

I see it has begun raining. Outside, the prostitutes press closer to the walls of the buildings as they shift from leg to leg to keep warm, half naked as they are. If Oscar had not saved his money and sent her to college, my Fulani could well be among them in these grim times. If I were back in my apartment, the rain would cheer me up. There are not many advantages to living on the top floor. As high up as I am there, eighty-eight painful steps, I still have only the buildings, the steel bars, the machinery hammering and whining, the continual smell of frying from the Chinese restaurant downstairs, so thick it gives me heartburn. Except, that is, when it rains. The tapping of the rain on my grimy skylight, and I'm a boy again in Vilna, in the hour when I have returned home from cheyder and my mother is busy cooking the evening meal while I sit at the window betting which drops will roll down the glass without breaking. But in this hotel, through these sealed-up windows, the gray rain flying past the street lamp leaves me stranded in this dismal room—and swells me up like a dead fish floating belly up in the harbor.

IX

There are two mirrors here, a big oval-shaped one in a wooden frame connected to the dresser and a medicine-chest mirror farther over on the opposite wall above the sink. I'm not so used to mirrors. I never look into them—except for the small lady's pocketbook mirror I keep on a shelf in my toilet for shaving. But that one is so small I see only a piece of my face at a time. Should I cover these mirrors with the sheets? That was my first thought when I checked in here yesterday, how come I didn't do it?

Late last night—I can't remember how it began—over and over I opened my eyes then I closed my eyes. I was fascinated with the street light shining in my face. It came in through the window and ricocheted from the small mirror across the room to the big mirror and then into my face. A light is one thing, I thought. A light reflected by a mirror is another thing. But a light that comes in my window and bounces from a mirror to a mirror to my eyes, that is unusual. Such a simple phenomenon became a mystery that gripped my mind half the night—as though a light that must bend and zigzag against its nature in order to reach me must be a light that is determined to find me. The bed sagged and creaked like an old woman. When I can't fall asleep at night, since I was a boy, my mind loses all its rigor and caresses me with its own thoughts. I blinked in what I am now sure was a random pattern, but last night it was like an urgent message—signals of grave distress from ship to ship. Beware, they warned, of the U-boats. A torpedo will tear us open from below, as a killer shark the belly of a whale.

Sometime before dawn, when it was I don't know—I had neglected to bring my watch with me, but it was still dark—I got up to urinate. Of course, as soon as I stood up the angles changed and the sharp light that was shining on me in the bed was now quieter. There is no toilet in the room, so I relieved myself in the sink. How many men and even some women have urinated in this sink before me? The metal grill over the drain is green from the acid. I turned on the tap to help me start and also to wash the urine down. I am a neat man in my bodily habits. As I stood there, on tiptoes so I could edge over the top of the sink, the enamel reaching like cold fingers through my pajamas to my thighs—a not unpleasant sensation—I plucked the string that lit up the small bulb over the mirror and I was confronted by my face. It looked no different than it does to my mind's eye, as they say. I noted that my hair was only slightly streaked with gray. Certainly, I thought, my final appearance will leave my family and colleagues with impressive memories. "How young he looks," they will murmur—"a tragedy." How, at a time like this, can I have remained so vain? Still, I was startled by the weight of my flesh. It is not that my face is fat. Au contraire, it is a gaunt face, pale, concave almost. It looked dense, like stone. The dark rings under my eyes would make an interesting sample for a geologist. My eyes looked exhausted just from the effort of keeping open places around them to look out from. As I looked, my neck began to ache from its burden. It was my face all right, only hardened, like the skin on an old elephant, or from a dinosaur. No. To be accurate, my face was the face of a prepared corpse waiting in its casket to be viewed.

Even my teeth were hurting now from the effort of keeping my jaw from dropping open. I forced myself—it seemed suddenly a matter of life or death, and in this, given my purpose for being in this room, I find a rather touching contradiction—I forced myself to begin moving my face. After all, I was not dead yet. I opened my mouth and moved my jaw from side to side. I stuck out my tongue and curled it up toward my nose, then down to my chin. I squinted and the light danced in my eyes. I closed my eyes and opened them. Then I began to smile, little by little into a bigger and bigger and bigger smile. I saw tears rolling down my stone cheeks. I am reporting this objectively.

X

Let me return to the pastoral atmosphere of life in a top-floor apartment dwelling. One day last summer the young woman from the second floor opened her door as I passed and stood facing me.

"Are you not the top-floor tenant?" she asked me. She was a tall woman, maybe six feet, a blonde, a German. I had seen her before, though we never talked, and I had even thought about her on occasion, in private. She was wearing a long, a very white nightgown, tied at the neck and ending at her feet. The strong sunlight from behind her lit up her naked-

ness. I was so astonished, and also a little breathless from the
steps, that I couldn't speak. But also, I couldn't take my eyes
from her. Yes, I nodded, as I stared at her. She smiled. Was
she showing herself to me? Her toenails were painted red.

"Could I interest you in a window-box of white petunias
for your fire escape? Not enough light gets down here and
they are beginning to die."

Not enough light? I could see even the delicate twist of
hair sticking down a touch between her thighs. Even now,
after all that has happened between us, it sends cold chills
throughout my body to picture it. The nakedness of women
had escaped me for so long I would have given her my most
valued possession, one of the few remaining Yiddish type-
writers, if she had permitted me for an instant to touch the
tip of my tongue to the tip of those secret curls.

Yes, I nodded a second time, even as I was already thinking, why does she want me to have this thing, the blonde
exhibitionist? Was there something illegal growing there
among the flowers? Marijuana, perhaps? Still I nodded yes.
Why? It could be that all I wanted was to watch her turn
around. When she turned I could see the sides of her plump
breasts through the openings in her nightgown. I noted how
the white gown ran down her back, past the slight rise at the
bottom of her spine, and then like a track between her diminutive buttocks. Why was she showing herself so to me?
Had she seen the numbers?

"There are only a few blossoms now, but I am sure that
upstairs, with all that light on your fire escape, they will
thrive, Mr. Solomon."

How did she know my name?

"How do you know my name?"

"Oh, I am glad you finally spoke. I thought you disap-
proved of me. From your mailbox—I make it my business to
know my neighbors, at least their names."

"There is more than enough sunlight here for you to have blossomed, Miss Dietrich."

"So you know my name too." She smiled, but otherwise she ignored my provocation.

"Yes. Miss K. Dietrich. I have always made that my business."

"Kristin. But let me carry them up for you. You have your briefcase."

"Yes, the briefcase is very heavy, so you carry the milk box."

"Yes. But let me put on my robe. I shouldn't run through the halls in my nightgown."

I do not know whether I blushed outwardly, but I felt hot flushes in my face. She never blushed, the whole time. Was I a member of her immediate family? She took a robe, a black robe, from a hanger in her closet and put it on over her nightgown, right in front of me. It was only after she tightened the belt that everything else came into focus. I noticed a white cat with long hair that was rubbing against my leg. I noticed that the floor was painted white also. I had no time to examine the rest of the room. My eyes were pulled to the woman running a comb through her blonde hair. To this day I do not know what that room looked like—even what kinds of books she had, if she had any.

"Put on shoes—slippers," I heard myself saying. "You never know what there is to step on in these halls."

I followed her up the five remaining flights. I climbed as fast as I could to keep up. She obviously walked more slowly. How did she know? I was forcing myself not to breathe heavily. Had she spied on me other times? Had she listened to my breathing? Had she watched me stop on each landing? Certainly if she lived above me I would be familiar with all her mannerisms, as they say. Or did I simply look to her like a man who had trouble climbing steps? I was too busy controlling my breath to observe her behind. And then I was too busy thinking how to keep her from entering my room. I felt that she was in control. But still, there were papers on the bed and on the table that I could not let her see. Perhaps even an edge of Fulani's panties would be showing.

When we got to the door I tried to make her leave the box outside. She wouldn't hear of it. She insisted that she herself should put the box out on the fire escape. What could I say? That my room was a mess? I said that. She laughed and said she had let me see her room, which was probably a bigger mess. After all, we were practically roommates. And she promised not to look at anything. She said she'd even keep her eyes closed, and I could lead her to the window.

So there we were in my room. Since I'd moved in almost seven years ago no one had come inside. Not even my son. Now this fräulein was traipsing through my room like some cleaning lady, or a mistress. Or a master. Maybe she was a policewoman. I was unnerved for a week. But I watered the petunias. Though first, right after she left, I dug them carefully out to make sure nothing was buried—like what? Like a tiny microphone listening—to what? Grunts, sighs, coughing? The solitary squeaking of an aging man exciting himself? After all, I did not talk out loud to myself. Maybe she was a high-class international thief and I was just what they call a patsy. When it is brutally hot, I am in the habit of taking off my jacket when I reach the building, to make the climb less painful. She must have noticed the numbers.

To tell the truth, I grew very fond of the white petunias on my fire escape. All during the summer I counted them. They were very changeable. One morning there were twenty-six blossoms, and the next morning there would be forty-three. In the evenings when I would come back from the donut shop—that was where I often took my dinner and a cup of coffee—I always looked to pass Kristin Dietrich in the hall.

It wasn't until I spoke to the Bulgarian super in front of the building that I discovered she had sublet her apartment to two other German women for six months. She had returned to her fatherland, he added, giving me a knowing smile, as they say.

"Are you familiar with her?" He continued to smile. I ignored his question. This Bulgarian refugee will never be a match for me, though I have always felt a drop or two of softness toward him. Bulgaria was a drop less tainted than her neighbors.

"What do you think of your new Archbishop?" I asked this Communist-hating super. "Is it true that he continues to seek rapprochement with the régime in your country?" I went on, innocently smiling back at him. His response was to turn and walk into the building without even a good-night.

The first Monday in September I received a postcard from Berlin with a picture of the University library. "I hope my petunias are blossoming grandly, for you," it read. "Affectionately, Kristin Dietrich."

The third Monday of September I received a second card from Düsseldorf, this one with a picture of Heine's birthplace. "I am traveling before settling in Freiburg for the coming months. I will help you plant new seeds in the box when I return in March. You will have many blossoms to count next summer. Yours, K." How did she know I counted the blossoms? Will my successor on the top floor continue the tradition?

XI

"Mr. Solomon," the young secretary tells me, "Dr. Hirsch is not in."

"You told me that when I called an hour ago, also two hours ago, also three hours ago, also four hours ago. . . ."

"I know I did, Mr. Solomon."

"Is he not in only for me?"

"Please, Mr. Solomon, don't ask me such questions."

Why do I want to contact Hirsch so desperately? I don't know. Of what help can he be? He has no choice but to deny his private agreements with me. He knows I have nothing whatever to hold over him. I would do the same. He'll tell the authorities he had no idea where I was acquiring the pages I was selling to him. Many people bring him papers to sell, occasionally papers that turn out to be priceless. Their need for discretion and even sometimes anonymity is often a most private matter—you'll get a dispute between brother and brother over rightful ownership of an historical study carried out in difficult circumstances by an uncle and buried inside a can in the backyard by their father: the one brother, into whose hands it has fallen, wants to donate or even to sell— he has a daughter to send to Barnard College; and his brother in Tel Aviv would certainly never forgive, maybe he would sue. The scattered papers of such a disrupted people as the Jews of Europe are bound to resurface in odd ways. His policy is not to ask questions. His first obligation is to the collection of which he is the custodian.

Maybe I have called so many times since yesterday only because I wanted to hear the voice of his secretary. The sound of my voice in the telephone makes her nervous, even jumpy, yet not unsympathetic. She is grateful that I don't get upset when I talk to her. I am sure Hirsch has said plenty to her about Solomon. Such a knot of emotions in her, I know she would give herself to me if she thought that would cheer me.

Maybe I should fly to her—a final junket on the shuttle.

No, I want to force that bastard, that pimp, to talk to me. I want to hear him scratching in my ear. I want to listen to the worthy gentleman pirouette like a ballerina in his perfumed English. I will speak Yiddish of course, slowly, ponderously; each word will force him closer to the floor—and he will begin, that piece of meat with his two small eyes that always plead like Adolf Eichmann's in his cage, he will begin to tell me his latest shikse joke in his half-forgotten "Austrian" Yiddish. I long for his joke. I will say, Hirsch tell me again, so I remember.

XII

I have just read this over. It is not so bad, but I can see that I am rambling. So I'll ramble. There is no dinner waiting for me. The prospect of a hot dinner and a passionate caress at home, or of sitting with friends in a cafe drinking an apéritif, has kept countless articles brief and to the point. But I am in no rush. There is plenty of time before my deadline. Maybe I shall discover something about my subconscious mind, as they say. Besides, I'll probably burn these pages when I'm finished. After all, I have more than one hundred articles to my name, collected into three thick volumes. Do I need another one? Should I finish my career as a writer of apologies? Why am I in such a fine mood? Insurmountable odds have always cheered me up.

XIII

Take the pale boy, for example, with the ears sticking out, who lived for a few weeks in the next apartment, the last one before the African moved in. Was he a Columbia student, this eternal yeshiva boy? An equally pale girl helped him move in his few pieces of furniture and liquor-store boxes filled, no doubt, with books. I kept stepping out to watch them from the landing, though I never let them see me. Half an afternoon they carried. She was above, stepping backwards up the steps, and he was below whispering commands. At every landing they stopped to rest. She would light up a cigarette and puff with a vengeance, as they say. And he chewed his nails, also with a vengeance. I could have moved in more quickly myself. For their pièce de résistance they carried up maybe a dozen blocks of concrete. This they managed holding one block between them, face to face, as they edged stiffly up the steps sideways. Together they looked like a wind-up toy. All the way to the top floor, eighty-eight steps and six landings, they carried, twelve times, like two young fools from Chelm, like slaves in Egypt before the coming of Moses.

She stayed with him a few days. Over and over they rearranged the furniture. At night, all night long all the nights she was there with him, they were whispering without a stop. What could they be telling each other, these two Americans, that they needed every second of the night? Their words escaped me. When people whisper it is difficult to tell their voices apart and I am an expert at such listening—I was trained, after all, in the most specialized of institutions—but I am positive that she did almost all the speaking. Maybe that is why his ears looked to be on fire.

After she left it was like a cemetery. What could he be doing in there? There was not even a single creak from the floor. Was he glued to a chair? He had to be going to the toilet, but I never even heard a flush. Maybe he walked in the air and timed his flushes to coincide with mine. Had he fallen into a coma just three feet away from me? I was so curious I was not able to concentrate. That weekend of waiting for his silence to break cost me maybe an article. Then, late the third night, the sobbing started. His bed was pushed to the same wall mine was against. Only a board separated us. Every night now he cried himself to sleep. Near the end of his crying when there was only left in him a repeating whimper, a squeak, I would fill up with a great nostalgia. Yes, a nostalgia. For what? For my nights at Auschwitz. I began to formulate an article (which I never wrote) entitled "Nostalgia for Auschwitz." (Perhaps I am writing it now.)

Every April, though I stopped attending eleven years ago when we were, all of us who still live, eleven years younger, we would meet—hundreds of survivors—in the Statler Hotel across the street from Penn Station, to commemorate the uprising in the ghetto of Warsaw, and to never forget. It tasted always to me like a reunion. And why not? We were youths together, mere boys and girls—and though there was then no future, that period now was the past of the various futures we lucky ones managed to creep into and become lost in: after all, the youth of a man is a precious thing, a small bird, an exotic bird with fluttering wings he carries his whole life in a chamber of his heart. After the speeches—disgusting speeches by politicians who buy votes by punctuating their paragraphs with the repeating flourish, "Never again! Never again!"—we would gather in a large reception hall for the highlight: We would eat bagels and drink coffee and note how much older we had gotten, and who was missing.

I never leaned the crier's name. He neglected to put it on the mailbox. Maybe he expected no mail. It is possible he didn't care. Could he have been a fugitive? A disgraced member of the underground, cut off first from family and childhood friends—though I imagine his bar mitzvah photograph still stands in its frame on top of the TV console, unless his father is one of those drastic men who disown a son—and then cast out from his cell for displaying certain regressive tendencies? Perhaps the girl had been his last link to the organization, a lover instructed either to bring him around or to abandon him, her Jonah, to isolation and remorse, ignorant of his comrades' ever-changing whereabouts (a phenomenon I am intimate with). But to put nothing on the mailbox, no matter what his mental state, was a mistake. If I were in hiding I would, to begin with, put a false name on the mailbox so as not to draw attention. Even right now, here, my final destination, I've given a false name, that of Werner Heisenberg, who verified what I already knew—the vital law, namely, that close scrutiny always changes the object we scrutinize so that the truth remains always a jump ahead of us. Of me. Maybe they will never discover my actual name and I will lie alone with a cross over my head in a graveyard filled with gentiles. Or better yet, a Heisenberg among the fallen burghers of Yorkville. What if a man could continue hearing from the grave? I would never hear Yiddish again. Only English. Only German.

Before Dawn the Third Day

XIV

Once more, as I sit writing in this alien hotel room, I sense that something here has happened to me before. Was it when I was a child in Vilna? But what exactly is it here that makes me feel that way? Could it be the sour smell of this hotel? Smell is certainly a sense that can open a man suddenly to forgotten moments. But no, as I breathe in deeply with my nostrils I know it is not this deathly fragrance. Could it be the brass pipes sticking out over the sink? Such pipes, I do remember, protruded, also with no present purpose, from a wall in my room in Paris where I first loved Inge in the days after my release from the D.P. camp. But it is not Paris I am sensing, either. Perhaps it is the iron legs holding up the bed: such iron legs held up my parents' bed. Why then do I feel I was at just such an ending before? I had permanently stationed a regiment of Pilsudski's Polish Legion under their bed. Many hot summer mornings, when my father was already at work, right after my mother shook out the sheets and laid the bedspread over the mattress like the flag covering the coffin of a hero—she was then pregnant with Malkele, but I didn't know it—I lay happily on my stomach beneath my parents' bed and commanded my thirsty troops as we pushed the Bolsheviks inch by dusty inch back to Kiev.

I considered myself a Polish patriot. I never doubted, the summer of my fifth year, that my father's questions were beside the point, or at best playful provocations, when he would ask me whether my regiment understood commands issued in Yiddish or whether I could guarantee that none of my tiny lead soldiers would scale an iron leg of the bed one night and slaughter my sleeping parents. After all, my father himself had served in the Fourth Regiment. These iron legs, then, are not responsible for this sensation that has seized my consciousness. Is it the gray rain plummeting down past the street lamp? Perhaps it is simply that I have always felt the nearness of the end—that everything in my life was a rehearsal for this. But this is not a rehearsal. Why Vilna? Of course—the pigeons. It is the pigeons huddling and gurgling on the windowsill.

When I was a boy of thirteen, I started helping my cousin Samuel from across the courtyard keep pigeons. For a time I spent every afternoon and sometimes an hour or two in the evening on his roof. He was older by three years, already a student at the Technion. He taught me to observe the habits of the pigeons—most memorably, how both the mother and the father fly off for food which they digest and then regurgitate into the upraised beaks of the ravenous fledglings. When I was in Auschwitz I spoke with a man about pigeons.

"Solomon," he whispered in my ear one night. The sound of my name summoned me to the surface, as it were. I had become detached from my name, like a minnow separated from its school by a sudden twist of current. It was the first word between us, though we had tossed and floated in half-sleep side by side on the same shelf for weeks.

"Solomon," he whispered with greater insistence, "have you seen a bird?"

"A bird?" My voice was not mine.

"Yes, a bird. Have you seen a bird since you came to this

place? Think." He was right. I could not remember even one bird. He had thought it through. His lips scraped against my ear, just as years later, in Paris, Inge's lips rubbed my ear to an unbearable pitch as she spoke to me of her girlhood in Bergen-Belsen. "It is this unending stench pouring from the smokestacks. What bird could live here with us? Not even those that feed on carrion."

"Not even a single pigeon," I heard my voice uttering. The constant rustle of the sleeping men reminded me suddenly of my cousin's dovecote in the evening when the fledglings were impatient to be fed. For a moment, right before my eyes, we were the fledglings pushing and squirming against each other on our shelves in the coop—awaiting, in vain of course, the return of the mother and father pigeons heavy with nourishment. Our beaks were opened, voracious, with nothing to swallow but the droppings from each other's withering bodies.

"Why do you keep opening your mouth in such a peculiar fashion?" His voice whispered inside my ear.

So I told him. I spoke of the dovecote in Vilna and of my cousin Samuel, the teacher. In what coop was he caught now? I lay on my back and spoke softly into the air above. He lay with his lips to my ear. He hummed and sighed inside my skull when I described how the babies were nourished.

"Like this—so!" I demonstrated how they opened their beaks.

"Like this?" He turned on his back and imitated me.

Side by side we lay, alternating between moving our puckered lips open then closed, then open, then closed, cooing and gurgling like the fledglings, and giggling with abandon, but furtively, like schoolboys over a smutty joke. I had not played so since boyhood when my cousin taught me to distinguish and to imitate the different calls of his doves. I was

never as convincing as he was. The pigeons adored him. He
had become, so to speak, an honorary member of the flock.

Suddenly, as though his very memory were attacked by
lice, my neighbor jerked to his side and leaned his lips to my
ear again.

"When one of us becomes too weak to even eat"—I could
feel his dry breath attacking my eardrum—"the other one
will chew and feed from mouth to mouth. Swear with me
that we will do so."

I kept silent.

"Swear," he commanded. His body trembled.

"We will see." I spoke calmly, too frightened to keep my
silence.

"Swear!"

"We will see," I hissed at him.

Not more than a few days passed and he was too weak to
eat. I chewed his crust of bread and tried to feed it to him,
not from my mouth as he had envisioned but simply with my
fingers. He turned his head away from me. Men, after all,
are not pigeons.

XV

Earlier, just when I finished putting the remains of Werner
Heisenberg among the burghers of Yorkville, my chest
started to hurt—very suddenly. Would it not be a good joke,
I thought, if, after all, I was found dead actually of a heart
attack? When the pain became fierce a panic seized me, even
though I know that soon when I take the barbiturates I will
not be afraid. Still, I heaved with terror. I almost fled downstairs to take a taxi to Roosevelt Hospital. Instead, I stopped
writing and lay down on the bed and tried to calm myself. It

seemed that my nature was crumbling. I could not pull my
brain away from my heart. I craved a single Valium. I berated
myself for not bringing any. I had decided that I wanted to
remain thoroughly clearheaded throughout the extremities
of these preliminary hours. Of course, I could have taken one
of my phenobarbitals, but I found the strength of mind to
resist this temptation to fritter away my fortune, so to speak.

As I taught myself to do in Auschwitz, I focused on an
event prior to my present predicament, a small event, an
inconsequential event, until my historian's mind began to
prowl on its own through the blind alleys of my memory,
scrutinizing even the tiniest of details, so that the event itself
lay before me finally like a mirage, and the remainder of my
corpus delicti started to calm down.

The last morning in my apartment, a mere forty-eight
hours ago, when I already knew what I must do, I was startled at dawn by a man's voice. Over and over with increasing
ferocity the voice groaned an obscenity, though I could not
quite comprehend. With no warning I was transported back
to my shelf at the moment of scrambling to get up, at the
moment of making myself as invisible as possible. Where, I
panicked in my confusion, were the others? Was I the only
one left? How, you should ask me, could a person of such
strong mind as myself be thrust so easily back to Auschwitz?
After all, that man wasn't the first to accompany dawn on
109th Street with groans and curses. Though it is undeniable
that I continue to refer back to the Nazis in these pages, in
recent years I have not dwelled on Auschwitz. The Nazi has
been but a minor character in my writings. Why, then, did I
respond so to the man's voice? My arrest and interrogation
the previous day, followed by the obliteration of a future, obviously played a key role. But it was just a few minutes ago,
when I lay in the bed here, examining the event, that I clearly
put two and two together, as they say. The man's voice dupli-

cated exactly the slurred timbre of the Ukrainian criminal
who functioned as the capo of my barracks until, that is, he
was fallen upon one night by a few Jews. We threw his corpse
into the cesspool, where we knew it would be found in the
morning—a warning to the other Slavic and Aryan criminals
who were our overseers in the spring of 1944. The SS were a
different matter. They had polished revolvers and Doberman
pinschers—they had the guarantee of a reprisal too drastic
for us to risk.

Each day at dawn this Ukrainian awoke with just such
a drunken repetition of invectives and punctured our exhausted sleep: we were never permitted—even then I understood it was by design drawn up in Berlin—we were never
permitted more than four hours' sleep. Most terrible, at least
for me, his crude and merciless awakening violated the few
moments of mental privacy we managed—and woe unto the
man whose slow response caught the Ukrainian's eye. His
name would certainly appear on the next day's list.

In spite of my need to go to the toilet and relieve myself, I
was drawn to the window. I unlocked the steel gate and
peered out over the dingy alley that looked shy and naked in
the gray light of dawn. It rained steadily. I considered, for
a moment, stepping out on the fire escape and plunging
headfirst at my fate. Even now I can picture the concrete,
strewn with pieces of broken glass, zooming up at me. Then,
too, my heart began to hurt, terribly, as though a hand were
squeezing it, and I fiercely concentrated on the scene before
me—the same scene I had brought before me in detail earlier in bed, and for the same reason.

A large, oval mound of wet newspapers, which lay just inside the torn fence that had once separated the alley from
108th Street, had begun undulating, stirred as it were from
within. The movements grew more violent. The obscenities
were coming from inside it. All at once a head broke through,

sheets of newsprint lifting and falling to the sides. Was the Ukrainian returning from his cesspool at this auspicious moment? If so, my soul would soon have to fly past him to its destination.

But I will not be rushed. It is merely the beginning of the third day. I have paid in advance for this room for a week, though they would have settled for three days. I wanted to be sure not to leave behind any debts and I do not want to be disturbed by the management. Besides, I am sitting shiva for myself before the fact, so to speak, because I do not expect there will be anyone sitting shiva for me after the fact. Perhaps I can still reach Hirsch. If I act soon and they discover me before the end of the week, they can send a refund to my wife.

The man lifted himself to a sitting position. He looked up, his mouth opened, and squinted into the down-flying rain. Immediately I pulled my head back. I was fearful that our eyes would meet. Maybe, I thought, he was merely searching the sky for his mother. When I looked out again, carefully, my eyes just above the sill, I saw that he now sat in a torpor, his head tilted downwards, in silence, as though his sluggish brain was unable to decide whether to go forth or to sink back into its blackness. Finally, with a slow, painful labor, testing one unsteady joint after the other, the man stood up. At that moment I realized that the pain in my chest had eased. This man was even more helpless than I was. I watched as he took out his member and pissed against the wall of the building. I was too far above the alley to see if the man was circumcised, but I did see that he had a strong stream. How had he managed to keep so fit? Maybe he was younger than he looked. He pulled a pint bottle from within his shirt, lifted it to his lips, and sucked at it for a moment. Then he held it up from his face and squinted into its emptiness. Would he smash it against the bricks as so many oth-

ers before him had done? He stood it carefully against the
wall of the building.

The man unbuttoned his pants, letting them drop heavily
to his feet, and squatted down. Not since I was liberated had
I watched a grown man defecating. I observed the act with
wonder—his stools were enviably healthy. Mine have been
twisted and paltry since the late fall of 1939. Still in a squat-
ting position the man folded a sheet of wet newspaper and
wiped his behind—carefully. He stared at the crumpled paper. Was he reading his future in the wipings? Then he put
his hand behind him and let the paper fall on top of the droppings. Did he imagine he was seated comfortably on a toilet
seat? He washed his hands in a puddle of water in front of
him, then slapped his face as though to awaken himself. We,
if any of us were lucky enough to have found such a treasure,
would have carefully rinsed the sheet of paper in the puddle
and hidden it someplace to dry. The man stood, pulled up
his pants, tucking in his wet shirt with care, and buttoned
them. I could see that his feet were swollen. He picked up
the bottle and stared at it. He lifted it to his lips for a moment, again stared at it, then slid it into his shirt. He hobbled
through the broken place in the fence and out onto 108th
Street. My bladder was bursting.

There were many things I had to do that day—I didn't
think again of the Ukrainian until I needed him, when a moment of mortal terror drove me to the bed.

XVI

A man's private fantasies, which have a rich life of their
own, end forever, and as though they never existed, when the
man dies—unless he confesses them to another. Or writes
them down. If he does write them down, even in a most dis-

guised manner, they become a part—an essential part—of
the historical record. With these fantasies recorded, a picture
emerges, not of an orderly society of impoverished creatures
imprisoned and entertained by a few glittering figures, but of
a world where we are all simultaneously kings and lovers,
avenging angels and groveling suitors. If we permit fantasies
into the historical record, we are transformed before the eyes
of the student, if he is smart enough to see what is before his
eyes, into a civilization of participants, participating always,
no matter how cautiously or with what abandon, at the edge
of an abyss.

I here offer my life as an example. Though anyone's life,
properly witnessed, could serve as easily. Even Hirsch's.

XVII

Later I will call Hirsch again. If I had his unlisted number,
I would walk down to the lobby and call right now. I almost
got it from his secretary. I could hear her wavering. Finally
she resisted me. Why didn't I push harder? Next time I will.
Hers may be the only sympathetic voice available to me. Perhaps I was afraid to push too hard for fear of losing her. It is
true, too, that if she had given me his home number I would
have no reason to call her again. Could it be she did not want
to lose touch with me? Alone in a room, a man can convince
himself of anything.

If I wait twenty-four hours, I could go down and call Fulani. She was just on the air—it was her voice, with her familiar theme-song behind her, that interrupted my reverie
earlier and sent me back to this table. For a moment the taste
of Patchouli literally dissolved the sour odor surrounding me.
A radio two rooms over was playing a prerecorded announce-
ment of her all-night Friday program. This time tomorrow

she will be there in the flesh. That was how I first discovered
Oscar's secret—I heard Fulani's voice coming from a radio in
the next apartment.

After the crier fled, an African political science candidate
moved in. We never talked. The few times I heard him opening his door to leave just as I was opening my door, I was
prepared to look right into his gleaming face. Maybe I would
bow to him—slightly. Maybe I would not. Certainly I would
gesture to him to walk down the steps before me. But he
never emerged. I am convinced that he slid back behind his
door when he heard me. I did watch him from my landing
one morning, stealthily of course, as he walked up the steps
holding a bag with a half-gallon of milk sticking out—and I
was positive as I climbed the stairs one evening that he was
observing me in the same way. The name he used was Mr.
Moses Chikema. He was a tall man with a Van Dyke beard,
who wore an African shirt over his slender frame. He received a number of periodicals on African politics as well as
several specimens of PLO propaganda. Except that he put
his name on the mailbox, and in two other important respects, he was no different from the previous tenant—silent,
impossible almost to catch a glimpse of, and always, I am
quite sure, alone. He never cried himself to sleep, however,
and every night he listened to the radio.

One night I heard Fulani's voice—on his radio. Clearly, it
was her voice. How could that be? Impossible. Unmistakably,
however, it was the voice of Fulani. At first the African's reception was no good, I could hear Fulani only in short bursts.
Hard as I concentrated, I could make but little sense of what
she was saying. I could distinguish few of her words. Once,
for a moment, I was positive I heard her speak the word
"Jewish," but in the next burst of clarity she seemed to be
speaking of a singer—a black man, the best, who, as I
learned in subsequent weeks, was named Wonder. Frustra-

tion started to unnerve me. I turned on my radio and began searching—no Fulani. When I turned it off I could hear her on his. Again I searched. There was no Fulani anywhere on my radio. On his radio—there she was, clearer now than before. She was talking to a man about the treatment of Arabs on the West Bank. It sounded like an all-night talk show, like Larry King's. That was all I needed, Fulani's voice all night from next door. Was it really a radio? Maybe she was there with the African, listening to records, talking. No, it could not be. Her words were measured and authoritative—certainly not words of love, nor the intimate words of bitterness whispered late at night in the darkness. Then there was music again, a man singing, probably the same one she had praised. "You are the sunshine of my life," he crooned sweetly. I almost knocked on Chikema's door.

I remained awake throughout the night. Her voice continued to mesmerize me, smooth and forceful for a moment or two, then for a few more moments inaudible almost—an echo, a whisper, a whispering echo inside the darkness that surrounded me. It is impossible precisely to describe the sensations in my mind and in my body that first night Fulani entered my room. To give flesh to her voice, to her fragrance, I filled out the panties with a cashmere scarf I had received once as a gift from Inge and not worn in many years. I listened and excited myself and then I rested a little, with my cheek to Fulani's lap, so to speak. I breathed in her fading bouquet. Everything from my Fulani uplifted me that first night. Even her late-night hatred of Jews. Even the oily voices of the black men who called to pant their agreement and to flatter. Even the hissing of the JDLers who called to threaten and to demean her woeful and poisonous heart.

On the other side of the wall, Chikema lay in his bed and adored Fulani. Had he been one of her callers? There were two or three who spoke as I imagine he speaks. Among all who listen to her, I alone know her secret name and her scent. There may be others—what of her African callers? What do I know of her private life? But certainly I am the only surviving Jew who can smother his face in her under-pants, as they say, as he listens to Fulani coming through the air—to me. Who among my colleagues would have had the imagination or the nerve to claim her intimacy? But even the panties are a counterfeit, are they not? They have never touched her body, and the odor has become more my own than hers.

XVIII

My last night in the apartment, with the tailor's move-ments my father taught me, I cut the panties into nine pieces and put all but one into separate envelopes to mail. I typed the addresses with my Royal, my American typewriter. The next morning I dropped them in different mailboxes—not by my building uptown but in the midtown streets around this hotel before I checked in. To whom did I mail them? Should I say? The spirit of these pages obligates me to reveal the names.

The first I mailed to our Madame Director, as a donation to the Institute. After all, there are no hard feelings. They had no choice but to request my immediate resignation—allowing me one last trip, under guard so to speak, to claim my personal belongings before barring me from the building in perpetuity. I am sure that they have already replaced the lock in the outside door. Beyond a doubt they are thoroughly compiling an inventory of my papers. Some items may sur-prise them.

The second I mailed to Detective Sawyer at the Manhat-tan South Precinct. He may be the first to arrive when the desk clerk dials 911 to report the corpse. This hotel is located in his district. I doubt that he will be surprised when he makes a positive identification.

The third I sent to Inge. Will she be able to distinguish my smell from Fulani's? When I bought my American typewriter in the summer of 1959—twenty-six years ago—a resurgence of passion had overtaken us. Emmanuel was not yet a year old. In the middle of the night I would bring him to her. While he suckled from one breast I would kiss and lick the sweetness from the other—and softly rub her wetness below. I had gotten the machine for next to nothing from a book dealer on Catherine Street who handled stolen merchandise on the side.

"Compose me a note on your crooked machine," she would croon in my receptive ear. Inge had never before been so unrestrained, even lewd. But more than anything else it was my words she lusted after.

Letter upon letter I typed in my impossible English, filled with graphic descriptions of what I would do to her body, what I prayed she would do to mine. "My dear Miss Luxemburg," I would begin each letter. Always I signed off with "Your ever-worshipping cunt cleaner and comrade, Karl." I would carry them to mail from the Institute in official envelopes. Before I left her I searched for those letters, in vain. Perhaps she threw them away. Perhaps she has hidden them well—who knows for what purpose? Certainly she should recognize the typescript on the envelope.

The fourth I sent to Hirsch himself. Let him tremble when he handles it. He is too smart not to know, even before he unseals it, from whom it comes. Will the secretary stand gazing over his shoulder? Will she smile at his uncomfortable perplexity when he pulls out the small piece of feminine silk? Perhaps he will place it in his private file.

The fifth I mailed to Mr. Moses Chikema, in remembrance of all the Sabbath nights we spent in separate quarters listening to every word Fulani whispered to us.

The sixth, the crotch itself, made of delicate lace, I mailed to Kristin Dietrich. She will know immediately what it is and who sent it to her. Will she also know why? Firsthand, last April 11th, a Friday night, she learned of my interest in Fulani. In the early hours of dawn we listened to Fulani, the German woman and myself. That night I didn't call to speak over the air, a counterfeit German Jewish professor from New York.

The seventh to Fulani. This was the piece that included the label—so she could see it was woven of pure silk by Lily of France.

The eighth part I addressed to "The Professor of Jewish Studies, The University of Arizona." It will take longer than the others to arrive, but he will throw it away without learning a thing. Maybe I should have included a piece of the lamb's wool. It is better that I did not—I need this comforting sweater a few more hours.

The ninth, the part that would have folded in slightly between her globes, I kept. I will leave it folded into this pad— as an illustration.

XIX

Outside there is light. The rain has stopped. At this hour, when I was a young boy, before my mother pressured my father into sending me to a secular Yiddish kindergarten, I would enter into the cheyder, closing the door against the pale light of the courtyard. We would begin by chanting the *Modeh ani.* The mystery of the Hebrew blending with the familiar Yiddish completing each phrase branded my brain tissue with greater permanence than these ghostly numbers on my wrist.

After *Modeh ani* we sang out the Yiddish "I am thankful." After *Lefonechoh* we sang the Yiddish "before you." After *Melech,* "O King." After *Chai vekayom,* "Who lives forever." After *Shehechezartoh bi nishmosi* we sang "Who has restored in me my soul." After *Bichemloh,* we sang "with mercifulness."

To this day I understand the world as just such an interweaving. All I have written attempts to penetrate a mystery by scrutinizing the familiar, where it dwells. As for the Hebrew language, I do not dispute that it may be the secret soul of Yiddish. Certainly the alphabet is powerful evidence, to say nothing of our history. Of what use is a soul, however, without a heart and a blood system? When I breathed in the Patchouli in Oscar's basement room, or when I studied the faces of the men restlessly asleep, or when I listened to Fulani's seductive voice in the pre-dawn dimness, or when I tasted the drops of milk from Inge's breast, or when I ran my finger from right to left, repeatedly, on the surface of a manuscript page four hundred and eighty years old, or when I whispered hoarsely into the ravenous ear of Kristin Dietrich, or even, as now, when I compose this simple list (with my German fountain pen)—all these things I have performed in Yiddish. Even a secret when it lies revealed before me has revealed itself in Yiddish. Even when Kristin Dietrich stood naked before me—I understood her nakedness in Yiddish.

I had just began to attend cheyder when my sister Malka was born. When we sang the Hebrew *Melech,* I always thought of her, since her name meant "Queen," the wife of the King. It gave me goose bumps, as they say, to think how I started each day in the cheyder by thanking my baby sister. Immediately, however, when we translated to Yiddish, "O

King," I thought for some reason of my grandfather Solomon, who lived in the apartment with my parents before I
was born, and whose circular picture my father had gotten
framed and then hung on the dining-room wall. In the afternoons, when my mother bathed Malkele, I would slip noise-
lessly into the kitchen and watch her. I loved it when my
mother bathed me. She would sing "Ven der Rebbe Eli Mey-
lach hawt gevorn zayr freylach" as she washed me all over
with the cloth. I pictured a jolly rabbi washing all his pupils
in a large tub as they squealed with delight. After she dried
Malkele, she would lay her on the table to powder and diaper
her. That was the best part—I begged my mother to let me
powder the baby. At first, she would shoo me from the
kitchen. One day she let me powder the baby. Then she let
me help put on the diaper. I never spoke of this to my father.
I knew he would put a stop to it. I knew he would talk to
Mother about it. She even let me stick through the safety
pins. She knew I would never hurt Malkele. I wondered
when that "King," my grandfather, was old and, they told
me, practically blind, whether she had bathed him as well. I
always thought of my mother when we sang "with mercifulness," I never thought of my father when we recited the *Modeh ani,* but I often wondered where he fit in the prayer.
Could he have practiced mercifulness in Hebrew? I knew he
wasn't the one "who lives forever." Whom could I think of
who would live forever? Not my father. Not even my merciful
mother out of whom my sister came. Not the teacher in the
cheyder. He had such fits of coughing he would have to run
from the room. We could hear him from his kitchen, coughing, gasping for breath, then coughing again, but a little
more softly. One boy claimed he heard his mother say the
teacher was dying of tuberculosis. Certainly not my newborn
sister. I could still vividly remember a time when she wasn't
yet alive. Once I asked my father if he knew someone who

would live forever. "The Jewish people will live forever," he replied with no hesitation. At that moment he planted in me a kernel which would turn me into an historian.

Keep in mind, however, that even if the whole world spoke Yiddish there would still be torture and killing. We would have raped our language, just as the Germans have raped theirs (to say nothing of the Russians, the Americans, the Arabs, and—we cannot leave them out—the Israelis). The glory of Yiddish flowers simply from never having had enough of anything else to rape it for. Dreams and desires have been its food, memories and the aroma in the kitchen of a piece of red meat slowly cooking with onions and carrots. Of course, we had no weapons with which to resist the naked power of the Germans, not even our own intimacy with their language.

To speak German as the German Jews spoke it—Inge, for example—was to speak a language almost as glorious and supple as Yiddish. Some Germans understood that. But what did they do to save us? They preserved their copies of Heine and Franz Kafka. They migrated to California and spoke out—careful, of course, to always distinguish the SS from the German people. They read Rilke aloud with their Jewish friends in apartments on Riverside Drive, and wept softly with awe and nostalgia. As for Heidegger, the great preserver of the German tongue who supported—but only for a short time, they always remind us—the national resurgence, they blamed his wife. In truth, if Heidegger had married a Jewess, as they would call her, rather than his pure Teutonic beauty, he would have encountered a richer German, a German whose words were not all similarly clad in brilliant uniforms and strung together like cadets crisply on display. But this is neither here nor there, as they say.

XX

The next morning, when Oscar finished sweeping my room and emptying my trash basket into a plastic bag, I asked him. I watched his brown skin redden as he claimed he never listened.

"But why not on my radio?" I pressed on.

"It is an FM station, Mr. Solomon." He said this after a pause more than long enough to show that he wished I had never discovered his secret.

"What station?" I knew he could not refuse.

"W . . . B . . . A . . . I."

I wrote these letters down on a pad—slowly. I too knew how to pause without releasing him.

"What type of station is that?"

"I don't know, Mr. Solomon." I enjoyed hearing him call me "Mr. Solomon."

"Every night?"

"No. No," he answered impatiently, and stopped.

I looked directly at him and waited.

"Only on Friday nights." He stooped to grasp the plastic bags.

"All night?"

Again he paused a long time before answering.

"I don't know."

"A good morning, Oscar," I said in Yiddish.

"A good morning," he repeated.

Oscar is a man who speaks English and Spanish, and more than a little Yiddish. The fools adore it when he addresses them in Yiddish. "A good morning, Mr. Zaslovsky." "It is exactly half past four, Mr. Rosen." "And how are your wife and children, Mr. Gellerman?" The few times Fulani waited for him to lock up, I watched her eyes narrow, murdering, maiming, when too many of my colleagues took leave of him in Yiddish. "A good evening to you, Oscar, and to your beautiful daughter."

In the two years since that encounter, Oscar has successfully avoided finding himself alone in a room with me—except once. He thinks I do not know when he empties my trash basket. But I have seen him take his opportunities. He starts up the stairs as soon as he spies me getting off the elevator on the main floor. A few times I took the elevator right back to the fourth floor and watched—carefully concealed, of course—as he quickly swept my office and emptied my basket. Twice I thought I saw him snooping through the contents of the basket. What could he have been looking for? Perhaps he feared I was writing an article about anti-Semitism among black intellectuals in New York, and naming his daughter as a leading proponent.

The one exception happened just this past Tuesday, at 9 a.m., bright and early, as they say, during my final stop at the Institute before I checked into this hotel. For the first time in almost two years, Oscar could not avoid occupying the same room with me and no one else for a few minutes. The director had obviously instructed him to accompany me and see that I didn't remove any materials from the archival boxes stored in my room. Oscar insisted on helping me put my personal belongings into the few cartons he had brought up with him. Of course I didn't permit him to touch a thing. Still, he would not leave. When I asked him why he continued standing in my room, he muttered that he was waiting to assist me to carry the boxes to the elevator. Where did they expect me to carry the boxes to? Of course, they could not know I was on my way to this hotel. I had no intention of returning to my apartment again. I asked him if he would be so kind as to store the boxes in the basement, in his room. Oscar, the specialist at hesitations, waited fully fifteen seconds before replying that he didn't know any reason why not. I added to the eight envelopes already in my briefcase a few other private items, as well as these five yellow pads—which I added one to the other after initially taking only one, as though I knew that each pad would prolong my life by one pad's worth of writing. I remembered to add a bottle of permanent black ink—and I left. The building looked deserted. None of my colleagues had come out to say goodbye. The director's door was closed, which surprised me: she had always, in her own businesslike manner, been a friend to me. Even Perl was away from the switchboard. The lobby was empty. The display, which I had organized, "Resistance among the Jews of Vilna," a collection of photographs and documents, looked strangely naked and abandoned, yet luminous, standing there in that hollow chamber.

"Don't worry about your boxes, Mr. Solomon. I'll take good care of them."

"Goodbye, Oscar," I said in English, more warmly than I had expected to.

"Goodbye, Mr. Solomon." He blushed.

My radio was AM only—for the morning news and weather on WINS, and occasionally, when I couldn't fall asleep, for a late-night talk show. I went right out and bought a new radio, a SONY—the best of its class, the man informed me. That night, after looking up its FM numbers in *The New York Times*, I located WBAI. It came in clearly. I left the dial poised at that spot. Every evening I checked to see if it still came in clearly. I would be prepared for Fulani the coming Friday.

XXI

I keep humming the *Modeh ani*. Every place in the world where there are Jews, the morning prayer is now being chanted. Jews are a people who continuously serenade their Lord. Even in our remembrance of the dead we love, praise, extol, and thank the Lord God of Abraham and Moses. We never ask why. But in our bones we know. Always we have known. When we stop singing, the Lord, blessed be His name, begins to slaughter. He opens His enormous eye and His creation trembles and closes its eyes in dreadful antici-pation. His blade never fails to drop. First among the people of the earth we have learned to defend our house by singing sweetly into His ear, reminding Him over and over how mer-ciful He has been, how forgiving He has been, how wise, and how, unworthy though we be, we love Him above all else.

Yet this singing is sweet, and the art of remembering that we have developed in our zeal to keep reminding the Lord is our greatest glory. When I would hear the morning prayer whispered in the pre-dawn stillness of the barracks, while the Ukrainian still slept, the apartment on Wiwulski Street where we lived when I was a boy appeared to me. I could see my sister again in the closest detail. Even the tiny scar above her left eyebrow that I caused when I turned up the kerosene lamp on the wall one afternoon so I could reread my year-old copy of the *New York Daily Forward*, my favorite reading matter in the spring of my fourteenth year. I had turned it up too high and Malkele, who was napping on the daybed be-neath the lamp, was hit in the face by the hot shards of glass when the lamp burst. I believed that I had blinded her when she shrieked and put her hands up to her bloody face. The whole time our mother washed her face and worked to stop

the bleeding above her eye, Malkele kept reassuring me that
nothing terrible had happened. She was wonderful.

How did I happen to have a copy—even a year-old copy—
of a daily Yiddish newspaper from New York? I expect you
have already asked yourself that question. Because of the
prohibition against profaning the sacred Hebrew letters by
stepping on them or throwing them out, the synagogue had
a room with a large bin where people deposited books and
papers they no longer wanted. Because of this prohibition, I
should point out, the Jewish historian has an incalculably
rich vein to tap. We boys would rummage through this bin.
The great prize would be a newspaper from New York. They
were few and far between, as they say. The few neighbors
who received an occasional paper from relatives usually held
on to them. My *Forward* from September 8, 1932, was my
most valued possession. Every day, for weeks and weeks, I
read every word. When I first brought it home, my father
read it with me. We had long talks about life in America and
about the labor movement in New York. He taught me a
poem by Morris Rosenfeld:

> Look for me not where myrtles green!
> Not there, my darling, shall I be.
> Where lives are lost at the machine,
> That's the only place for me.

> Look for me not where robins sing!
> Not there, my darling, shall I be.
> I am a slave where fetters ring.
> That's the only place for me.

> Look for me not where fountains splash!
> Not there, my darling, shall I be.
> Where tears are shed, where teeth are gnashed,
> That's the only place for me.

And if your love for me is true,
Then at my side you'll always be,
And make my sad heart sing anew,
And make my place seem sweet to me.

I dreamed then of emigrating to America. My father did
not. Even if he wanted to, he told me, we would not be permitted to enter. The doors to America were closed. Things
there were not so good, we both agreed. This hotel was already, then, what it is now. It was already a proper stage-set
in which to take leave of this world. Still I dreamed.

It is growing brighter outside. This time tomorrow, Fulani
will be getting off the subway in East New York. She will
enter her basement apartment, which she rents in the house
her father owns there and has slaved for a decade to fix up. I
have often timed her so. Of course, for all I know, Yasir Ara-
fat's private limousine whisks her through the city. For all I
know, she lives in the house and her father in the basement.
For all I know, Fulani is the sunshine nestling around Stevie
Wonder's wondrous loins.

XXII

The third Friday that I listened to Fulani I started to call. I
was clever not to conceal that I was a Jew. I introduced myself
as Professor Lewis Schorr, a Jewish refugee formerly of the
university city of Freiburg. Where Kristin Dietrich had gone
for the year. From my years with Inge and unavoidable contact with her circle of superior German Jews—they commu-
nicated with me only in English, they knew no Yiddish,
of course, and I pretended not to understand their beloved
German—I had become an expert at mimicking a German
speaker's English accent. I told Fulani that I was a part-time

lecturer in sociology at the New School. Particularly, I presented myself as an expert on Émile Durkheim. Heady stuff, as they say. I improvised a personal history as I spoke—afterwards I had to write down what I revealed, my counterfeit past, so I would not contradict myself the following week. Yes, I began to call every Friday night, late usually, not before 2 a.m. I kept a separate notebook on the details of Lewis Schorr's life. It could be judged as an abortive attempt to write fiction—doesn't every historian indulge that whim at one time or another? Schorr's opinions, on the other hand, were most often my own. Who among her listeners could know that no German Jew, particularly one from the university city of Freiburg, would claim, for example, that the Nazi ideology was a natural outgrowth, as they say, and not a grotesque perversion of nineteenth-century German philosophy; a natural outgrowth of the music not merely of the obviously Teutonic Wagner, but of Beethoven, of Schubert, of Schumann, of Brahms. What obligation did I have to defend European civilization? Oh, Fulani loved it when I made that claim and honored me with Stevie Wonder.

Certainly I wanted her to recognize no connection between her lovelorn German Jewish caller and the Institute where her father toiled daily for his aging white masters.

As sharply as I looked, I could never be certain when I encountered her at the Institute that Fulani had not made the connection. I found her glances quizzical—as though she were keeping a secret between us. That possibility thrilled me. Perhaps she was simply responding to my staring. As hard as I tried, I could not stop myself from staring whenever she came by to visit Oscar, and I always arranged it so we passed each other more than once. Each time I marveled with new eyes at her height and the dignity of her posture. Did she tell her father funny stories about her suitor, Lewis Schorr? It occurred to me that if Fulani were a nightclub singer I would attend all her performances and probably end by joining her company. Would I end up crowing like a rooster on a stage in Vilna during her whirlwind tour of the Soviet Union? Did she know even about the cream-colored panties I kept stuffed with a scarf beneath my pillow?

One time I found myself in the elevator with her. I did not plan it. She swept in after me on the top floor. What was she doing up there? I trembled from the power of her fragrance. She pressed Basement. I pressed Lobby. I knew that it was time again to rub the panties through her coat—or perhaps even a new pair. This pair would be black but a little more modest. She stared right into my face the entire way down— or maybe I should say she glared. For years I have been able to make others shift their eyes away when I look at them, particularly in a small enclosure like an elevator. This time it was me—I could not meet her terrible eyes. My eyes fixed themselves on the hollow of her throat. I had to speak. I had to force myself not to use the German accent.

"You are Oscar's daughter, Ruth?"

I spoke in so strong a Yiddish accent it sounded to my ears like a caricature. I had looked up at her carefully when I uttered the name "Ruth." She was excellent. She betrayed no emotion. She remained poker-faced. What a wonderful partner she would have made.

"You support PLO murderers?" My accent had grown even thicker.

Just at that moment, when the elevator had reached the lobby with its familiar shudder and the doors were preparing to open, I saw that she was not glaring at me at all. She was looking through me as though I did not exist. She saw only my absence—just what we prayed the SS would see when their eyes raked our bodies.

I wanted to throw myself to the floor and kiss her shiny brown shins. Instead, I clicked my heels like a German,

turned briskly, and as I began stepping from the elevator, in
my finest imitation of a German accent, I spoke, weakly I
admit, the precise words I had heard a drastic young black
caller say to her the previous Friday.

"I'm leaving. I don't like to lower my standards. I don't like
to be at the bottom of the barrel. I don't like to beg. I'm just
leaving."

"When?" She demanded with the same sharp tone she
had used with him.

"Soon. Before summer. Yes, before next summer," I answered with his shocked hesitation.

When I called the following Friday, she did not reveal that
she knew my true identity.

The elevator was not wholly empty when I rode back to
the top a few minutes later. It was full of her fragrance. I rode
it down to the lobby and back to the top three more times. I
got off only because Gellerman rode up with me the third
time. We had not spoken in nine years. He was insulted at a
reception when he overheard me calling his wife a stupid
fool. He didn't hear all of it. What I said was that for remaining with a man so ridiculously her inferior, Reyzl Gellerman
was no less than a stupid fool. It was one thing, I went on, for
a girl alone in the world to marry a distant cousin who had
enough money to have brought her over from the D.P. camp
a decade earlier, but to remain with him all these years . . .

"You call my wife a stupid fool!" He must have overheard
me from the next room. His cheeks were trembling. He
slapped me across the face. "Your wife is a German whore."

I laughed in his face. He was led away. We have not spoken
since. Whenever I happened to ride up with him, I always
remained standing in my spot, compelling him to get off before me. One time he tried to force me to leave before him.
He stood still. I stood still. The door slid shut. We rode down.
Others rode up. I listened as they chatted with him. I kept

silent. They got off. Still we held our ground, as they say. The fourth time up, the Director joined us. She nodded to me and I to her.

"Gellerman," she said to him, "I was just coming up to see you."

He waited for her to leave, then he followed. I followed him—another small victory.

This time I got right off and left Gellerman agape. The shock must have been powerful because the doors closed and the elevator took him down again. Could he smell the absence of Fulani? If Hirsch had been in the elevator with me, I could have torn him to little pieces and dropped the pieces down the shaft. A year ago the Gellermans were honored by their son and daughter on their silver anniversary.

XXIII

Hirsch must be in his office by now. Certainly the secretary is. I will go down and call again. I'll buy coffee to go and a buttered bialy, just like a man going to business. Did my venerable colleague, the director of the Judaica Room at Forty-second Street, not suspecting Hirsch, speak to him of his suspicions of me? Could Hirsch have warned me that they had started to secretly film me at my usual table in the Judaica Room? There I am on film—a regular home movie, candid-camera style, as they say, for the police to laugh at. And for posterity.

"Look, children, there is your grandfather performing research in the library."

"But *Oma*, Grandpa is not even looking at the book."

"That is how he thinks, *mein schöner* Bengie."

"What is he doing now?"

"Why, he must be taking a pad and a pen from his brief-case."

"But why are his eyes moving around so fast? His nose looks funny."

"Your grandfather was a good man, children."

"That is not a pen, Grandma."

"Emmanuel, what kind of film are you showing the children?"

"*Oma*, look at Grandpa. He is cutting the book with a razor."

"Emmanuel!"

"Look, he just took out a page."

"Emmanuel!"

"*Oma, Oma*, Grandpa is putting the page into his brief-case."

"Emmanuel, what are you doing to the children?"

"Look, *Oma*, who is that man who is putting his hand on Grandpa's shoulder? Why has Grandpa closed his eyes? Is he sleepy? Why is his forehead so wet?"

"Emmanuel, in the name of God, he was your father."

"Why is Grandpa giving the man his briefcase? Who is the other man holding Grandpa's other shoulder?"

"Emmanuel, stop this!"

"*Oma*, why is Grandpa looking down at the floor?"

"Emmanuel, please."

"*Oma*, where are those big men taking Grandpa?"

"Emmanuel, I command you to stop this."

"Let the children see what he was—a thief. The bastard-bitch."

"He was a wonderful man. He was handsome and smart. He was a savior of our people's precious archives."

"He was nothing but a sick little Yid, Mother, and you know it."

"Emmanuel, *Kind.*"

"Don't twist the past. He berated you all the time. 'The German,' he called you. 'Fancy lady,' he called you. He never let you be. Always he beat you down. He treated you like dirt under his feet."

"He never laid a hand on me."

"With his vile tongue, *Mutti*, with his jargon, his Yiddish. And he never gave me the time of day."

"Herr Schwartz also spoke Yiddish."

"But Ben was different, *Mutti*, he wasn't arrogant. He took me to Yankee games. He, not Father, gave me Chanukah presents. He, not Father, bought me my first Gillette. Maybe they were childhood friends from their precious Vilna, but Ben wasn't sick. He hugged me, *Mutti*. He didn't smell."

"Emmanuel, *komm hier, mein süsser.*"

"*Mutti, Mutti, meine schöne Mutti, ah du bist so alt. Aber schön, du bist schön. Dein Parfüm ist süss wie die Blumen.*"

"*Oma*, Dad, look—the screen is empty."

What else could explain why Hirsch began to avoid me weeks before I was arrested? Three times I sent him messages that I had a number of items of interest. Then I went so far as to call. I gave the message to his secretary. When I called back the next day, she had a return message. I remember it exactly. "Mr. Hirsch is very busy, but he encourages you to continue your good work. He said that he will respond to you shortly with interest." She spoke as though she had written it down and was now reading it. Why was she so careful? In spite of her nervousness, or actually because of it, that was the first time I felt her presence. Why did he say that I should continue? Was he helping to set me up? He could easily have sent another message. "Now is not an opportune moment," is how he could have worded it, "financially speaking, of course, to buy even the most interesting items.

Perhaps, at some future date the situation will change." That sounds like Hirsch. Would she have sounded less tense, perhaps even relieved, to have read me that message instead? Certainly I would have understood that. After all, my price was cheap and Hirsch is too greedy to resist a bargain. So how could I have misunderstood? He would in no way have implicated himself. I underestimated his treachery. He must have heard, informally of course, rumblings from Forty-second Street. How was it to his advantage not to tip me off, as they say? Certainly, he could have cut himself free without helping to entrap me. He must have concluded that he would be safer with me completely removed. Perhaps he has other dealers to protect and he decided that by throwing me to the dogs they would be satisfied and his larger operation could continue untouched. He must have concluded that I had nothing on him. He was right. How could I have left myself so exposed?

Except for the secretary. If I want Hirsch, I must get to the secretary. But do I want him? He is, after all, a first-class custodian. He is also a meager man. I would not even have to do very much. If I spoke to the police about him, they would be sure to question the secretary—I do not think that she would lie to save him. Yes, he is vulnerable. Simply a letter to Detective Sawyer would get the ball rolling, as they say. He is a smart and thorough man. I don't even have to talk directly with him. He was looking for more. This case clearly interests him, it even seems to tickle him. I would be an informer. Or simply, these pages here, if they fell into the right hands after I am gone. No! A Jew doesn't inform on another Jew—even posthumously. Of course, if I made it known only in selected Jewish circles I would not be an informer. But what would they do? They would say the trouble-maker is at it again—even as he sinks, he wants to drag another one down with him. They would simply cover it up.

Hirsch will remain where he is. In nine years he will retire. He will be honored at dinners in Boston and New York, and in Jerusalem, for his unparalleled contribution to Jewish research. I must talk to him. I must hear his voice. This time I will extract his home number from the secretary. He won't be home when I call, but I will talk to his wife. What could I tell her that she will understand? To her I am another of her husband's pitiful refugees. Her father owned a factory. Her grandfather came from Russia in 1882 and grew fat in the ladies' garment business. Her father inherited the business, bought out his brother, and built a factory in Fall River, Massachusetts, where there were no unions. I have done my homework on Hirsch. She will regard me as a fool.

The secretary is a sweet girl. I would prefer to talk to her. She must be Emmanuel's age. I imagine her with brown hair—cut short—and very round brown eyes. Her body is slender, but she has large breasts. She has had maybe a single lover—in college. A white Anglo-Saxon Protestant. She studied literature and anthropology in one of our better schools. She writes stories, or maybe even poetry. Her grandparents, on both sides, spoke Yiddish. She is a Polish Jew through and through. Why do I go on like this? I do not even know her name. Perhaps I could bring them together. It would straighten the boy out to marry such a fine girl. What am I thinking? Let his mother find him a proper match. Maybe I should introduce him to Kristin Dietrich or to Fulani. Fulani wouldn't even spit on him and Kristin would be unable to hide her disappointment when she discovers that he speaks German like her father, and knows less Yiddish than she does. Let his mother envelop him with her fragrance and her whispers—he is hers.

XXIV

If Inge's lover had been one of the German Jewish professors who surrounded her—the one-armed musicologist, for example—I could have overlooked it as more of her sentimental German weakness. But with a man who was born in Vilna, whose father played chess with my father—never! What did it matter that I had dabbled a bit? Neither of those two widows was from Inge's German circle. Esther had been a classmate of my cousin Samuel but a year older, and a Communist. And Rivka was my sister's best friend. Many afternoons I watched them play house. Most often Malkele was the mother and she would put on our mother's shoes with high heels. Sometimes it was the other way, and Malkele would put her finger in her mouth. I was amazed how, with a sudden gesture, Malkele could transform herself into an infant. Rivka simply remained a girl sucking her thumb. But Malkele abandoned herself to the part. Right before our eyes she was newborn. I would pretend not to know that they made believe I was the husband and father—a rabbi no less, they decided, because I was always with a book in my hands.

Mine were affairs of no importance. You don't believe me? It is true that with each of them there were memorable moments. Esther, may she rest in peace, talked without a stop when she made love. Yiddish poured out from her even more dramatically than it does from me. She told me what to do and for how long to do it. She would climb on top of me and heave herself up and down, and always the words came. She would moan and shriek and at the same time she would tell me in minute detail exactly what she was feeling. And between her numerous explosions, while we were still coupled, she would babble of the past. She told me, for example, that she knew just how much I hated her when Samuel brought

her to the roof to help with the pigeons. She even told me
how more than once when I was not there she and Samuel
took off their clothes and embraced right inside the coop. I
didn't tell her about the time I watched them from the next
roof, where I had hidden myself. Then she told me that she
knew it when I hid on the next roof spying on them. Did
Samuel know? Did Samuel know? Yes, she told me, of
course he knew, but he made her promise to say nothing.
Was he angry? "No, Samuel loved you too much to be angry
at anything you did. He said it was time for you to learn
what's what. He would even have given me to you if he had
had the power to—which he didn't have, naturally. Though I
liked it—your schoolboy eyes greedily watching my naked
body and hating me."

Such things she told me the few times we embraced in a
hotel room not far from here. She died of lung cancer three
years later, while Inge was pregnant. If I had not gone to the
funeral and then followed the hearse to the cemetery on Staten Island, if I had not gotten out of the hired car and stood
looking into the black waters of the harbor while we crossed
over on the ferry, I might never have been so weak as to have
made the mistake of confessing this trifle to Inge. Though
for a few years this confession helped draw us close. It
brought passion back to our marriage.

About Rivka, the first one, I said nothing. Rivka accused
me one afternoon of always calling her Malkele in moments
of intense passion while we embraced. Was that so terrible?
If she had called out "Hershele," the name of her brother
who died pathetically of dysentery and resignation right in
my barracks while I watched from across the room not knowing he was breathing his last, I would have held her in my
arms and smoothed her hair with my hand. And Hershele
had not even been my friend. He was a bully—more than
once he knocked me down in the snow. Once he even

punched Malkele. Rivka told me she could not bear it when
I called her Malkele. So I stopped myself—for a few times.
This, remember, was only 1951. We were still washing the
stench of the camps from our bodies. Why did I lust so after
Rivka those few spring afternoons? Inge and I were still practically newlyweds. Was it simply to hear Yiddish whispered
into my ear again? The next time I called out my sister's
name, Rivka wept the whole afternoon and refused to look
at me. Finally, I sat quietly in a chair and read a book. With
one exception, I have not seen her in thirty-four years. In
1953 she remarried—a surgeon—and moved to Phoenix,
Arizona. She has two sons and a daughter named Mandi—
after Malka. Are you surprised I know all this? I also know
that Mandi has recently married a young man who is studying to become a rabbi with the Reconstructionists in Philadelphia. Do you want more? Both sons are doctors and the
husband is now a bigshot in the American Medical Associa-
tion. Yes, I know his name—but I won't reveal it here.

But with Ben Schwartz, it was different. I introduced him
to her. The boy was not yet ten years old. Schwartz was a
senior fund-raiser for the UJA. His territory was the garment
industry. I would often meet him for lunch in a bar on
Thirty-eighth Street. He always took a London broil sand-
wich on a club roll and a bottle of Rheingold. He had a car,
and in the summer he would drive us to Brighton Beach. He
was a single man. I should have been smarter when I saw
how much Inge and the boy loved it when he sang Yiddish
songs. At first, Inge wanted to introduce him to one of her
Germans. Why in the world would he be interested in a German woman? I teased her. To whom do you want to introduce him? To your friend the Hebrew teacher? Do you think
a little Hebrew makes her kosher? I was merely teasing her.
Though I hated her German crowd, in those years we had
a truce.

It was through Schwartz that I knew what had become of Rivka. He was in her class as a child and they had remained in touch. For a time, when they were children, Malkele and Rivka made fun of him without mercy, because he had crooked teeth and sticky eyes. A year later he was constantly in their conversation. They discussed him in detail, so to speak. Malkele was in love with him.

"What about his crooked teeth and his sticky eyes?" I asked them one afternoon.

Malkele wouldn't speak to me for three days. She was shocked that I had listened to their conversations. He began to come over to listen to her practice the piano. She would immediately stop her scales and begin playing only Chopin when he was there. I too loved to hear her play Chopin. My favorite, and Ben's too, was the Second Polonaise. Malkele, much wiser than either of us, preferred the Fourth Prelude. Little by little I grew fond of Ben. I even took him to the roof and introduced him to Samuel one afternoon. Now he was having an affair with my wife.

For months I said nothing—though I knew without even the smallest doubt. Don't ask me how. Schwartz still joined us for dinner three, four times a week. Inge dressed up slightly on those nights—and she wore our perfume. Was she so up in the clouds, as they say, that she didn't think? Or was she paying me back for Esther, more than a dozen years later? He continued teaching the boy to play chess, and every other Sunday that spring he took him to a baseball game—Schwartz had free access, through a business connection, to a box in Yankee Stadium. Why hadn't I thought to teach chess to Mennele? I was a greatly superior player.

I still slept with Inge every night, but I didn't touch her even once. She must have noticed, but she never said a word. One time she tried to entice me. She wore my favorite nightgown—a cream-colored, silken gown that reached in long sweeps to the floor. It had three small buttons at the top of the bodice, one of which she kept undone as an invitation to me to unbutton the other two and expose her breasts down to the tops of her nipples. Was she inviting me to take her back from him? I turned away, but my mind began to think of Schwartz undoing those buttons. It pictured his fingers grazing her breasts as he opened the bodice. It pictured him licking her magnificent nipples until they became long and upwardly curved, and ready for his lips to suckle. It pictured his fingers reaching under her gown and slowly moving in circles on her smooth thighs and then on her mound and deftly parting the hairs. It pictured how she raised her body slightly permitting him to lift the nightgown up to her waist where he sensuously let it remain. It pictured him lifting himself above her, holding himself up slightly so as to not press his entire weight on her all at once. It pictured him spreading her legs with his own. I watched her take his large penis with her hand and caress it and begin to rub it around the top of her open vagina, then push it into her body. In the smallest detail I saw his penis pulling the glistening lips of her vagina slightly up as he pulled slowly out, and then pushing them slightly inwards as he plunged his wet penis slowly into her. Their shiny hairs brushed and entangled. She began to move in a slow circular motion upward to meet him as he plunged in, and then down again, in a continuing circular motion, as he pulled out in preparation for the next slow thrusting—deeper, deeper than I had ever entered into her. I had to run to the toilet and relieve myself to keep from seizing her. I could have won her back that night, for regardless of all else, my soul was more passionate than his. Why hadn't I tried? Why did I abandon her? After that night, every time I saw them in a room together I became aroused.

I must admit that imagining them in such ways became my keenest pleasure. On one or two occasions, I must admit further, my mind transformed Inge into Malkele—Ben's first beloved. I would have been happy to watch them through a window or to listen to them from beneath the bed—in whatever cheap room they went to. Could they have come to this hotel, to this very room? Are you surprised that I never followed them?

One evening I challenged Schwartz to a game of chess. Emmanuel's face turned red. Why had he become so agitated? What did he know? I defeated Schwartz with ease. We played again. Once more I defeated him with ease. Again we played and again he lost. He was a sucker for every cheap trick. The fourth game I beat him in four moves. Emmanuel's eyes were on me the whole time. Was he proud of his father? No! His eyes were sharpened with hatred.

There had been a time, there is a photograph that records it, when Emmanuel looked up at his father proudly, as they say. In Riverside Park there is a tunnel that goes under the Drive to a promenade that runs along the river. I knew how to find the precise pitch to make the tunnel vibrate. When he was still a small boy, I would take Mennele on walks along the water, but going through the tunnel was the highlight. I would say to him, "Listen," and begin to hum and soon all about us the concrete walls would tremble and call out. Mennele loved it. His hand would clutch mine more tightly when we approached the tunnel, his face gleaming with excitement. He never grew tired of asking how I did it. I taught him that every enclosed place in the world had a sound that could make it tremble and sing. All he needed to do to discover this sound was to listen carefully as he patiently hummed up the scale. Over and over Mennele tried to find the precise pitch of the tunnel, but his voice was not yet deep enough. I would join in the humming and soon we would have our "concerto for tunnel and two voices," as I helped him name it.

His favorite story when I put him to bed concerned that tunnel and all the stray cats of Riverside Park in the wintertime. Every night these cats would gather in the tunnel for a little warmth. There was one cat who had learned the secret pitch by spying on us on our secret walks. This cat would begin to hum. The other cats would help out by meowing. Soon the tunnel would begin to vibrate and purr, just like another cat. Then the walls would heat up and glow, and all the stray cats would be saved another night from the bitter cold. All night long this cat would stay awake and hum. He didn't dare catch even a wink of sleep for fear the walls would darken and the tunnel grow cold and damp. The others would all sleep snugly and comfortably, almost as though they were home in their apartments, in delicious beds, under the warm covers. When daylight came our exhausted cat just had to go to sleep and the other cats would watch over him, protecting him from dogs, and even gather delicious scraps of food for when he woke up hungry. For some reason Mennele never grew tired of this story.

There is a picture that Inge took of the two of us standing at the mouth of the tunnel, all bundled up in our thick winter jackets. Mennele is holding my hand and looking up at me expectantly, glowingly. Our lips are puckered, for we are humming in unison. In the background there is a stray cat with its mouth open. It may be hissing in fright at the sudden vibrations surrounding it, but it looks as though it has joined us in our concerto. I wish I had made a copy of that photograph to look at now.

Mennele's eyes were on me again, but in a different way, as I defeated Schwartz for the fourth time. What had gone wrong? Had Inge stolen the boy away from me? Or was it that I had grown too harsh, too remote, even for my own son?

"Are you going to play me next?" I spoke suddenly to the boy.

He remained silent.

"Speak up. Are you ready to play me, now that I have defeated your teacher?"

He continued staring at me, but said nothing.

"Have you lost your tongue?"

"Leave the boy alone, Leon," Schwartz commanded with an intense whisper.

I stood up, put on my jacket and left the house. That night and for two weeks following, I slept in my office. Every night I dragged an old mattress up from the basement. Every morning before Oscar showed up, I dragged it down again and went out for my coffee.

The fourth day after I left I received a short letter from Schwartz. "I am sorry, Leon," he wrote, "if you think I am interfering in the way you have chosen to raise your son. Inge is very upset since you left. I do not want to disrupt your family. I will be very busy with this year's fund drive in the coming weeks and I will not be able to visit. Please go home to your family, my old friend."

I lived for three years more with Inge and the boy—though I spent most of the time in my office. Occasionally we ate together. Long after the boy went to sleep and Inge was closed in her bedroom, I would open the sofa in the dining room and go to sleep. All that time she carried on with Schwartz—and she involved the boy as well. One time I saw the three of them together. Emmanuel was already sixteen years old. I had just left the Forty-second Street Library for the long walk back down to the Institute when I spied the three of them walking south on Fifth Avenue. I followed for a few blocks. It was near Christmas, and they were shopping.

They carried packages, just like gentiles. They stopped in the crowd watching the Christmas display in the windows of Lord & Taylor's. He held one arm through hers—right in front of the boy. They resembled the other gentile families soaking up the Christmas spirit. Long after they left, I stood there watching a tiny village with twinkling lights. A horse and wagon filled with innocent peasants slid around and around a tall church. A priest with a red sash pulled a string that made the miniature bell in the church tower tinkle. Small children of landowners skated around a rotating Christmas tree, tall as the church, with a star on top. Snow fell gently. The children were orderly. The boys wore impressive black uniforms with silver trim. The music was by the elder Strauss. Somewhere, where we couldn't actually see it, a synagogue was packed with noisy Jews.

I never saw Ben again. Three years ago I went to his funeral. Half the garment center turned out. The Israeli U.N. Ambassador, or his aide, was there. He died suddenly of a coronary. Was Inge with him when he collapsed? She and the boy were there. They were grieving as though for a husband and father. It seemed as though everyone there paid his respects to her and consoled the boy. Rivka was there. She was the only one besides me who did not go over to Inge. She smiled sadly at me, but we did not talk. I was watching the funeral I would never have. I am sure that they sat shiva for him in the apartment. I discovered that he left a trust fund for the boy. What he left Inge I do not know. She dresses immaculately and she never asks me for a penny, though she works only part-time in an antiques shop on Madison Avenue. I am convinced that she made Emmanuel visit me once a month. Why else would he have come? Will he be surprised when he discovers that I too have left him a modest amount?

XXV

Are you wondering how I knew so soon and without the smallest doubt that Inge was having an affair with Ben Schwartz, may he rest in peace, without having followed them? You will never be able to figure it out, not in a million years, so to speak, but I have decided to tell you.

When Malkele was in love with Schwartz, in those few short years after she was no longer a child and her body was not yet twisted by arthritis, she invented a certain phrase to let Ben know when she wanted him to kiss her. I overheard them when she presented him with her proposal. These were her words, exactly: "Every time I say to you, 'To what are Chopin's Preludes preludes?' you will know that I want you to kiss me and embrace me—and you will follow me to whatever private place I choose. If you fail to follow me even once, I will never let you kiss me again—and I will never marry you." Malkele was then a very bossy and dramatic girl, and Ben was totally her captive. One day I heard Ben say those very words to Inge, when they and the boy were talking about their favorite composers: "To what are Chopin's Preludes preludes?" My eyes immediately flew from the book I was reading. He was looking right at her. She was actually blushing and smiling. Did they think I was blind and deaf? Did he think that I had lost my memory? It is true that he never knew that I had overheard Malkele make her dramatic proposal. But if he thought at all he would have remembered that I had at least heard Malkele utter that phrase to him— on a number of occasions—and from that I could have started deducing. The phrase didn't sound right in English. I am sure that Inge would have loved him to say it in German, but Ben never had an ear for the difference between German and Yiddish. He would have sounded just like Malkele if he had tried. A moment later she walked into the kitchen and, of course, he followed. They remained in the kitchen for three minutes. I watched Emmanuel mouthing the speech for his upcoming bar mitzvah—which was held in Temple Emmanuel, where the Germans go. I had once said those words to Rivka, but she didn't respond with any knowledge. I was more shocked that Ben had remembered all these years, and that he had so cheaply violated his intimate memory, than I was that together they were violating me in my own apartment while I sat there watching my son prepare his bar mitzvah speech without my help. Why cheaply? Perhaps he was honoring his memory of my sister, his first beloved, by repeating her phrase to my wife, his last beloved.

Every evening Mrs. Hirsch prepares gourmet dinners for her husband. She has cookbooks that guide her on tours through all the cuisines of the world. Their Passover seders are among the finest in Brookline—her haroshes has become famous, Hirsch told me once, as though I were interested. Hirsch talks, talks, talks, and like a prince he loves to lead his family and guests through every word of the Haggadah. Once, when I was flying to Boston right before Passover with some items for him, did he invite me to his home for the seder? No, he asked me to bring him a dozen pieces of blessed matzos from a Hassid in Williamsburg who owed him a favor. Their children Rachel and Daniel have already spent their junior years in Israel, studying at Hebrew University and learning about life during six weeks on a kibbutz. Their youngest, Jonathan, is there now, a philosophy student. This Hirsch told me the last time we spoke. Jonathan, he also assured me, has not grown ashamed to ask the four questions—in Hebrew. In a few years Rachel will marry and have sons and they will begin asking the four questions. Hirsch is a proud man and a collector. I imagine how he examines the identifying marks on the bottom of every plate and the underside of every spoon when they dine at a friend's home. An original Moses Soyer hangs on their dining-room wall. If Ben were truly his father, Emmanuel would have been good enough for Mrs. Hirsch's daughter—or even for Mrs. Hirsch.

If he were still alive, Ben would be sixty-two. He was only forty-nine when he took away my wife. Inge was still a young woman then. If Malkele were alive, she would also be sixty-two now. If she hadn't been crippled by arthritis, perhaps she would have survived. She would be entering the twilight of a great career on the concert stage. Inge would admire her and Mennele would adore her. My brother-in-law Ben and I would still meet for lunch on Thirty-eighth Street. Every year they would come with their daughter to my house for the first seder. At the end of the seder, Malkele would always smile at her husband and say, "To what are Chopin's Preludes preludes?" A moment later Ben would follow her from the room. Naturally I would have told my wife the secret meaning. She would smile at me and blush. Our son would smile at the two of us smiling and blushing at each other. His favorite cousin, named Bess after our mother, Basia, would smile at how handsome her cousin looked when he was so happy—and she would sit down like her mother at the piano and play Chopin.

Late Afternoon the Third Day

XXVI

After I called Hirsch's office, I went for a walk. The late morning sun had come out and the wet streets were beginning to dry. You could see the wet spots shaped liked continents shrinking on the pavements. I laughed at the thought of a shrinking globe, a shrinking economy, a shrinking people, and, of course, my own rapidly shrinking options. I had slept so little my eyes burned. I bought a pair of the best sunglasses—Ray-Ban, they are labeled—in a drugstore on Lexington Avenue. I had decided to walk to the Belmore Cafeteria, where the taxi drivers go. I knew it was on Park Avenue somewhere below Thirty-fourth Street. I discovered that it had gone out of business—a recent casualty in the relentlessly shrinking cafeteria world. The sign in the window, which must have been more than a few years old, thanked all its patrons for sixty-seven years of loyalty. The Belmore lasted longer than I will. Once New York City glowed all night from the lights of those cafeterias. In any neighborhood you could find a cup of tea, a Danish, and a conversation of some nature. Now, instead of Dubrow's and Garfield's, instead of the Belmore, instead of the Automat on Fourteenth Street, instead of my old haunts on upper Broadway, there are Burger Kings. How can the soul linger and know the wonder of its own isolation in such places? Only desolation unencumbered by self-knowledge waits to embrace us now. Despite the June sun above my head, I felt cold. Perhaps the rain was still in my bones. But my yen for a cafeteria grew, so I did what was next best. I walked four blocks west along Thirty-first Street to a dairy restaurant near Seventh Avenue. The food would be better, but full waiter service would make lingering difficult and conversation impossible. Every bite of my lox-and-onion omelette tasted unforgettably delicious. My bialy, with a smear of scallion cheese, was fresh and crisp. The aroma from my two cups of coffee was wonderful, and the warm taste on my tongue almost brought me to tears of gratitude.

After my second cup I fell into a reverie and began formulating a plan. Perhaps it was inspired merely by the Ray-Bans I continued to wear for the sake of anonymity and the self-enclosing serenity exhaustion brings me in a busy room. Rather than simply dying, why not disappear to perform one last task? By the time the bondsman caught up to me, I would have accomplished it. What task am I referring to? Simply put, to execute the "Angel of Death" himself, Doctor Josef Mengele. What did I have to lose? I would travel to Paraguay with a false identity. I can easily arrange to be a German Jewish rare-book dealer from Paris. Why not? My German is just right. Even my French, which is, I admit, a little weak, I can speak with a German intonation. About rare books I know a thing or two. What better than a German Jewish businessman looking for action, as they say, to ferret him out? Rare-book-dealing could be perceived as a cover for a variety of other, larger dealings.

In the midst of my strangely comforting fantasy, I was shaken to the bottom of my soul. "Is This the Angel of Death?" From more than one table this headline glared up at me. Below it were two pictures. One, taken in 1968, was clearly of Mengele—and there was no diminishment of arrogance in his face that now intruded itself into every corner of this restaurant packed with Jews eating their midmorning delicacies. The mirrors on both walls reflected his face, back and forth endlessly. I was growing dizzy. I closed my eyes, but I could smell him. The stench of his domain was starting to overpower me. In the middle of Manhattan? In 1985? Had we never been liberated? Was I still up there on my shelf waking in a panic from an uneasy dream of a delicious meal and decades of life lived so badly? Would I now have to live through this unbearable dream once more? No. It was merely a picture, next to another picture, beneath a headline on the front page of a reckless newspaper. But his hideous face must be staring up from every newsstand in the city. He must have come into my mind because I had spotted that headline on my walk without knowing it. A dozen times I must have passed that face smirking up at me. How could I have been so self-absorbed? Was I blinded by the sun? And if there were no headlines, no *New York Post*, would he not have come to me? He has never lost his hold over me. Even in these last few hours of my life, while I enjoy my last tasty meal, even as I lick my lips for the last salty traces of the smoked salmon, as Inge would call it, Mengele can creep in at will and take over my consciousness. Still, the last thing I needed was this headline, this hoax cooked up behind closed doors in Berlin and Asunción. Could I really have outlived him?

The Brazilian police claim that the second picture is also Mengele, taken in 1979, an aged and altered Mengele who had changed his name to Wolfgang Gerhard and lived a simple life in Brazil. It is the corpse of this man Gerhard that has just been exhumed. Should I believe these officials? Could eleven years have robbed him so totally of his Nazi arrogance? Where had he learned to neutralize his gaze like a hunted thing? From his private collection of youthful twins with whom he played such deadly games? From Brazilian victims of his updated methods? Torturing emptied a man of everything, but not of the arrogance in his face. The face in the second picture is not Mengele's.

It is the oldest trick in the book, and Mengele has had decades to perfect his plans. All he needed was the right kind of corpse and a few years to let it rot in a Brazilian swamp while he continued to live his comfortable life in Asunción. Even his dental profile could have been transferred to the other man. Why not? Are there not still Nazis dedicated to these leaders in hiding? Who, more than the Angel of Death, would they want to serve? His children are wealthy and loyal. Officials could easily be bought off, and even eliminated at a later date. They are counting on a world that wants to close the ledgers, as they say. They are counting on the remoteness of the location. But a man like Mengele would live only in Paraguay, in Asunción, within that self-satisfied circle of pure Aryans that rules that small outpost of the fatherland. Never would he have agreed to live a simple life in Brazil, servicing a ruling bureaucracy made up of half-breeds, of mongrels, of inferior types little better than Jews. For a fee he might help them develop a more efficient system of inter- rogation. He might have heard of a German recluse, almost his double, living in the Brazilian rain forest. He might have visited the man once or twice, seducing his simple soul. He might even have brought him to Asunción for extensive den- tal work. The double may then have drowned, accidentally, in Mengele's private swimming pool before he was returned to Brazil, not to his simple home but to his fragrant swamp. Why not?

No, Mengele is still in Asunción waiting for the dust to settle, so to speak. Waiting for the world to forget all about him, as it will. Soon it will be too late for anyone to get to him. He will be out of reach in the fatherland, enjoying his old age in comfort, amid his children and grandchildren, surrounded by a small but powerful and efficient circle of admirers.

But a great opportunity may have presented itself for the moment. He is an arrogant man and therefore a careless one—particularly when he is on the threshold of such a great triumph. Best of all, Mengele is already officially dead. The mutilated remains I leave behind me will be quickly and secretly buried and forgotten. Those who have conspired before will conspire again, this time to protect themselves. The family will have no choice but to accept the fraudulent corpse from Brazil as their father, Josef Mengele. The recluse Wolfgang Gerhard will have more in death than he had in life. Now is the time for me to travel to Paraguay and perform this sacred act. Mengele will be intrigued by the silent Jew in sunglasses and he will have himself introduced to me in his favorite *Wursthaus* in Asunción, where I will have, coincidentally of course, begun taking my lunch. Then I will begin to charm him.

There are four key rules a Jew must follow when he sets out to charm a German of influence and power. First, he must begin to ingratiate himself—not too obviously, and with just a touch of challenge. Second, he must hint that he has something of great value to offer—for a fair price, of course. Third, he must never in any way whatsoever refer to German women—but he must continue to drop clever remarks, and not always such subtle ones, that convey a wide and intimate knowledge of Jewesses of all stripes. Last, he must be exceedingly careful to act ever-so-slightly less intelligent than the particular German he has set out to charm, and at the same time ever-so-slightly more intelligent than the other members of this German's circle. This could prove quite dangerous. The last rule I refer to as the Jewish seal of approval—a distinction all Germans crave. I have formulated these four basic rules up close, as they say, and I consider myself a foremost expert in this field.

Yes, I thought almost happily, my life has prepared me well to be the instrument of Mengele's last-minute downfall. Procuring a visa for Paraguay should prove easy enough. My papers as Siegfried Lowy remain intact—even the passport is updated. The key to my safe deposit box is right here in my pocket. The cash I still have access to should prove to be just enough to accomplish my task. Whatever needs I have left afterwards will certainly be taken care of.

For a Jew, the secret of a good disguise is to remain a Jew. Better still is to be disguised as a Jew who is further disguised—a touch carelessly—as another Jew, so that when they have unmasked his second disguise he has managed to authenticate his first disguise. I should present this principle to my soul brother, Moses Chikema. I'm giving away my secrets free of charge. I won't be needing them myself. For my second disguise I could have Lowy pretend to be Hirsch. That would let it seem for a day or two at least—but the rumors will persist—that Hirsch was part of a conspiracy to smoke out and execute the still-living Mengele. Without doubt, he will turn this to his advantage—and his retirement banquets will be even grander. The one time I passed as a non-Jew came to a disastrous end. Of course, there was no choice then—all Jews were fair game, on the Aryan side of Warsaw. There were no exceptions—not one. Even the most valuable lackeys were soon disposed of for new lackeys. Perhaps it is important to be always prepared with one well-practiced and thoroughly thought-through gentile identity—just in case, as they say. For myself, I am no longer interested in posing so, no matter what the circumstances. If I live, by some miracle, to the next act, I will go to my death with a *Sh'ma Yisroel* trembling on my lips. When the world is business as usual, however, it is vital for a Jew to hide as a Jew.

How many others have been nourished by this fantasy of torturing and killing Josef Mengele? I have contemplated it often—in detail. Was I simply letting my fantasy of killing the Angel of Death protect me from the glare of his face? But now was certainly the last chance. Soon he would be home free, as they say, and I would be gone. So how could I not go and get it over with? I asked myself while I drank my coffee on Thirty-first Street, among still-observant Jews who also tried to ignore the face in the newspaper as they talked business on their late-morning breaks for blintzes, or hot borscht with a boiled potato. For them I will do this. What do I have to lose? For them I will urinate on Mengele's face in his private suite while he slowly bleeds to death from a wound in his stomach where the bullet, muffled by the silencer on my pistol, has entered his body. For them I will tear off his scrotum while he still lives and stuff it in his mouth for him to chew on or choke on. For them I will push my thumb into the sides of his eye sockets until the eyeballs are forced out, one at a time.

Enough. I do not want him in my consciousness, taking it over—not at this juncture. As soon as I started to repeat "for them," I knew I had struck a false and dangerous note. My friend Ben Schwartz must have frequented this dairy restaurant on his rounds, lunching here with the moderately large contributors from the ladies' garment industry. Judging by the turnout at his funeral, he was certainly held in high esteem here in the garment center. I left the waiter a two-dollar tip.

XXVII

The afternoon sun has just dropped behind the top of the Metropolitan Life Insurance Tower. I am beginning to sense the slow approach of the Sabbath. The streets are filled with men and women rushing to subways and buses. It is my last chance to call Hirsch's secretary again. Soon she will leave for the weekend—and I will be cut off forever from her sweet voice and from Hirsch.

I have devoted my life to recovery—a task with grave limitations. It is not possible to fully recover what was lost. The restored collections help give us a certain picture; our scholarship aids us to understand this picture, and serves as a guide. But only the memory holds actual bits and pieces of what is gone. This memory, however, selects out, just like the doctors in Auschwitz, sentencing some images of the past to the perpetual half-life of sentimentality and official versions, and dooming the remaining (and, I have learned, the more vital) images to immediate oblivion—almost.

This memory does permit us to survive, but it has made day-to-day life nearly impossible. For the oblivion I refer to here is nothing less than a lower portion of our consciousness—where we are ceaselessly tormented.

Only action has kept me from drowning in this unseeable darkness where all the fish have teeth like razors. Only danger has saved me. Only having to look behind me when I walk from the Library has rescued me from walking permanently backwards to the years before 1939—as so many of my colleagues do without knowing it. When you walk backwards toward the past, you see nothing but the illusion of a future always receding.

Every day I see them walking backwards through the halls of the Institute, just like a movie in reverse. I see them back

out of the elevator. Then I see them back into the elevator.
The more they walk backwards the more fiercely they begin
to fight with one another over their differing and fading versions of what was—trivial things, such as what Tlomackie
Street looked like in 1931, or what store replaced what other
store on Wiwulski Street in 1927. These things have life-
and-death importance for them, and that is as it should be.
But they do not go far enough. To find what has fallen into
it, you must be aware that this oblivion is always right behind
you—and you must often look over your shoulder, suddenly
alert for any opportunity to make a lightning raid into its
blackness to rescue a single image: Malkele's patent leather
shoe poised to press down on the pedal of the piano. Or the
simplest of forgotten sounds: my father clearing his throat in
the morning while it is still dark outside. Or a particular
odor: the aroma of a chicken roasting in my mother's kitchen
in the spring of 1923, while the baby cries. Or the feel of a
certain piece of fabric: Rivka's dress when I put my hands
around her chest from behind and squeeze her and she
screams and Malkele consoles her and convinces her to say
nothing.

The chief technique I have discovered to make such retrievals possible is to live always with one foot outside the
status quo, as they say. Too much respectability sedates us
and we begin to walk backwards without knowing it. The
whole time we are blinded by a vision of a false future as we
back away from it toward our lost world, our hearts stuffed
with nostalgia, until the oblivion behind us pauses, then
closes around us as we back into it unawares. Persistent
research is important, organizing our materials with in-
telligence is vital, writing our articles with clarity is indispensable—but only when we haven't forgotten how to twist
our necks and surprise the blinding darkness perched behind
us do we make a significant contribution to our children.

One foot outside the status quo is the best technique I know for keeping our neurons alert, our muscles prepared, our intuitions poised, and our dignity intact. But this powerful technique works only if we avoid, at all costs, crimes of violence against other people. For the memory of such a crime, both the sweetness of it if it was an act of vengeance, and the guilt, will begin to swell inside our brains and squeeze out forever the little ghosts of those actual moments that our memories had almost doomed to oblivion.

I have had these fantasies about Mengele before, though this time, thanks to the *New York Post* and the dead end I have backed into, they were unusually vivid. If a Jewish historian becomes an executioner, he perpetuates the crimes against our people by this act of forgetting how to perform his sacred work.

XXVIII

When I left the dairy restaurant at noon, I walked up Fifth Avenue to the main entrance of the Library. I stood outside and gazed up the wide stone steps. Why was I standing there? Doesn't every culprit return to the scene of his crimes? Let us just say I was there to say goodbye. In the spring the steps are a marketplace. There were umbrella salesmen, their hapless faces squinting at the sun. Others were selling ladies' pocketbooks. One man sold windup toys—little drummer boys who beat their miniature drums and travelled in circles around their master. Of course, there was a sprinkling of young black men whispering "good smoke" and other more exotic phrases such as "ecstasy" and "black beauties" (yes, of course I thought of Fulani)—this is commonly referred to as the five-and-ten-dollar trade. I myself engaged only in the sixty-five-dollar trade. Perhaps I should

have hawked my pages in front of the Library rather than to
Hirsch.

The Moonie in his navy-blue suit, chalk in one hand, an
eraser in the other, shifted from foot to foot before his large
portable blackboard. For years now it hasn't stopped him that
no one pays any attention. He spoke rapidly while he constructed diagrams demonstrating, to himself at least, that his
master was truly an avatar. Over and over his divinity was
proven and then erased. In past years this Moonie had subtle
competition from the "Mitzvah Mobile."

"Are you Jewish?" the young Hassid would inquire suddenly in my ear when I passed him. The question always
made me shiver. Perhaps it was merely the sharpness of his
whisper against my eardrum. I always looked back at him
impassively. Occasionally I saw him leading a young man
into the trailer, to teach him to pray properly. After a time he
stopped inquiring. In his eyes I was not a Jew. Probably I had
become part of the scene, as they say, a member of the sales
force. God knows what I was peddling from my briefcase. He
was right. Only God did know what I was peddling, and
Hirsch of course, and probably the librarian already had his
suspicions. Now everyone knows. Even Fulani. I am sure Oscar has filled her ear. Will she wonder aloud tonight why
Professor Schorr hasn't called? Inge and the boy know. I am
sure that they have discussed it fully with their Germans, another example of the excessive behavior of *Ostjuden*. Does
Kristin know? I cannot even begin to speculate about what
Kristin knows and when she knew it. In every important library in the world they know. I will never be permitted to set
foot in a library—anywhere. Even my small library in Vilna,
if it still existed, would ban me from its shelves.

The lunchtime crowd on Fifth Avenue separated like a
school of tuna when they passed me, as though I were a dangerous reef or perhaps merely a sandbar. Inside the Library,

derelicts were now enjoying the exquisite luxury of sitting stupefied in chairs. Others, the self-made researchers and compilers of New York City, concentrated on freeing another few moments for their lifelong investigations before returning to jobs in the main Post Office and in the stockrooms of midtown.

Again I felt a powerful sensation that all this had happened to me before—in Vilna. Was it the slender, raven-haired violinist in front of the northern lion planting the tenderest of kisses on the lips of her breathless cellist with red cheeks and curly hair? Obviously he had just shown up— late as usual. But, after all, is it the simplest of tasks to make your way through midday Manhattan with a cello in your arms? They were working their way through Juilliard—as we were informed by the neatly lettered sign—by adding some Bach duets to the midday sunshine.

Could I have been returned to Vilna by the joining of these sorrowful adagios of Bach, through two hundred years of bloody history and ocean voyages, to the even more sorrowful dissonance of the aging young saxophone player at the other lion, a porkpie hat (as I now know they are called) on the pavement before him—his sign reading "Thank You," as he works his way through life?

Certainly it wasn't the aggressive portable radios drowning out these mysteries with disco music.

This time I knew what it was without having to rummage in my brain. The girl looked just like Malkele when she sat every afternoon at the piano practicing her Bach "Inventions." I dropped a five-dollar bill in the open violin case and looked up at her quickly, discreetly. She had the same reddish black hair—and more particularly, the same command in the way she kissed the young cellist that Malkele had with Ben, with Rivka, with Father, with me, with everyone who knew her, except Mother and Samuel. I could imagine this young woman throwing a temper tantrum, and her young man would blush and do exactly as she wanted him to—I could see how utterly he was hers the moment she kissed him and forgave him his lateness.

Beginning when she was seven, Malkele practiced for at least two hours every afternoon and often again in the evening when she finished her homework. I would sit and read, but I also listened. She started playing the same year our mother had her first seizure. For weeks Mother stayed in her room. She let no one in except Father. It was my responsibility to take care of my sister until my father came home.

When Rivka and Ben would come to the apartment, they too listened to our little genius until she finished. The teacher once told my mother that Malkele was destined for the concert stage. It was after a lesson. He sat drinking tea with my mother, Malkele, and me—and he became a little carried away.

"She is destined for the concert stage of the finest cities of Europe."

"And New York?" I asked, seriously intrigued.

"Certainly New York—in the great Carnegie Hall. And you, young man, because you are so attentive to your sister, you will go with her on her tour. You too will see all the great cities of the world."

Malkele loved it when he said I would go with her as her manager, her valet. She smiled at me and I pinched her under the table. It was her secret, brazen smile no one but me ever saw.

During Mother's periods of withdrawal, as we called them, I always stayed in the house when Ben came over. If Rivka was there, I would go sometimes across the courtyard to see Samuel. Those days Malkele didn't like Samuel. She always asked me where I was going and she gave me a dirty look when I said I was going to see Samuel.

"Why don't you go to the library?" she would say. "Aren't you tired yet of those smelly pigeons?"

Malkele never talked about Mother when she was sick. She wouldn't even practice the piano softly. When our mother was sick, Malkele simply ignored her presence in the next room. Mother must have put cotton in her ears. Rivka would speak in a whisper, Ben would hardly speak at all, but Malkele would go on—laughing, gaily laughing and singing, shouting—as though there were no one suffering in the next room. She told me later, when she herself was crippled and living with me in Warsaw, that she was convinced that our mother needed to hear her carrying on so gaily—that she brought her back to us by her laughter and the sheer force of her piano playing. I knew she was not speaking the whole truth, but I said nothing.

When Malkele was eleven and I fifteen, our mother left for almost a year to live with her mother in the town of Smargon, where she was born. Her father, Grandfather Spivack, drove a cart with a horse for a living. We almost never saw them, because her father was a severe man who disliked my father. He considered Father a fraud and an apostate, and when Mama started having her nervous seizures he blamed it on him. He belonged peripherally to a small Lithuanian Hassidic sect. My mother had had six older brothers—but three were killed in the First World War and one disappeared. The other two worked in a tannery. I met my Uncle Itzrak one day when I found him in the house with Mama, drinking tea. Malkele was still a small child, and when she tried to climb onto his lap he pushed her away gruffly. Mother flinched but said nothing. When she introduced me he looked me up and down, as they say, and scowled. For years I dreamed of Uncle Itzrak. In my dream I ride with him, against my will, in his cart to Smargon. Over and over he whips the poor beast into a lather. Suddenly the horse snaps its powerful neck and catches the whip between its bared teeth. Neither one lets go of the whip. They are consumed by their struggle. The whole time we race forward blindly. Neither master nor beast is in control. I keep punching my uncle in his arm with my small fist. He only laughs and roars. Then we are in Smargon, where I am held captive in a dark room with a dirt floor. I have nothing to read. My mother comes in and out with bunches of dry hay for me. She does not recognize me. All night I hear dogs howl outside the window. Uncle Itzrak and Mother lie sleeping in a large bed across the room. I crawl under the bed for warmth. I can hear them crying in their sleep like two orphans.

I met him only two other times. In some ways I think I take after him.

Now that Mother was gone, I was responsible full-time for Malkele. When Father took Mother to her own mother, I was afraid she would never come back. How could Father have been so weak? I thought. What would they do to her, those terrifying men? When she was happy, my mother loved to sing. She knew more songs than anybody, except Father. Every Friday night she lit candles—with Malkele's help. Now Malkele insisted that she could light candles all by herself. Of course, Father let her. She was marvelous. She had the voice of an angel, as they say, and her green eyes flamed. She began cooking the Friday night meal alone—though I helped her. All through that time I made sure she kept practicing the piano—she seemed to have lost some of her ambition.

Malkele and Rivka knew exactly how to upset Ben. Together, they were devils. "My brother, Hershele," Rivka once said to Malkele in a whisper just loud enough for Ben to overhear, "told me to tell you that he will wait to walk home

with you after school tomorrow." Malkele looked agitated—
she actually turned red in the face. On and on they chatted
about Hershele. Ben turned white. Tears came to his eyes.
Malkele was merciless. She began to tickle him and make
him laugh and bask in her attention. Then she began to play
a Mozart sonata and his eyes filled with gratitude. But she
didn't tell him that she had arranged the conversation with
Rivka as a joke. The next day Ben threatened Hershele. Hershele was three years older than Ben, and he beat him black
and blue—and came away with a sudden interest in Malkele. The following day he truly waited for her. "Your stupid
puppy told me you are in love with me," he boasted. Malkele
slapped his face. Hershele grabbed her and put his hand inside her skirt. Malkele kicked him in his shins and ran
screaming hysterically to find me. I immediately ran, without
making a plan, to find him. We were the same age, but Hershele, despite his sweet name, was more like a bull than
a deer.

"If you ever touch my sister again, I will kill you."

"What did you say?" he asked almost politely.

Foolishly I repeated my threat. Before I could finish he
swung his arm and punched me right in my face, knocking
me down. My face bled and bled. My nose was broken. But
he never bothered Malkele again. It took a week for Malkele
to calm down. She said we should make a plan to kill him.
Every day she had a new plan. The doctor said there was
nothing to do about my nose. It would heal by itself—but a
little crookedly. He suggested I push on the bone with my
thumb every chance I got, to help move it as much as possible back into place. Twenty times a day Malkele reminded
me. Twenty times a day she kissed the bump on my nose. It
took her another week to console Rivka, to make her feel
forgiven for having such a disgusting brother—and still more
than welcome in our house. She even reminded Rivka that

Hershele had not done much more to her than I had to Rivka
when I squeezed her chest.

There was a short time, during the first period that our
mother was away, when Malkele always wanted me to go to
the library while Rivka and Ben were over. She knew I
wouldn't leave her alone with him, so she wouldn't ask when
Ben was there by himself. Probably she didn't want to be
alone with him, anyway. But as much as she wanted me to
leave, still she would do anything to keep me from going to
Samuel's roof. Why was she so anxious for me to leave? With
both Rivka and Ben, what harm could come to her? So I
often went. I was then flying through the novels of Charles
Dickens. But what mischief was she up to? I doubled right
back, as they say, more than once, but I never caught them
doing anything unusual. Years later Malkele told me that she
had invented a new version of "house." Ben was the baby boy.
Malkele was always the father and Rivka was again the
mother. She told me that once they had gotten Ben to take
all his clothes off, down to his underpants, and then the two
girls diapered him. She made me swear never to tell Ben that
I knew. In the time he was first involved with Inge, while I
still lived at home, I was tempted to bring it up—but I didn't
want to violate my memory of my sister. And I could think
of no way to bring it up without making myself look like a
bastard-bitch.

Until she was almost thirteen, Malkele and I shared a secret. No one knew. Not our father, not Ben, not even Rivka.
Our mother knew, but she never said a word about it. Maybe
she never thought about it. Starting with our mother's first
breakdown when Malkele was seven, I began to bathe my
little sister. I continued to bathe her, twice every week, even
in those periods when Mother was better, until she was almost thirteen, when she herself stopped me. She didn't tell
me why, but I discovered through a bit of detective work that

she had begun to menstruate. I continued to massage her legs, which began to hurt her when she was eleven, until the final days in Warsaw.

When I bathed her, I told her an ongoing story about a bird named Poopik. Poopik was an adventuress. She flew everywhere in the world: America, Australia, Africa, Asia, the jungles of South America, Palestine, but she remained loyal to Malkele and always sent messages to her—through me, naturally. Poopik's best weapons were her quick wits and her eardrum-piercing screech. Her messages were the stories I told Malkele, and they were filled with advice and encouragement.

"How you will love Sydney, Australia, when you give a concert in this concert hall. I am above it right now. The people are going in to hear Jascha Heifetz. I will make caca on their heads. Don't stop practicing and don't let any boy marry you and trap you in Vilna."

Every time I bathed her I had a different story. Poopik was always in peril. She was arrested for making caca on the king of China, she was caught by a fierce eagle in Tibet, she was swallowed by a boa constrictor in Brazil, but always she managed, not only to escape, but to free all the other small creatures as well. She screeched and pecked the bottom of the eagle's talon; it released her and the mouse that it clutched in its other talon. Poopik gripped the mouse's tail with her beak and slowed its fall from so many miles up—enough so that they both landed softly. She worked her way, painfully, through the long body of the serpent and out the other end, leading to freedom six baby rabbits and an old toothless fox who promised to raise the bunnies, its mouth watering as it spoke.

I looked down at Malkele expecting her to ask in alarm how Poopik could have abandoned the bunnies to the old fox. She smiled back contentedly.

"Do you have any questions?" I sounded like a school-master.

"I have one question." Her voice was far from alarmed.

"Well, what is it?"

"Do snakes have tushies?"

"Of course, of course," I answered. "All animals have to make caca. Poopik knew this and it gave her faith."

"Does it face up or down when the snake crawls?"

"Does what face up or down?"

"The tushie."

"Everyone knows a snake crawls on its belly. So where do you think the tushie faces?" This Malkele found very funny, though my voice was cross.

"Just like my tushie. Does it make peepee like me too?"

I blushed that my naked little sister should speak so freely of her private organs.

"Don't you want to know why Poopik abandoned the cute little bunnies to the treacherous old fox?"

"Because the poor old toothless fox was very hungry."

"Is that what you think of Poopik?"

"No, silly, Poopik knew that the fox would try to eat the bunnies, but without teeth all she would accomplish would be to wash the bunnies, and then she would grow to love them just like a mother—just like you love me."

Poopik told the mouse what ship to stow away in to travel to Vilna. She gave it our address and said that Malkele would take care of it. I had bought a soft little stuffed mouse which was waiting for her in her bed. It brought an important message from Poopik: "Next year I will return to Vilna to visit you." I showed her the mark I made on the tail where Poopik had gripped it. "And the tail is so long because it has been stretched," Malkele added. To the very end Malkele loved playing the baby sister with me. She kept that mouse the rest of her life. She even brought it to Warsaw with her in that last year. She told me how lucky for everyone that Poopikle was such a musical mouse. She named him Poopikle in honor of Poopik.

Malkele always shouted and cursed me when I washed her long hair—she threatened to cut it all off. But she loved it when I would brush her hair after it dried. Even before she noticed, I could feel the slight swelling of her breasts when I soaped her. I said nothing—but I knew that soon she would no longer permit me to bathe her. I loved to soap her long little body. She was perfectly shaped before her affliction, but her long legs would remain very thin because the arthritis gripped her just when she started filling out. She had green eyes that could shoot arrows, and a large mouth that frowned more deeply and smiled more foolishly than anyone else's. She was a clown and a tragic princess rolled into one person, a breaker of hearts.

Every night, after the arthritis began tormenting her, except for the short time before she joined me in Warsaw in 1939—and for one other very short period—I rubbed her legs, until the end.

XXIX

All these things I thought about in front of the Library. Suddenly I couldn't wait to return here to this dismal room so I could write it all down. Why did I rush away from the sunny afternoon to write down this foolishness? What has this to do with my present purposes? Some men's natures unravel when they face death. I do not want to be such a man. But let me repeat—what we call puppy love, what we remember as the self-important illusions of childhood, remain as safety valves, so to speak, in our consciousness that must be kept open—a little—or we become men like Hirsch: politicians and diplomats. Diplomats rearrange the past to suit their temporary goals. Their inner lives—the ground for their deepest perceptions—are pure mud. An historian is a man who must discover the past by recovering what it was like to be particular people alive in a certain time. What better technique for staying alert than continuing to remember the bits and pieces of his own previous history? A true historian is interested in much more than the decisions of prime ministers and the moves of generals.

XXX

The four years between 1934 and 1938, when I did little else but read books, prepare for examinations, and take care of Malkele, were the best years I have had—equaled only by my courtship of Inge in Paris while I was ferreting out bits and pieces of our plundered collections. There were also my visits to my cousin Samuel. Samuel was very strong and his brilliance always startled me. Beginning in the spring and lasting almost until October, he always took his shirt off during the summer afternoons on his roof. His body was the color of bronze. He had hair on his chest and even on the backs of his shoulders. In all of Vilna there was not a boy more muscular than Samuel, or more resourceful—Jew or gentile. He knew how to heal the broken wings of pigeons. He knew how to embrace a girl—he always knew just what to do. Best of all, Samuel trained a pigeon to carry messages back to the roof.

"Wait here," he would tell me, "this beauty will soon fly back to you with an interesting message." Off he would go with the bird. Fifteen minutes later or an hour later the bird would fly over the roof and land on the top of the coop. I would remove the tiny can from its foot and pull out the message. Samuel's messages were always very dramatic.

"There are three Jew-hating bullies here by the Talmud Torah on Gdanska Street," he once wrote. "I am about to take care of them. I will see you shortly, Samuel."

When he returned he had only a few scratches on his face, and he told me in great detail just what he had done to them. Hershele, I remember thinking, would have cried and begged them to let him be. I wondered how I would have responded.

The most dramatic message that he sent to me with his carrier pigeon he sent years later, in the fall of 1937. I was visiting him less frequently that year. I had graduated from the Yiddish Gymnasium in June and had started at Stefan Batori University. Samuel was already working as a chemist. Malkele was that year in constant pain, especially in her legs and her fingers—yet she forced herself to practice the piano and she had begun to give lessons. Mother was home with us and Father traveled a great deal to tiny villages where he stayed for days at a time in the simple houses of peasants while he cut and sewed garments for all the inhabitants. I was by then a member of a Communist youth group and Samuel was a leader in the Labor Zionists. He was glad to see me that October afternoon in 1937—I had seen pigeons circling over his roof and I climbed up to wish him a happy birthday. He wasted no time telling me to wait for a message. When the bird alighted on the coop, I loosened the tiny can and removed the message. It read, "Tell your sister that if she let herself stop hating me so much for just a second she would fall in love with me—as I love her." When Samuel returned, we did not say a word about it to each other, but I knew that he knew I would deliver his message to Malkele. I wanted to choke him. The only man that my obscure heart

permitted Malkele to be touched by was Ben. At the same
time I wanted to embrace him with the happiness that suddenly overflowed throughout my body. And what of Ben? I
knew Samuel to be a force that could not be stopped. Malkele would meet her match in him. And what of me? What
of my woeful heart? I would be lost without her. Did he know
about her arthritis? Of course he did. His parents must have
talked of it often. Samuel would not let such a thing stop
him. In any case I felt honor-bound, as they say, to give Malkele his message.

That evening, without a word and with dread in my heart,
I handed Malkele the piece of paper. I had often in the past
told her about Samuel and his carrier pigeon. I watched her
read it. Malkele never mastered the art of the poker face. She
turned red and her lips curled into a frown, then into a smile,
then—though this time I could see her force herself—once
again she began to frown.

"And what of that loose woman, that Esther?" she demanded. "What of her?"

Though I managed to leave out the more brazen details, I
had told her about the time I spied on Samuel and Esther
embracing on the roof. I could keep few secrets from Malkele
in those days. Many times she asked me to tell her about
Samuel and Esther embracing. Every time I told her she became angry. Once she slapped my face. She also knew, for
example, that I loved Rivka. She knew how hopeless that love
was—Rivka had been promised to a wealthy cousin of hers
who lived in a town fifty miles away. There was nothing
Rivka could do about it—nor I. Rivka knew it was bravado
when I asked her to run away with me—what would become
of Malkele without me? I knew Malkele would never marry
Ben, no matter how long he waited for her. He was more like
a brother. I was more like a man to her—was that how I
wanted it? But now there was Samuel and suddenly I felt as

though I were Ben—and I vowed, though in futility, to defend his interests.

"Tell him that if he wants a response he must teach his pigeons to fly to my window—no, tell him he must come here and tell me to my face what he wrote on this piece of paper." She folded the paper into quarters and then into eighths and put it into the pocket of her dress.

"So it is true."

She glared at me and said nothing.

"What about Ben?"

"Ben is a child—and swear to me you won't tell him anything of this."

This time I glared and said nothing.

"Swear," she almost screamed.

I kept my silence.

"Swear," she whispered slowly with forced deliberation.

I swore because I could see how agitated she was becoming. Every time she grew so agitated, her legs would begin to ache even more and her fingers would involuntarily turn in like claws.

Before a month passed, however, Samuel suddenly married a woman from his Labor Zionist club. She had become pregnant and Samuel did the right thing by her, as they say. By that time he had started coming daily to visit Malkele. Every day now it was Samuel who rubbed her legs and then her fingers, as he spoke in a quiet voice, but rapidly, of the wonders of a pioneer life in Palestine. He told her how the hot dry desert air would flow in over their kibbutz and would relieve the pain in her fingers. He told her how her responsibility on the kibbutz would be to teach the piano to the children and to perform on the Friday culture nights—and how she would earn money for the kibbutz by her performances in the concert halls of Tel Aviv and Jerusalem. Every afternoon for those four weeks she sat huddled on the sofa, covered with blankets, warming her hands under a lamp while she slowly caressed her fingers, one by one, so she could play for Samuel when he came to our house in the late afternoon. Her eyes burned and grew narrow and focused with concentration. She could still break my heart with the Fourth Prelude—but I knew she would never be a concert pianist. Now she always started her small concerts with "Hatikvah," which she made me sing, along with Samuel and her. Even Mother joined us for the singing. Mother, too, loved Samuel's visits. She made tea for them and her eyes, like Malkele's, beamed with desire.

The day after I gave Malkele the message I gave Samuel her answer. That evening he came to the apartment. He faced the chair where Malkele sat, held up his arm, and the carrier pigeon he had concealed inside his shirt flew with a breathtaking flourish across the room and perched on Malkele's arm. She pulled off the tiny can but her stubborn fingers couldn't pull out the piece of paper with the message. She stamped her foot, threw the tiny can to the floor—the pigeon fled back to Samuel's shoulder—and her face darkened. We stood dumbfounded. I knew that her fingers were about to curl and tighten in agony. Before I could run over to help her, Samuel bounded to her side, knelt, lifted both her hands to his lips, and kissed each finger. I was sure she would slap him across the face, but she didn't. Instead she emitted a small giggle and her lips of their own volition curled into their widest clown smile. He picked up the tiny can and, guiding her fingers with his own, they pulled out the message. After she read it, without a word she reached into her pocket and handed him a message that she had prepared beforehand. He actually blushed when he read it, and then the two fools, she sitting, he kneeling, smiled directly at each other for more than a minute. They looked up at the sound of the door closing when Ben left, but she took no notice of his absence. Malkele had experimented to get the note just right. Among her things I discovered a neatly folded sheet of paper with almost the same message written a half-dozen times—first in Yiddish and finally, though haltingly to begin with, in Hebrew. "Before you leave me this evening," it read, "we will know, with our souls and with our bodies, if I am to be yours forever."

It was true that Samuel had made the woman pregnant a month before and didn't know about it until a month after he sent me to Malkele with his first message. What good did that do? Between the rheumatoid arthritis and the sudden rupture of her passion for Samuel, a deep permanent furrow appeared overnight on my sister's forehead—and she was not yet sixteen. It was a vertical furrow that ended between her eyebrows and seemed to divide her face into two sections. From then on she was a tragic clown. I resumed rubbing her legs, but I could have been an elderly nursemaid rather than the brother she had possessed for so many years—body and soul, so to speak. Ben again started to come over, but not so often. Rivka was being prepared for her wedding. Mother lived by then in a world of her own—as far as we knew, she thought Samuel was simply an attentive cousin who was now making an impressive match. Father came back from his visits to the countryside fattened by the bread and potatoes of his peasants—but his heart was growing more and more threadbare. Except when she gave lessons, Malkele never sat down at the piano. In one moment, Chopin and "Hatikvah" were banished from our lives.

XXXI

It is too late to call Hirsch again, or Ellen Meyers. When I called this morning, again she informed me that Mr. Hirsch was not in. Then, after a moment's hesitation, she said that there was no way she could help me.

"What is your name?" I asked.

"Why?" She asked with great hesitation.

"Simply so I know what to call you in the future."

"Ellen." Her voice sounded relieved.

"And your last name?" I continued.

"Meyers. Ellen Meyers. O.K.?"

"O.K.?" I mimicked her. "What is so O.K.?"

"Mr. Solomon, there is no way I can help you. Please understand that."

"Are both your parents from Poland?"

"Yes."

"You are a child of survivors, no?"

"Yes, but why are you asking me?"

"Do you belong to a group?" I went on.

"Mr. Solomon, why are you asking me these questions?" Her voice was angry.

"Please, Miss Meyers, answer my questions. You are Miss Meyers, are you not?"

"Yes, that is my father's name. I am not married."

"Do you belong to a group of children of survivors?"

"I did, but I left it."

"Why?"

"It seemed too . . ." She paused, looking for her words. "Too self-congratulatory."

"Do you think so?"

"Yes, Mr. Solomon, is that O.K.?"

"O.K.? It is fine. I agree with your assessment. My son belongs to such a group—I am a survivor of Auschwitz, you know." I could not believe I had said that to her. She said nothing in response.

"Hello."

"I'm still here, Mr. Solomon."

"My son—" I continued talking because hanging up seemed suddenly beyond my power. I was beginning to crumble again right before this young woman, but I simply could not terminate the conversation. "My son belongs to such a group in New York. His group leader tells him that he is haunted by the Holocaust. He told him that it would be better if I, his father, spoke openly with him about my experiences—'The Auschwitz Experience.' I could lecture under that title to his group. He would be proud of me. I could tour America lecturing to children-of-survivors groups."

I could hear her breathing on the other end of the telephone. Was she impatient? I could not stop. You might say it was a filibuster.

"'And who is your group leader?' I said to my handsome son. He is, by the way, a handsome boy, just twenty-seven, not much older than you, I imagine. And he said, 'A psychologist who is himself the child of a survivor.' 'A psychologist who is himself the child of a survivor, is that right?' I was making sure I heard him accurately, you see. 'What is wrong with that?' he asked. 'And what is wrong with being haunted by the Holocaust?' I asked. 'It depresses me,' he said. 'It depresses you?' I repeated. 'Yes, it depresses me,' he said. 'Life is not a joke, my son,' I informed him. 'Look,' he shouted, 'why can't you just talk to me? And don't tell me to read your articles.' That is what he said to me. 'And why would I tell you that? I know that you do not read Yiddish. Of course, we could have them translated into English, or maybe even into German.' 'Now, look,' he shouted. 'Look, Father,' I replied. You see, he has avoided calling me 'Father' since he was a young boy. 'Oh, shit,' was all he could say to me. 'Ask your mother,' I said to him. 'She has talked to me. She came and spoke with my group.' 'Yes,' I said, 'about the "Bergen-Belsen Experience."' 'Stop it,' he shouted. 'Stop it, Father,' I shouted back. 'You are no father to me.' 'Too bad your *Uncle* Ben is

dead. He could speak to your group about the "Maidanek
Experience," and then perhaps your psychologist can ana-
lyze just exactly in what way a son is haunted whose mother's
boyfriend is a survivor of the Holocaust. He could start a new
group for children of women who bring male survivors into
their bedrooms.' 'Fuck you, bastard-bitch,' he shouted so
loud all my colleagues could hear him, and then he rushed
out."

There was silence. I no longer heard her breathing.
"Why—" I was now shouting—"don't you write down my
number. Tell Hirsch that number 69636 tried to reach him."
I could not stop myself. She was listening to me as I
crumbled. "A rather interesting number, no? Notice the three
sixes."

"Mr. Solomon."

"Hello."

"Mr. Solomon, I am here—why are you saying these
things?"

"Ellen, may I call you Ellen?" I said quietly, trying to col-
lect myself. My throat hurt.

"Yes, you may, Mr. Solomon."

"Do you know why I am trying to reach Hirsch?"

"I think so."

"You know a thing or two about my present difficulties."

"Yes, I think so."

"You do know, don't you?"

"Yes, I do."

"Thank you, Ellen, for your truthful answer. Now let me
ask you if I have any chance of reaching Mr. Hirsch at any
time?"

"No, I don't think he will speak to you."

"Is he in his office right now?"

"Yes."

"Is he listening in to this conversation?"

"No, I don't think he is."

"Are you not positive?"

"No, I am not positive—but I don't think he is."

"You are a brave and bright young woman, Ellen."

"I certainly didn't expect this job to turn me into a good German."

"That is very perceptive and kind of you, Ellen. What will you do about it?"

"I have given my notice."

"Will you give me Hirsch's home number, if I ask you? It is not listed, you know."

"Yes. I know it is not listed."

"Will you give it to me?"

"Yes, I will. Do you have something to write with?"

"No, don't give it to me now. Think about it. If I want it, I will call you before you leave today."

"I said I would give it to you. So why don't you take it? Why do you keep testing me?"

"It is not that, Ellen. I am not sure that I want it. I am not sure that I want to continue thinking about Hirsch at this particular time. Do you understand that?"

"Mr. Solomon."

"Yes, Ellen."

"Be nicer to your son. He wouldn't have spoken to you about his group if he wasn't searching for a way to draw closer to you."

"Thank you, Ellen. And Ellen, there is no need to quit your job over this. Good jobs are hard to find. Hirsch is simply protecting the Collection."

"Stop driving me mad."

"In his position I would do the same thing."

"I wouldn't." Her conviction was actually quite moving when she spoke these words.

Now it is too late to call Ellen Meyers again—unless I wait

until Monday. Perhaps I should wait until Monday. Why not? She will grow sick of me. This time she said good-bye so softly—and soulfully, as Fulani would say. No one has said good-bye to me in just that way for many, many years. In the early days, before she regained confidence in the future, Inge would whisper her last good-bye every time I left the apartment. Now that it is the Sabbath and the prostitutes are beginning to station themselves outside, perhaps I will put on my new Ray-Bans again and go out into the darkening street and find a dark lady and pay her to say good-bye to me properly—but money cannot buy what I heard in Ellen Meyers' voice, thank God. Still, it is no simple journey I will take on this Sabbath. I need all the good-byes I can get. If I had a radio, I could listen to Fulani tonight—I could even go down to the phone and have Professor Lewis Schorr take leave of her. Surely she would give him a proper good-bye. But what of Leon Solomon? I can call Emmanuel. If Inge answers, I'll simply hang up—I've done that enough times to her. Why is he still living with his mother, a young man of twenty-seven?

XXXII

Will I never reach Hirsch? Can I simply leave it at that? I must think it through. Certainly he knew that they had me under surveillance, but clearly he was not the one who originally tipped them off. It would not have been in his interest. The librarian deduced it. He saw a pattern—years of complaints by other scholars of missing pages, almost always, he noticed, in volumes previously called for by Solomon. He called the police and voiced his suspicions. As many times as I've gone through this in the past three days. I've been stuck with the same question. Why did I make it so easy for them by always sitting at the same table—in the same chair, even?

A man who permits himself the luxury of sitting in the same spot in a public place every day is a man who has grown too comfortable in this world—turning himself into a sitting duck, as it were.

In Warsaw I would never have sat in the same place twice. If one day I sat at a table in the late morning in the near end of a café, the next day I sat at a table in the late afternoon at the far end of the café—and the third day I would already be in another café, where I also had business to attend to. I was careful not to follow an easily discernible pattern. I remembered carefully and I improvised.

All they had to do was train a hidden camera onto my end of my table and wait for 12:30 on a Monday or a Tuesday or a Wednesday, when I always showed up. They even knew that I always left at 4:30, in time to walk back to the Institute before it was locked up for the evening. Detective Sawyer could go on coffee breaks or set his watch by me. I had turned into a German. I had begun walking backwards without knowing it—just like the others. All the time I was living with the illusion that I still knew how to look back over my shoulder. There was a time when I knew what I was doing. When did I lose my edge? Sawyer even knew how to get more out of me than I needed to give him. Why did I lead him back to the apartment and give him the other pages? I told myself I was protecting the Institute—they would see that this was a one-man job, as they say. But really, I lost my nerve. I had forgotten how strong the desire is to ingratiate oneself with a particular authority—as though he will then protect you. I had forgotten the simplest of rules—never volunteer real information. The police understand this need the perpetrator has to ingratiate himself. The smart game is to use that expectation against them—with subtlety, of course. The trick is to volunteer plausible and extremely false information—to send them on tantalizing wild goose chases, to lead them to commit themselves fully to a route that will eventually lead them nowhere. The trick is always to play for time.

All I have against Hirsch is that he didn't warn me—but even there I was a fool not to have anything that I could use, so that it would have been in his interest to warn me immediately. Could it have been my affair with Kristin Dietrich that had so loosened my grip on myself? It would have been so simple for Hirsch to warn me. I refuse to continue thinking about him, and about his American wife, and his two sons and a daughter, and his secretary. Will the foolish girl really leave her job? I wonder how often Hirsch has made a pass at her? Perhaps she has succumbed to his persuasive enthusiasm? Perhaps right now they are in the office. Everyone has left the building. She feels compromised, a little, but flattered by his solicitous attention, and even a little consoled by his reassurance that nothing terrible will happen to Solomon. She wants to linger, but he must hurry—Mrs. Hirsch has organized a late-evening dinner party at a delightful new spot that specializes in nouvelle cuisine. And Ellen will eat alone in a cafeteria on Harvard Square, hating herself for being such a fallen young woman. If I had had a daughter instead of a son, my life would have been a drop sweeter.

XXXIII

I admit I was confused when they arrested me. Like one of those who had scraped out the eyes of his mind, I stopped thinking. I simply handed them my briefcase. That I would have had to do, in any case—but it is all a matter of psychological edge. When they took me to the precinct house, Sawyer immediately started asking me about the Institute. Had I brought any of the Library's property to the Institute? Over

and over I repeated that when I returned to the Institute I
never took those pages from my briefcase. Where did I take
them, then? Did I take them to my apartment? I simply nodded. Ironically, I did keep from telling them where I sold
those pages. Strangely, however, they never asked me. I insisted that I merely took them home so I could study them
carefully. I kept mumbling that the Library closed too early.
I was almost happy that I had accumulated a number of
items because Hirsch hadn't responded to my messages. I
invited them to my apartment to see for themselves. I never
even called a lawyer. All the way uptown in the police car all
I thought of was Fulani's panties. What if Sawyer found
them? I became obsessed with the panties. I was humiliated
at the prospect. Of course, he displayed no interest in anything but the "stolen property." I don't know whether he noticed the panties. He said nothing, but he is a sharp man.
When he received his piece in the mail today, did he immediately recognize it? In any case, I was so grateful to him for
not finding the panties that I congratulated him on being
such a thorough investigator. I told him that if I had to be
arrested I couldn't have chosen a finer man to arrest me. I
told him that I had always admired intelligent police techniques. I offered him a glass of cognac. He seemed amused
with me—underneath his words lurked a laugh. I can see
now that underneath the laugh lurked contempt. And why
not? I became the Jew he thought I was. But why am I here
now? Why am I fulfilling his expectations? He won't be surprised or even sorry. Can I remember exactly how I came to
this decision? Was it the shame of getting caught? Was it fear
of a court case and a prison sentence? I have, after all, served
enough time, so to speak. But these are not fully my reasons.
I will be banned from libraries. I will never again be permitted access to any of our collections. An historian must remain an active agent. His vitality depends on remaining

active, on never allowing himself to be forced to simply watch history pass before his nose, as they say, as he ages and withers.

XXXIV

Perhaps I pretended too long that I was an Émile Durkheim specialist.

"He wrote extensively about anomie," I lectured to Fulani's listeners.

"Come again, Professor," she demanded.

"Anomie"—I spoke with my nasal and sharpened German pronunciation—"a state of goallessness, rootlessness." I rose to the occasion, actually believing as I spoke in my authoritative, clipped German style that I was serving her listeners, so many of whom clearly suffered from anomie. "'A' means 'without' and 'nomie' derives from the Greek 'nomos,' which means 'law' as well as 'order.' For example, in 'astronomy,' which means literally 'star order,' the laws of astral movement." She let me go on when I began to lecture in this manner—impressed perhaps with my air of knowing and certainly giving me enough rope to hang myself.

"So you are saying that this rootlessness comes from a lack of laws?"

"In a manner—and a lack of arrangement and order."

"O.K. Now translate."

"Simply, I mean a lack of purpose, given the absence of order. Many people suffer from this, and it is a dangerous state, often leading to suicide—particularly in the summer, as Durkheim demonstrated so well in his monumental work. . . ."

"Can whole groups of people have this affliction?"

"Precisely—large segments of black people, for example,

suffer from anomie. Anomie can be produced in whole societies by depriving them of cohesion and purpose. The Gestapo was expert in creating this phenomenon. The young man who called earlier, who said he never bothers to look at himself in the mirror except in the morning when he washes his face and combs his hair, he suffers from anomie. Every week he calls and every week he sounds listless. Of course, the fact that he calls so faithfully means that he is not totally resigned to his affliction."

"Like you, Professor?" She asked in a quiet voice. She had never spoken to me so directly before. I chose to ignore her question, but I was so shaken I almost fell into Yiddish.

"The important thing for this young man is a project—but a project connected to something larger than himself. His people, for example. You, Fulani, are an example of a person who has refused the magnetic pull of anomie. But here let me caution that the project cannot be one of vengeance. Vengeance does, it is true, provide a person a goal, a purpose, an identity—it provides law and arrangement to a man's life, if you will. In that way vengeance can even save a man's life— but it destroys his personality, and leaves him eventually with a more severe anomie—do you follow me?" She said nothing. One of her cleverer radio techniques was to say nothing, letting her caller move on ahead or begin to stammer and contradict himself. I continued lecturing.

"I repeat. Vengeance is not a proper project. Nor is any sort of violence to others—such activities will leave him even more bereft. Bereft of himself. When the young man said he felt like the man in the film *Taxi Driver*, he was identifying with the main character's sense of mission. His exact words, and I jotted them down, were, 'I saw this movie on TV Sunday, *Taxi Driver*. That's how I feel too, like that guy. It gets a little violent, it might turn your face away, but that's how I feel, like that guy.' The main character, as I learned in sub-

sequent discussion, turned his rootlessness into an obsession
with killing evil. This will not do. It is a form of spiritual
suicide rather than physical suicide—there can be no destiny
worse than that. I know of what I am speaking. I was a victim
of such phenomena on a grand scale in the 1930s, when the
German nation started down its path of spiritual suicide."

"Like Israel today, Professor?"

"It is unworthy of you, Fulani, to inject Israel in this way
just while I, a Jewish survivor, speak of Nazism."

"If the shoe fits, Professor."

"I am not speaking of shoes. What if I said that blacks who
mug innocent and rather helpless elderly people are no different from the government of South Africa, for example."

"So you admit that Israel mugs its Palestinian population?"

"Fulani, we snarl at each other like two starving dogs over
a single bone—while the master laughs."

"Why do you avoid any discussion of Israel, Professor? You
talk, talk, talk about everything under the sun but you won't
talk about Israel."

"Why should I talk about Israel with a Jew-hater?"

"You are baiting me. I never said I was a Jew-hater. I only
happen to believe that Palestinians have rights. You do remember the importance of human rights, Professor? If Beethoven and Bach can be part of a conspiracy to deprive you
of your dignity, why can't I speculate whether or not you are
part of a conspiracy to deprive my Palestinian brother and
sister of their dignity?"

"Fulani"—I stayed in my German accent and controlled
the passion in my heart—"you are speaking foolishness. Of
course I worry about Israel's treatment of Palestinians living
on the West Bank. I worry about what occupation is doing to
Israeli, to Jewish, consciousness. Yes, I do worry that we may
be forced to commit spiritual suicide. But understand that we

are the only people who have not yet committed such suicide. And by the way, Fulani, Palestinian men and women are not necessarily your brothers and sisters. Many are certainly racist. Did you know that?" She seemed to want to ignore me, so I stopped speaking and waited.

"Professor, has it occurred to you that you yourself are spreading anomie through these radio waves?"

"Do you want me to hang up?"

"I didn't say that. If you want to hang up, hang up. If you want to keep speaking, you may do so for another minute or two. Then I want to play some music. We need it."

"Let me end with a theory. It is a simple theory. It explains Germans and black nationalists and, yes, many Israelis—at the same time. All men are in the military. I might add, all men except a significant proportion of Jewish men, but you will object, so I will leave that out. All men are in the military. Some think of themselves as generals, some as colonels or majors, others as captains. Many think they are sergeants. Of course, the overwhelming majority see themselves as simple foot soldiers. There are three types of foot soldiers. The largest group are the bent ones whose eyes look down at the ground and they, of course, beat their children. Then there are those who strive and strive to become corporals and maybe even sergeants, if they are lucky. 'Yes sir,' they say, 'yes sir'—and they become taskmasters, mean sons of bitches, as they say. The third group are those who become rebels, as most of your callers are."

"I like to think so."

"But even the rebels, my dear Fulani, are trying to rise in the ranks."

"That's a rather cynical thing to say, Professor."

"It is the truth. And their way of rising in the ranks is to replace the army with another army, where they are the generals. If they had only dreamed of becoming sergeants, or even captains, they never would have rebelled."

"Are you saying that even revolutionaries don't want to get rid of the military?"

"Oh, of course not. We have always loved the military."

"So you're saying you don't care about oppression. You don't care about hungry children. You don't even care about genocide. You don't even care about your own people." She was impatient, but strategic, and therefore content with herself.

"Yes, we care a little, but that other, the lust to rise in the ranks, is much greater in us." And then I whispered the words that finally upset her. "We use even the little caring we have inside of us as stepping-stones. That is my theory. It is simple and almost universal."

"Even our caring?" There was almost, for a split second, a plea in her voice—perhaps I imagined it.

"Even our caring, Fulani. I know what I speak of," I whispered, feigning and yet not feigning a certain hopelessness.

"But what of the women? The women have never been in the military?" She snapped, punishing my serpent's heart.

"The women, my dear, are our only hope."

"Do you support the women's movement?" She snapped again, demanding a response.

"Support the women's movement? Why should I do that?" I could not pull back from my folly.

"Because, Professor, you just said they are our only hope."

"Hope is no concern of mine."

Why Fulani welcomed my weekly telephone calls I'll never know. But she did. She treated me as an expert—though it is true that she often used me as a foil after I hung up. She often mocked my words, seeing in them proof perhaps of the decadence of white people—of Jews. Many of her callers imitated my German accent—an imitation of an imitation. All night I would lie in my bed, my nostrils breathing in her fragrance and my brain drowsily dancing to her curiosity about Professor Lewis Schorr.

When she persisted in demanding that I tell her why hope was of no concern to me, I proceeded to invent for her a Christian wife, who was named Inge. A proper name, after all, for the wife of a German Jewish Professor.

"My wife died eleven years ago, Fulani. I have been left all alone since then. Inge was an angel. She took care of me and she taught me to care again about the world." I made no reference to my time in Auschwitz. I simply went on as though they all knew that. I knew no one would interrupt to ask. "Most important, Inge made me feel that I didn't have to rise in the ranks. I loved her more than I loved becoming a sergeant, and that love spread into other corners of my life. I cared more to understand Durkheim than I did to be the world's foremost Durkheim specialist. I didn't see it with such clarity then, but I do now. . . ."

"So how can you say that human liberation from the military cancer is no concern of yours?"

"Because she left me. Do you understand that? She abandoned me." I was suddenly truly touched by my own words—and all the listeners could hear that. "She was in great pain. I tried to help her. She said, 'Leave me alone, you filthy Jew.' Those were her last words."

"Thank you, Professor Schorr," Fulani whispered after a pause where I am convinced I could hear her breathing. "Now I'm going to play some music."

If she hadn't called me "Professor Schorr," the moment would have been perfect. Fulani, I suddenly sensed it throughout my body, was whispering in her most intimate voice, to me—in a moment when I was truly bereaved over my loss of Inge, and God knows who else. What if she had

shifted to "Leon" at that moment? She did, I am almost convinced, know who I was. I would have wept openly and lux-
uriously as Leybele Solomon, in full hearing of Fulani, in
full hearing of her numerous black admirers, in full hearing
of her loyal contingent of young Jewish men who fervently
wished her dead. And maybe, just maybe, as they say, I
would not now be in this terrifying predicament. Why did
this speculation pass just now through my mind? I do not
know. Why did I refer to my predicament as terrifying? I feel
no terror—just yet.

I have twenty-four phenobarbitals and a bottle of bourbon—a combination that should prove as deadly, I am told,
as a basket of asps. They will assume that Werner Heisenberg was simply a lush. The prospect of drinking the bourbon
continues to gall me. A Jew is not a man who drinks himself
to death. The phenobarbitals are more appropriate—to
simply fall asleep of ennui and dream oneself out of this life.
It is likely that this poison was invented by Jewish chemists.
Samuel was not the only Jewish chemist I have known. There
was a man in Warsaw in the early days of 1940. Perhaps the
phenobarbitals are enough—twenty-four is a rather large
dose. But I cannot take a chance. The first swallow of bourbon should feel good. Even the second swallow. Soon my
stomach should be empty of this morning's meal. I feel enor-
mously hungry just now.

Fulani played one of her favorite pieces—"A Love Supreme," by the saxophonist John Coltrane. Over the past year
I had grown quite fond of it. I often discovered myself humming its melody—sometimes I even discovered myself singing the repeating phrase—"a love supreme, a love supreme,
a love supreme, a love supreme." In Yiddish, of course. I felt
honored that she chose to play it at that particular juncture.
Professor Lewis Schorr's cup had run over, as they say. Leon
Solomon, alias Werner Heisenberg, was left chastened and

breathless and enveloped by her almost completely dissi-
pated bouquet.

XXXV

The best time was the Friday night meal in the years before Mother and then Malkele became ill. Starting when she
was still a baby, Malkele loved being Mama's little assistant,
as they say, when Mother lit the candles and made the Sabbath blessing. In her last years, when she lived in Warsaw
with me, Malkele continued to light the candles every Friday
night and chant the blessing with the voice of a world-weary
angel. But in those early years the two of them, mother and
daughter, sounded truly like angels—though Malkele soon
became a little devilish. In the beginning, whatever Mother
did Malkele did. Then she began to do more—she varied her
chanting a touch, creating a kind of harmony, an echo that
haunted Mother's sweet traditional singing—just as Malkele's green eyes, in which the flames flickered, highlighted
the poignancy of Mother's rich brown eyes. Father and I
never interrupted or attempted to comment on their constantly varying duet.

Those Friday afternoons I helped Mother prepare the
meal. I loved cooking when I was a boy. I haven't cooked a
real dinner in many years now. In the early years of my marriage, and again in the years following Emmanuel's birth, I
often prepared the Friday night meal. I tried to teach Inge
my mother's Vilna recipes for carrot tsimmes, potato kugel,
and gefilte fish, but she never quite achieved the correct
taste. Inge is a gourmet cook. Her leg of lamb is simply su-
perb, but her brisket is too dry. Her candle-lighting ceremony is also gourmet. She holds a lace kerchief over her
head—it looked to me that each week she had a new one.

The words are the same, but the sound is different—a foreign sound, classical, operatic, European. Did she light the candles tonight? Is Emmanuel home with her? Where else would he be? Has he tried to call his father? Are they worrying?

Soon she will have yet another occasion to light a candle.

This is almost the anniversary of Ben's death. She can light two memorial candles at once—and let their flames dance on the refrigerator, side by side. Ben and I will be in the same cemetery—only three streets apart, as they refer to them here in America. He can be found on Maimonides Boulevard, and I will be located on Spinoza Street. If she steps carefully, so as not to disturb any graves, Inge can simply cut across two courtyards of Vilna Jews and place a pebble on my gravestone whenever she visits Ben. My pebbles should accumulate as proudly as his.

A year ago I visited Ben's grave. I counted twelve pebbles on his monument. Ben left no one besides Inge and Emmanuel. I am sure all the pebbles had her fingerprints on them. I added two more—one for Malkele and one for myself. Would Inge notice and wonder? The wind cannot add a pebble. There is still a plot reserved for Inge and me. We are not divorced. Will she find a way to be buried next to Ben? Will Emmanuel have the nerve to put her there? More power to him. In less than a year she will send the boy a significant signal. Will she have the will to buy a single stone for my unveiling, rather than the more economical and imposing double stone, half of which will shimmer blankly like a mirror a few more decades? Do they have queen-sized stones? King-sized stones? Stones for three? Enough! I will get more than I deserve.

While Mother and I were busy cooking, Malkele played the piano, preparing for her Friday evening concerts, for Father. On Friday afternoon the three of us were alone.

Malkele's friends were in their own houses helping their mothers. Soon the fathers would arrive home. But now the gefilte fish cooled in its juice, the tsimmes and kugel simmered with a piece of meat in the oven, the chicken slowly boiled in a broth. Malkele was playing her heart out. After dinner was her recital, as we called it. To our applause she would enter the parlor in her white Sabbath dress and curtsy smartly. She would seat herself with the poise of a beautiful woman. She would announce the name of each piece with the accomplishment of a professional. Everything she would play she played by heart, just like Artur Rubinstein. Her teacher, Mr. Gordon, always said that if only he had Malkele's long, graceful fingers he would have been a great master, giving concerts in Vienna and Saint Petersburg. He always said "Saint Petersburg," as though he lived still in the old Russian Empire. We called him Saint Petersburg—a name I invented one evening to amuse Malkele and it stuck to him. Malkele loved him and found him funny. He was very stout and his shirt collars always curled up. Before she was ten she was already well beyond him. When he stayed for tea, in the years that Mother was well, he drew pictures for his star pupil. Malkele forgot them after he left, but I put them all in a box to save. My favorite one was of an elephant rearing up on its hind legs, in deadly battle with an enormous serpent that had wound itself twice around the elephant's body and faced its fierce tusks with its terrible fangs. I named it "Saint Petersburg and the Serpent."

The Moonlight Sonata was Father's favorite and Malkele, who adored him, always ended her concerts by playing it. Except during their mysterious and charged female ceremony on Friday night, Malkele and Mother were never very close. She was always Daddy's little girl, as they say. I hated it when she wound him around her little finger. I hated him even more the few times he became angry with her. I could have stuck a knife into his heart one time when he smacked her on her behind. She was so shocked and humiliated that she became hysterical and ran to the piano and pulled the top down on the fingers of her left hand. Her own reflexes saved her from a terrible self-mutilation. She pushed her hand in and the top came down above her wrist, doing no damage. I was the only one who saw that. Both Mother and Father thought she had broken all her fingers and Malkele did nothing to disabuse them. Mother screamed and dragged Malkele to the sink, yelling to me to run to get Dr. Szabad to the house immediately. Father was beside himself. His face whitened and he stood in the middle of the room wringing his hands. I felt a great sorrow for him then, but I could say nothing. They would not have believed me if I had spoken. I left the apartment and stood outside in the courtyard. When I returned, Malkele was sitting on Father's lap, comforting him. Mother said it was a miracle that her fingers were spared. Malkele knew that I knew. She winked at me over Father's shoulder. Her green eyes flashed, daring me to betray her.

But on Friday evenings such things never happened, even when Mother was on the edge of a breakdown. She lit the candles and chanted and looked peaceful and even motherly all evening. Only in the period when Mother was away did Malkele take charge of the blessing. When she finished her concerts we always applauded and shouted "Encore, encore." Malkele always obliged. Each week she played a different small piece, often one by Chopin. The piece that remains clearest in my memory, however, because it was practically the only piece she continued to play the last year in Warsaw, was Ravel's "Pavane for a Dead Princess." She would play it slowly and painfully. Her fingers struggled to solemnly announce her forthcoming virgin death.

During the meals Father would speak to us of his week's

doings. Though he spent his days and often his evenings in the back of a fashionable shop on St. John's Street, altering women's dresses and coats, he was an active listener, as well as an avid reader. He knew always what was going on in the world. And he knew many of the secrets that the rich Polish women talked about as he fitted them. But the times I liked best were when he had returned just in time for the Sabbath from a week of sewing for the peasants. He smelled always from the smoke of a wood fire—and he would look scrubbed like a peasant boy. He was filled with stories the peasants told him and with new songs. He taught them Yiddish songs and they taught him Lithuanian and Byelorussian songs. Mal-kele always wrote down the words and notated the melodies in her school pad. From the time she was eight she knew how to transcribe music. By the time she was twelve, we had quite a collection in the apartment. She could have become a first-class ethnomusicologist—of the stature of Béla Bartók, a national treasure. Even with such a painful disease as rheu-matoid arthritis racking her body, she could have become a great collector and composer, cross-fertilizing, as they say, the Jewish and the peasant folk sounds.

I tried to preserve Malkele's notations of the folk melodies of the peasantry of northeastern Poland, as they called it then. But they were seized later by the Warsaw police when the Gestapo was informed that I was a Jew and not the Cath-olic Pavel Witlin, an expert employee in a small bookstore on Świetokrzyska Street, recently expropriated from Jews, of course. My identity had been switched with a dead comrade whom I had never met. Leon Solomon, Jew, was now offi-cially dead. Malkele's new papers identifying her as Maria Witlin were a pure forgery. I was informed against by the janitor of the courtyard where Malkele and I—as Witlins, of course—had rented a small apartment. The man's wife heard Malkele lighting the candles one Friday night. She must have concealed herself in the hall outside our door. Isn't it ironic that that was exactly how she would have thought to catch Jews—in the act of celebrating the arrival of the Sabbath? Malkele the rebel who often cursed God for her fate, Malkele the apostate who once when she was twelve stood calmly before the City Synagogue on Yom Kippur and ate an apple—it was that night that Father smacked her—Malkele the solitary sister who had no one's love but her brother's, Malkele the tragic concert pianist with twisted fingers who knew more about German and Polish musical developments than about Jewish religious traditions, Malkele the ethnomusicologist who in a most precise fashion recorded the words and the music of the Polish peasantry, Malkele whose socialist mother lit candles only as a concession to her sentimental husband—this Malkele, this baby sister of mine, was responsible for our downfall because she insisted on her right as a Jewish woman to light the candles and bless in her throaty voice the newly born Sabbath. And I, who otherwise traversed like the true professional the alien boulevards of Warsaw, even stopping occasionally, like any other Catholic, in the large cathedral—was it on Marshalkowska Boulevard?—as I spent my days buying guns and smuggling them to our boys in the ghetto, I had not the will nor even the desire to forbid her this perilous activity. By that time Malkele obeyed me when I insisted, but I never then said a word.

The janitor blackmailed me dearly—and in the end he turned us in. Perhaps his wife nagged him into his betrayal. I should have foreseen that he would eventually do precisely as he did, but what choices in any case did I have? It is interesting that the man's daughter, a sixteen-year-old Polish patriot to whom Malkele had given a few piano lessons without charge, came that morning to the bookstore and warned me of her father's intentions. I ran home but I was too late. The janitor himself, innocent creature that he was, met me at the gate to the courtyard and warned me not to enter. He told me that Malkele had been taken away by the Polish police.

"They carried her out like she was a royal lady—on a chair. She waved good-bye to my wife and commanded the collaborators like they were her private servants. A royal lady." I can still see how his half-closed eyes opened toward me for a second when he referred to the Polish police as collaborators. When he finished speaking he smiled sadly at me, as though he felt my fate, and waited expectantly for me to question him further. I knew he was stalling because he expected the police to return at any moment, but I also saw that at the same time he meant what his lips said and his eyes expressed. Central European Christians have always enjoyed the humiliation of their shameful behavior, and a consoling empathy has grown in them, like a cancer, toward the Jews they revile and betray.

I didn't tell him that I knew of his perfidious role. I shrank away, as though in slow motion, holding him frozen in place with my eyes, and I disappeared and saved myself—temporarily.

Though I tried desperately—I was possessed with the idea—I wasn't able to rescue Malkele's careful copies of the folk songs, nor her own compositions, nor the many volumes of her diary. I waited near the shop where the janitor's daughter worked. I told her exactly what boxes to look for and where they were in the apartment. I had thought it through with that special clarity a fugitive is graced with, and concluded that the girl would not betray me as her parents had. She didn't. When we met later that afternoon on Matejki Street, she told me that the boxes were no longer in the apartment. She had also searched the room in the cellar where her father had concealed some lamps and other small items he had stolen from us—but the boxes were not there. The Gestapo must have carted them off. For years after the

war ended, I searched for any remnant of Malkele's work—I
have found nothing. I advertised in newspapers in New York,
in Paris, in Tel Aviv, in Warsaw—nothing. I have given as
detailed a list as I could pull from my memory to every Jewish archivist in the world. Nothing has surfaced. Somewhere
something may exist. If anything does surface, Hirsch will
probably gain possession—the diaries alone would be a tre-
mendous capstone to a great career. He will be the first specialist to edit the most intimate of details of my family's life.
No doubt he will dedicate his introduction to my memory.

The girl gave me a gold watch she had taken from her
father's pocket, an inheritance from his father, and a silver
crucifix that she had taken from their bedroom wall, an inheritance of her mother. It was only fitting, she told me, that
I use these things in my attempt to buy Malkele away from
the police. The girl I was able to locate after the war. She
returned the stuffed mouse, Poopikle, that I had given her as
a gift. She said she had kept him safe for me. I wrote a short
article about her brave attempt to help. She is now an influ-
ential member of the Communist Party hierarchy.

I was able to warn the others in the bookshop on Świetokrzyska Street. They immediately abandoned the shop and
set up, I have no doubt, another front for their operations. Of
course, they abandoned me as well. My sister was taken. I
was wanted. I was no longer in a position to be trusted, and
I could not count on them for any help. The Communists
were scrupulously careful, as they had to be. Would they
have demanded back my gentile identity if it hadn't been
tainted? I discovered that the Polish police had handed Malkele over to the SS. It took a great deal more to bribe the
Germans than I had. If I had had a fifty-pound sack of
smoked sausage and had moved before sundown on the following day I might have been able to save her—temporarily.
During the next two days I did see Malkele again—on six-

teen occasions that I shall never forget. Even beyond my death I shall remember. In the very cells of my body decaying in the grave these memories will remain—locked for eternity into the atoms themselves, that never decay. Even beyond the Apocalypse they will lie buried, waiting for God to acknowledge His responsibility.

When the Communists abandon a man, they do it thoroughly. Even my good friend and working partner Josef Kleuzewski dropped me like a hot potato, as they say here. I hadn't thought of him in over a decade until recently—until, to be precise, I became suddenly interested in Fulani. Then Josef began showing himself in my mind. But why? Why Warsaw? The first time I enveloped myself with the panties alone in my apartment I knew the answer. It was in Warsaw in October of 1939 that I first entered the apartment of a gentile—and I encountered the smell of patchouli. Josef had taken me for dinner to the apartment that he shared with his brother and sister-in-law—another proof of my new identity. He introduced me, of course, as Pavel. Perhaps the sister-in-law used patchouli, though I associated the odor with Catholicism. I was interested, I remember, that the apartment had so many pictures of Christ. Even Josef's bedroom had one—was it just part of his cover? Once I made the patchouli connection, almost a year ago, my own apartment never again felt entirely Jewish. Though to inhabit always a world that is not totally Jewish is, of course, a basic Jewish occupation.

There is but a single photograph of Malkele that survived the Holocaust. It was taken for the Yiddish daily *The Vilna Times* before her first public piano recital when she was eleven. In 1953 I had two reproductions made from the Institute's copy of the newspaper. One was eight-by-eleven, which I framed and kept on the wall to the side of my desk. When I cleared out my office on Wednesday morning, I took the picture from the frame and left it right on top of the filing cabinet. On the back I had glued a photocopy of the caption that appeared under it in *The Vilna Times,* as well as a photocopy of the date, "20 September 1933." "Malka Rachel Solomon," it reads, "serious eleven-year-old pianist performed publicly for the first time last night. She played sonatas by Mozart and Beethoven for a highly appreciative audience of family, friends, and music lovers. Her teacher, the well-known pianist Itzhak Gordon, predicts that Malkele will make her mark on a world scale. Not only is he arranging recitals for her in Warsaw and Cracow, he informed us, but also in such distant centers as Leningrad, Jerusalem, and New York." The reporter clearly took his liberties with the words of our beloved Saint Petersburg. I also stamped "Property of the Jewish History Institute" on the back. By leaving it so, I can rest assured that Malkele's picture will enter the archives of the Institute and be there for another to wonder at and study one day.

The other, a wallet-size copy, I have kept with me for thirty-two years now, transferring it faithfully when I've changed billfolds. I am looking at it now.

The child is wearing a long black dress (the color I remember, of course) to highlight her green eyes. Her black-reddish hair, which I myself had brushed and arranged earlier that evening, is swept up into a bun—soft and lush rather than severe—and tied with a bright red ribbon. She is posed sitting at the piano but turned sideways a drop, towards the camera. Her hands are poised over the keyboard. You can see each one of her supple ill-fated fingers. She is looking right into the camera, as the photographer must have demanded. He got more than he bargained for, as they say. He must have told her to smile because she is scowling, her eyes bristling with scorn and with pride at the same time. A few loose hairs have fallen in front of her eyes. She has her pursed lips a little to one side as though she is about to blow on the loose strands.

Both Father and Malkele were angry with the picture. Malkele said the paper was purposely making fun of her—simply because she was a pupil of that clown, Saint Petersburg. Father said nothing, as he didn't want to inflame her any more than she already was. I can't remember that Mother voiced any opinion at all, though I saw her weeping silently during the slow movement of Beethoven's "Pathétique"—perhaps it was only in gratitude that Malkele had refrained from playing the "Moonlight." I myself loved the picture. It looked exactly like Malkele and, more important, it reflected her awesome defiance. I am looking at it now. What should I do with it? Whosoever receives these pages, let him also be stunned by her beauty and torn to pieces by the immense waste. I loved her more than my life.

XXXVI

When a man avoids bringing up a painful subject, he is assuming that there will be time later. I must talk right now about the death of my sister, Malka Rachel Solomon, aged nineteen, in the late morning of July 12, 1941, after two days of agony.

There was a certain man, a pharmacist, who lived also on the Aryan side with a father who had rapidly grown enfeebled after the Nazi occupation started. Like me, this man smuggled guns into the ghetto, though he worked with the Zionists rather than the Communists. I am withholding his name because I am about to reveal his darkest secret (but not so dark as my secret), a secret that, except for me, he took with him to his mass grave. I sometimes visited him in his apartment to talk. He spent most of his evenings there because he could not leave his father alone too long.

He began to talk to me of his plan to poison his father before the Nazis took him. Nothing but indignity and certain painful death awaited Jews who were in any way enfeebled or handicapped. He paused when he said the word "handicapped," for he knew what I was thinking and I knew that he had planted that thought. If I believed in the supernatural, I would say that at that instant the spirit of Malkele flew between us like the shadow of a passing night-bird thrown in against the wall by the lamplight outside. This man whispered to me of a substance that would kill painlessly. If he gave it to his father at night, in a glass of tea with milk, the old man would simply fall asleep and not wake up. Of course, he could not be buried in a Jewish cemetery—those days had vanished forever. He would have no choice but to abandon him and disappear. Still, better to leave the dead body of his father for the authorities to bury than to allow them to take his father's life in whatever sadistic manner they chose.

"They will be even more brutal with your sister," he suddenly said—which is precisely what I was thinking when he said it.

A current of electricity passed between us. These terrible crimes would fuse us through all eternity. Within two days he would have enough poison for both of us and on that night, we agreed, we would act.

The next morning, when I helped Malkele dress, she saw right away that I could not look directly into her eyes. When I wouldn't tell her what was wrong, she began to scream at me. Was that when the janitor's wife first started spying on us? Malkele accused me of detesting her because she was a terrible burden. She accused me of desiring to desert her for

a Polish woman who could save me and give me what I
wanted. The following morning, the morning of what I
thought would be our final day together, she only smiled at
me when I couldn't look into her eyes. She had me help her
put on her finest white dress, which she usually wore only on
the Sabbath. What had she figured out?

That evening my friend poisoned his father—may they
both rest in peace. But I could not poison Malkele. Again she
smiled tenderly at me when I helped her bathe, and again
she put on her finest nightgown. I told her another install-
ment of my ongoing story when I massaged her fingers and
legs—a story she found funny, of how Poopik cut off Hitler's
mustache with one sweep of her knife and then, as he stood
there naked and shivering, she cut out his heart, without
mercy, and threw it to a pack of dogs. Our stories then were
filled with retribution. But I could not put the poison into the
hot milk. She seemed to be almost disappointed when she
woke up the next morning and found that nothing had
changed. The next three nights I tried to commit the act.
Every night I prepared the milk and the third time I went so
far as to put in the poison but I spilled it down the sink. I
simply could not kill my sister.

It was because she had grown so crippled that the Warsaw
police handed her over so quickly to the Gestapo—before I
could buy her back. She was among a group of very old Jews,
small children, and cripples, whom the Nazis decided to brutally beat and leave to die slowly in the hot sun and the cold
nights on a public square beside the Saxon Gardens at the
edge of the Ghetto. They did it to instill terror in any Poles
still harboring Jews.

It took Malkele three days to die. I saw her lying there on
the cobblestones. Her face was crushed. I could do nothing.
The square was surrounded by troopers. I think I even heard
her once, but I could not tell whether she was whimpering or

humming. It is a peculiarity of the human mind that it invents what the ears may not have heard—and then does not let go of its invention, regardless of how often you may command it to stop. Over and over those three days—and at odd moments on each day since then—I found myself humming Ravel's "Pavane for a Dead Princess." Just now I was humming it. You must understand that I am not demeaning my sister's final agony by telling you this. I am simply giving an accurate account.

I left and returned sixteen times those three days. I couldn't stay more than a few minutes. There were plainclothesmen everywhere, Poles as well as Germans, and they would soon figure out that I was a Jew. I did see her dead body. Two Poles were about to throw her into the back of a truck already half-filled with corpses. I saw her fingers sticking out beyond the man's grip. Her miraculous fingers remained twisted, even in death.

Sabbath Eve

XXXVII

I stood looking from the window a long time. I cannot tear Malkele from my mind on this the eve of my departure. I watched three young women—children still—waiting on the street corner. Their long brown legs were made even longer by mini-skirts and high heels. They paced and chatted. They shifted their weight from one naked leg to the other. With each passing car they provocatively thrust their pelvises forward and looked up, their expressions, for a split second, filled with fright when their faces were caught in the glare of the headlights. I was struck by how much they resembled three deer startled from their grazing at the edge of a highway by a passing car, their elongated but supple legs their only defense in a world of predators. Before she was thirteen, Malkele had such legs. By the time she was a young woman, arthritis had deprived her even of that meager defense.

In her last year in occupied Warsaw I began to bathe my sister again—just as I had when she was a child. Every night, after she moved in with me, as I continued the saga of Poopik, I rubbed her legs. Occasionally I would receive special notes from Poopik, in Malkele's labored handwriting, delivered by Poopikle the mouse, between whose gentle jaws I'd find them lodged. "It is unsafe to stay out after dark," or

"Don't forget that tomorrow is your sister's eighteenth birth-day," or "I forbid you to grow a mustache." One evening I received a note that read, "The time has come, Leybkele, for you to resume bathing your baby sister." After I rubbed her legs, I filled the tub with warm water. Malkele came into the bathroom with a thick towel wrapped around her. Without a word between us I undid the towel and helped her into the bathtub.

Every night after that I carefully soaped Malkele from her long graceful neck down to each and every toe. Though her limbs were atrophied and her spine bent slightly backwards, her small breasts remained girlish and as lovely as her face. Soaping Malkele, slowly, gently, quietly, became for us our kaddish for our obscured childhood and for our dead mother and father. This soaping was our only defense against the looming Nazi death machinery. During the day we longed for those few moments of slippery tenderness. My own muscles craved it as much as hers.

Yes, yes, we were, after a fashion, Malkele and I, lovers. But we obeyed the final taboo—we never, to be cold and German about it, fornicated. I washed her hair. She still cursed and threatened me. I soaped every inch of her body. I caressed her pointy nipples with the palm of my hand. I dried her and helped her into her nightgown. I carried her to her bed. I brushed her thick reddish black hair in the candle-lit bedroom. Once she whispered to me, "To what are Chopin's Preludes preludes?" and I kissed her. Sometimes, after that, I lay with her. We kissed each other's lips and we embraced, but I never entered her. That restraint, which I adhered to religiously—Malkele, I am sure, would have welcomed me, though even she was never bold enough to ask, either di-rectly or through a message from Poopik ("Malkele is ready to experience her womanhood," it could have read)—that re-straint of mine was a crime against my doomed sister. I consider that lack of defiance against the Nazis, and against God too, if you will, my gravest sin. That is what I should have confessed to when Detective Sawyer interrogated me.

If we should omit these most private details from the historical record, there is no way to appreciate fully the richness of life for two young Jews, surviving temporarily, with false identifications as Pavel and Maria Witlin, on the Aryan side of Nazi-occupied Warsaw. I watched the three girls for almost an hour before one, and shortly afterwards a second one, drove off with their buyers. Then I watched the third one for more than another hour. Now that she was alone, she stepped back into the shadow of the building. The cars passed without even slowing down. I ached to go down to her—but how could she receive what was then in my heart? She would simply have considered me a degenerate and impotent old man if I brought her here merely to slowly massage her long grief-stricken legs. I continued to watch until she walked off with a slight limp, alone, into the darkness of East Twenty-eighth Street.

Late Sabbath Eve

XXXVIII

Again I stood looking for a time. The girl was nowhere to be seen. Was she sitting, defeated, in the back of a bar somewhere in this neighborhood? Would she dare return to her room so early with no earnings? I would be foolhardy to search for her now. Perhaps she does have the capacity to see what I need from her. What do I need? Certainly the janitor's sixteen-year-old daughter—against all historical odds—met me with courage and clarity. I had never been more than remote when I passed her in the courtyard, or suspicious, hostile even, when I encountered her in the dining room playing Malkele's piano. Yet she did, for example, retrieve one very significant personal item for me from the apartment. Unless she had eavesdropped on us, she was a very intuitive girl. She brought me the remains of Poopikle the mouse. The Polish police had torn him almost to shreds, pulling out his stuffing, clearly searching for jewelry—prizes all Poles assumed Jews possessed. It may even have been the janitor himself—or more likely, his wife. "This was all I could find that might mean something to you," the daughter told me. "I am so sorry." Ellen Meyers reminds me of her.

In the days after Malkele's death, when I should have been moving decisively, finding my way down to Lodz, perhaps, or

up north to the partisans in Rudnicki Forest near my home,
all I did was sit in the small piece of a room I had rented
from an aged Polish baker—for the price of one of the two
items I had inherited from the janitor's family. Luckily it was
the gold watch rather than the silver crucifix I gave him, or I
would not have had the time to stitch together the remaining
shreds of Poopikle until he was a whole mouse again, criss-
crossed with seams and scars, but whole. Sitting there sewing, across the room from the baker who spoke occasionally
of his son, a corporal in the cavalry, and now a prisoner of
war working in a labor gang inside Germany, I felt like my
father among his peasants. Many times he asked me to read
the one short letter he had received from his boy. He said his
eyes were weak. It is more likely he could not read. One more
time I waited for the girl, just a block from the apartment. I
asked her to accept the reconstructed Poopikle as a gift—it
was all I had. Again, with her youthful, straightforward intuition, she asked me if the mouse had a name. I blushed
when I told her. She said she was delighted with her new
companion, and that one day she would return him to me. I
had not even a picture of Malkele and every time I tried to
picture her with my mind the image of this girl, Maria, flickered before my eyes. Even now I can't bear to write her family
name. Though I trusted Maria, I didn't tell her where I was
now residing, or what plans I had. She didn't ask. Two decades would pass before I saw her or Poopikle again.

Of course, I could simply ask nothing of the girl. I could
approach in the darkness of the bar and give her cash, discreetly of course—twenty dollars, or fifty, maybe even a hundred. Without a word I would retreat, leaving her sitting in
the darkness, glowing with an emotion she had forgotten existed in the world. Why do I fool myself so? She would take
me for a particular kind of crank who would return to exact
his price. Still, there remains with me more than three hun-

dred dollars in cash. Why should I leave it for Detective Sawyer? I am sure he is not incorruptible. If only I had a boxcar
filled with sausage.

I was now cut off even from the slim network that remained. I was on my own, as they say—and I was rapidly
becoming a walking dead man. With Malkele's death, which
I did nothing to forestall, I simply ran around in a useless
panic, I became my father after the suicide of my mother. It
is the supreme irony of my life that my incarceration in
Auschwitz saved me—first, by putting me back with other
Jews, and second, by reawakening in me my sense of purpose
as an historian. Living with the baker, I was disintegrating.
After a few weeks he told me that he needed another item of
value from me. Perhaps he thought I had an inexhaustible
supply of gold watches. I gave him the one valuable possession I had left—the janitor's silver crucifix. It was a deadly
mistake. If a Jew was going to present a silver crucifix to an
illiterate Polish baker in Nazi-occupied Warsaw, he might as
well have tossed all caution to the winds, as they say, and
baldly bragged of his intimate knowledge of German women
to a German official in Gestapo headquarters. Where did I
get it? the baker wanted to know. How did he know I was a
Jew? Poles know. They are bloodhounds when it comes to
Jews. The tailor sitting across the room from him stitching
was my father. If I had hummed Yiddish melodies as I sewed,
the picture could not have been clearer. Should I have told
him that it was a family inheritance? It was all I had, take it
or leave it, I hissed at him. I knew I had not managed to
intimidate him.

The following morning, before dawn, I disappeared from
the baker's rooms. I was convinced that the Polish police
were about to come for me and hand me over to the Gestapo.
Now I was completely alone in the streets, in a city of hunt-
ers. Should I appeal once more to the janitor's sixteen-year-

old daughter? How could she save me? Could she hide me in her father's secret storeroom, among all the boxes of gold he had appropriated from my apartment? Should I quietly slip into the Ghetto, to starve, to grow diseased, but to hear, at least, a sentence spoken in Yiddish? In truth, after what was done to Malkele, I could no longer bear even the sight of Warsaw. Should I attempt to travel home to Vilna? Without Malkele, that was impossible. Besides, what could I do there, the only one left of my ill-fated family? Return to the university and resume my studies of history? No. Better a new beginning. Better to go south—to Lodz? Perhaps I could make it to Lodz.

Somehow, after days of walking and hiding, I managed to reach the city of Lodz, where I was stopped by two Jewish policemen who spoke the first Yiddish words I had heard since Malkele was taken from me. They turned me over to the Gestapo, who were engaged in a roundup of Jews—perhaps I helped fill a quota (I have written about this phenomenon elsewhere)—and the Gestapo delivered me finally to my own people again—to Auschwitz. There were even a few familiar faces from Vilna in my barracks. What roundabout way brought them there I never learned. A Jew who was young and strong and lucky stood a slight chance of staying away from the gas. Was I one of the lucky ones? I could have been spared more than forty years of bad dreams and failures, but my son, my son Mennele, would then never have been born.

XXXIX

Why didn't I poison Malkele? I have tormented myself with this question countless times, particularly in the days after her gruesome death and again in the years since I left

Inge. I never spoke with anyone about it, not even with Inge
when she was my life's companion. Even during those years
when I was permitted to let that question sink into oblivion—
a temporary oblivion—it remained active in its own way. In
Auschwitz it was a vital component of my secret agenda that
kept me working—absorbing to the best of my strength the
beings of the men around me before they disappeared. Afterwards, it entered my articles between the lines, so to speak,
adding a tension to the lucidity of my style—a combination
that many have found penetrating, as they have told me. Perhaps it was an urgency to escape the renewed attack of that
question, in the years after I left Inge, that drove me to begin
taking pages home—to study.

Why did I start to sell them to Hirsch for sixty-five dollars
a page? Would you believe me if I told you I was accumulat-
ing a substantial sum in order to make one last effort to locate Malkele's papers, if they still exist, and purchase them?
I could still do it. I could take the money and travel to Israel
as Lowy. The sum is not yet large enough—it won't get any
larger now. Still, I could do it. You believe this explanation?
But not entirely? You remain skeptical? I cannot be accused
of stealing to support my affair with Kristin—that is what
Hirsch would immediately conclude, but I met her long after
I started trafficking with him. Perhaps it would be useful to
ask that question differently. How could I have sold them to
Hirsch? How could I not? How could I, given the history of
our collections and the retrievals that have made my life useful and bearable, not have begun removing papers from one
temporary storage terminal and shifting them to another?

Why didn't I poison Malkele? Just as I did not have the
moral fiber, as they say, to commit incest, likewise I did not
have the moral fiber to commit fratricide. For these two sins
of omission, to borrow Christian terminology, I deserve to
burn in their Christian hell eternally. I remain convinced,

given my intimate familiarity with the German obsession to file all documents, that Malkele's papers still exist—and will resurface. Even without me, her compositions will be performed one day in piano competitions. Her Byelorussian folksong notations will constitute a significant contribution to the field of ethnomusicology.

XL

I thought also of Inge when I gazed again into the dark street. It has become nearly impossible for me to remember her naked body in all its particularities, without also seeing Ben Schwartz possessing her. Parts become quickly blurred. Only with the greatest concentration can I eliminate Ben from the picture and see again her upturned nipples, for example, those long succulent nipples I loved so much to taste and lick. If for a moment I should try to move my focus to her flat belly or her resilient globes, Ben reappears and takes possession once again—and together, his hands pressed to her belly, his groin to her buttocks, their faces smiling, they fade away from me. For a short period last April, without any attempt on my part to conjure her image, Inge came again before the eyes of my mind—as she looked when we were first together in Paris after the war. To what did I owe this dangerous gift? To nothing less than the sudden presence in my life again of Miss K. Dietrich.

The Bulgarian janitor told me she had returned, but I didn't see her. Every evening for a week I hesitated when I passed her door—once or twice, you might say, I lingered there, unable to knock. One time I spotted the Bulgarian watching me. When our eyes met he smiled, in triumph so to speak. I planned and even rehearsed a few opening sentences. "It is time for us to plant new seeds." What if she didn't remember? I made sure that my sleeves were rolled up, lest she had also forgotten who I was. "Is your floor as white as you left it?" I could hardly picture what she looked like, but my mouth watered. I did remember vividly the sides of her plump breasts and the miraculous twist of the hair between her thighs. My mind had reconstructed her face into Inge's—but with blonde hair. Why was I permitting myself such foolishness, such illusion? This is a mistake, a breach in discipline, my brain insisted. Wasn't my life full enough, what with my work, my dealings with Hirsch, my nocturnal affair of voice and nostrils with Fulani? Even the super laughed at me. "You have continued to blossom, Miss Dietrich—grandly." This was my pièce de résistance. Would she recognize the two allusions?

I even bought a small bottle of Joie de Patou: in twelve years its price had risen from sixty-five to one hundred and forty-five dollars. I would have it to give her at the appropriate moment. Though, at first, I imagined spending time with her in her immaculate apartment, I prepared my own. Or, at least, so I thought. I swept the rug. I hid Fulani's panties at the bottom of my underwear drawer. Twice during that first week of waiting I put clean sheets on the bed. I read and reread her postcards. I reconstructed my previous encounter with her. Kristin, it became clear, specialized in dramatic entrances. I knew that she would come to me. All I needed to do was to prepare myself and wait.

I opened my windows to air out the apartment. On Monday I went to Macy's and bought a new type of electric fan, with blades of blue plastic that spin silently. I wanted to rid the apartment of its lingering staleness. I also bought a bottle of after-shave lotion by Ralph Lauren, the finest and most intriguing, so the salesgirl assured me. Also a pair of black silken sheets and pillowcases—to create a fitting contrast to her Nordic brilliance. The first three nights she did not come.

I put the white sheets over and under the black ones when I went to sleep, and shook out the black ones each morning to keep them fresh. I left Fulani's panties in the bureau, though I had grown very attached to them. If Kristin had not come by then, Friday would be the acid test, as they say. Would I be able to resist Fulani when her voice came to me through the night air? Looking back, I think if it had been Fulani whom I awaited, I would have been more excited. She would have been, after all, a healthier match for me. Her understanding of power is similar to my own. She need not be innocent to be good. She would claw and kill for those she loves, yet her nature is wonderfully suspicious and bitter. She remembers everything. Her aristocratic spirit is so fierce, she reminds me of Malkele. Her body is more mysterious than Kristin's, darker, yet more direct—the black fuzz on her mound leaves her more naked. How often have I felt my lips, my nose, my cheeks, luxuriating there, wetly, her clitoris exposed to my tongue licking tenderly in small circles? Perhaps if it were Fulani who had come to me, I would not be in this room tonight. Together we would be searching the historical record for all links between African and Jew. Together we would fill the airwaves with our findings and bring an end to the growing hatred between the Jews and blacks of New York City. But it would have taken much, much longer than I have for Fulani to come to me. I would have been smarter to expect a Martian. As for the giant ravishing German—she I knew would come.

XLI

Why was I so confident? Of course, I am not unattractive. My full head of curls contrasts neatly, as they say, with the lines on my forehead. A woman would find my green eyes

dignified by the crow's feet around them. My old suits, which
I bought in Paris, still fit me. I have kept them clean and
always pressed. The elegant double-breasted coats and the
pleated pants have become the latest style again. Soon my
son can begin to wear them—to his late-night soirees with
the other liberated children of survivors. They will admire
the luxurious feel of the material and the classy European
lines. I imagined stepping out with Kristin to fine French res-
taurants just as I had with Inge, on two occasions, thirty-
seven years earlier in Paris. I knew all along it was not my
dignified physical charms but my elegant numbers that
would bring Kristin to me—certainly, however, my appearance would not violate her Freiburg sensibility.

True to my intuition, on Friday of that second week, at 10
p.m., two hours before Fulani was due to come on the air,
Kristin knocked. I was sitting in my armchair waiting. My
black shoes shone like glass. My gray pleated trousers were
sharply pressed and spotless. It was too warm to wear the
coat but my white shirt, the fourth one I had worn that week,
was freshly starched. My sleeves were rolled up and I wore
no tie. Why was I so warm? It was still April and my windows
were open. I held a book written in French in my hands so
she would not think I was simply waiting. The Joie de Patou
sat on the bureau in its ribboned gift-wrapping shaped by the
salesgirl to resemble a flower. All that happened after she
entered was like a dream of love being performed on a stage.

Kristin came to me dressed all in white, just as she was
when I first saw her. She took off an elegant jacket and hung
it up in my closet before she said a word.

"I have decided to come to you." Why was she wearing a
cabaret-style hat, a top hat, over her upswept hair? I could
play the same game.

"Take off your boots." We both spoke with quiet intensity,
like two performers confident of our parts but neither of us

knowing the other one's next move. She lifted a leg to me. I went over and pulled off one boot, then the other. Even in her bare feet she was half a head taller than I.

"What next?" she demanded.

"Unbutton your blouse and give it to me." She obeyed. I folded the blouse carefully and placed it in the top drawer of my bureau.

"Now your skirt." She unbuttoned her short pleated skirt that hardly covered her long legs and let it drop and stepped out of it. I lifted it and hung it in the closet, on the same snap-on hanger as my other pair of French trousers.

She stood before me with nothing on but her matched white and delicately flimsy brassiere and panties. I could see the outline of her broad nipples and the slight rise of her mound. Her blonde hair remained swept up under the black top hat. I looked her up and down, as they say. My mouth was dry. I saw that she had makeup on her face, making her complexion very white. Her bright red lips matched her long fingernails. Was she about to sing? Only the fishnet stockings were lacking. Still, my mouth was dry. Still, I felt a weakness in my knees.

Kristin smiled suddenly, truly like a pale angel, so to speak, and undid her bra, which was hooked in the front, and let it fall behind her. Her nipples were wide and light in color. Then she lowered her panties past her hips and slowly down the length of her slender legs to her feet. Her mound was almost as blonde as the hair on her head. Her curls were not so wiry as Inge's—soft they were, and moist, and ending just as I had remembered in a slight twist. Had she prepared herself so beforehand? Or was it the natural inclination of her nether curls? One foot stepped out of the panties and with the other one she lifted them up to me. I plucked them from her toes with my two hands and pressed them to my face.

In private, I have thought about these few moments numerous times, though I am not positive I have not embroidered my version. The odor of her white panties was so sweet and female, so intoxicating, it was all I could do to keep from weeping. Why weeping? Two years ago I took a bus by myself to the White Mountains of New Hampshire. I stayed two days in a tourist house in the village of Franconia. The first night I walked for miles in the blackness along a dirt road— though I held a flashlight in my pocket. I stepped into a field where there were no houses, no lights, and I looked up. I had not seen the sky so brilliant with stars since I was a young boy and the four of us—Malkele was just emerging from infancy—took a short holiday in the Ponari Woods outside Vilna. The Lithuanian sky was stitched with stars, each one distinct, a being shining and flickering in the blackness, yet eternally interwoven among themselves, like the Jewish people to whom my baby sister had just come. I wept a long time that night in the White Mountains, unseen by any others. My heart was lighter than it had been since I was that boy in the Ponari Woods, since before Mother became terminally distraught, since before Malkele's fingers twisted into claws, since before Father began carrying his obscure defeat in his heart like a tumor.

For a moment, with Kristin's panties pressed to my nostrils, my mind was flooded with the taste of Inge—as she was in Paris the night we became lovers—and my soul was grateful to this Teutonic giantess, and in the very nuclei of my body's cells I lusted as I had not in thirty-seven years. Yet in the front of my brain—I can locate the particular spot, between my eyebrows but back an inch—was the question, Why was she giving herself to me? All these reactions Kristin saw. She reached her hands to my head and pressed the spot over the bridge of my nose with her thumbs and all doubt disappeared, temporarily. She removed her hat and shook her head. Her blonde hair tumbled forth, longer, longer even than I had remembered it.

"For you alone I have not cut my hair," she whispered hoarsely, like Marlene Dietrich, and enveloped me with her nakedness. "I am very, very wet, Leybele, for you," she hummed in my ear as her hands reached down to the buttons of my gray trousers. How did she know to call me Leybele? My suspicions were easily put to sleep by her arousing enchantments.

Very Late Sabbath Eve

XLII

By Hirsch's standards, Kristin Dietrich was extremely inexpensive. She wanted nothing more than to receive what she so desperately needed to give me. It was more than a question of guilt with Kristin. It was her creative instinct, so to speak. Her techniques were a reenactment of shame and debasement—but with the players reversed—and love. For Kristin did love me, purely, playfully, greedily, with passion. Her genius was her capacity to keep her arrogance and forcefulness intact throughout. Her goal was nothing less than our mutual redemption. It is impossible almost for a German to drag himself up from the slime of German history between 1924 and 1945, even if he wasn't born until a decade and a half later. Kristin's attempts were noteworthy and even touching. I could go to her even now, but she is more than I can afford. How could I permit myself to be rescued by the daughter of a Gestapo officer? In order for her to satisfy her hunger she would need me to treat her as her father treated one of his *Juden*. Even that would not work. If I wore steel-tipped boots and stepped on her face, she would still feel responsible—for turning me into a monster. Both of us would sink together, a double suicide, so to speak. She would turn into a Jewess, but with her hunger for shame un-sated and her German arrogance pushing her on to even lower depths. And what would I turn into? Still the love was sweet and nourishing. If only it could be separated from that other drama, a little, we could still . . . No! Some things are not possible.

XLIII

Before, when I spoke of Kristin's nakedness that first of three nights last April, I had to pause at the most dramatic moment in order to caress myself. I stripped naked and lay down on the bed and relived, after a fashion, a number of highlights of that first night. What does it mean that at this penultimate moment I had no trouble bringing myself to or-gasm? Shouldn't I reconsider my general plan? What does it mean that while I thought intently about Kristin, a picture of Inge, as she was our first night together in Paris thirty-seven years ago, wavered in and out of my consciousness—the way in the late night a distant radio station will slip in and out over the one you are listening to?

That night Kristin taught me how to love a woman again. After a time I began to whisper words of passion into her ear—in Yiddish. It was my voice, my Yiddish, more than my body, that brought out from her, over and over again, an ec-static womanly response, more intense than I have ever wit-nessed. Cheek to cheek we lay—sometimes I was on top, sometimes she was on top—whispering love-words. Like a deep echo, in her hoarse whisper, she repeated my Yiddish words back to me. She had hardly a German accent—she was better at it than Inge. Had she practiced? Perhaps she got it from her father who had mastered it, for the comic effect at Gestapo banquets, by mimicking his *Juden* or his

Jewish sexual-slaves. But then Kristin's passion was so forceful that these assailings did not have a chance to grip me.
Twice I had an orgasm that night. I remember them both in
detail—almost, even, the actual sensation. The first time was
in her body. "Leybele," she cried, "Leybele, come inside me,
Kind, kum." The way she said "come," in Yiddish, so sweetly,
so imploringly, softly, brought tears from my eyes, and for the
first time in nearly eleven years an explosion of semen from
my body into the body of a woman. I did not turn away from
her. The Yiddish kept coming from me as though I had not
had a soul to speak to for those same eleven years. Did I call
her Malkele? She never said a word about it even when I told
her of my encounters with Rivka. Little by little, I told her
almost everything those three nights together—like a young
boy I babbled and babbled. I almost spoke of Malkele's and
my deepest secret. To a daughter of an SS officer I almost
spoke of that sacred, intimate secret—but I didn't. Nor, of
course, did I tell her of my dealings with Hirsch. Though
perhaps I hinted at them. About my half-life with Fulani—
that was another thing. The second time, Kristin did to me
what Inge never would, what I could not convince Rivka, nor
even that shameless, talkative spirit Esther to do to me. Kristin received my climax, which to me felt like a flood, in her
mouth. That has become the third most popular in my small
repertoire of intimate memories when I relieve myself.

Why do I write so graphically of my encounters with Kristin? It is not simply my responsibility as an historian that
drives me to reveal such intimate details. I write this way
because it is all I have to offer myself, at this most crucial
moment in my life, of life itself. I have learned to take keen
pleasure in the products of my memory. Call it fantasy if you
like, I have taught myself to be a voyeur of my own past. That
has become my specialty.

XLIV

The second evening, Kristin came up carrying a large bag from the Red Apple. Had she come to prepare a late supper for two? I had a bottle of Beaujolais. Dinner candles I didn't have—a yohrzeit candle would do as well. She wore old jeans and a Columbia sweatshirt. Her blonde hair was loose, rippling down to her breasts. She could easily have been taken for a Barnard girl who has thrown caution to the winds, as they say, and embarked on her first Manhattan adventure. But why with a Jewish refugee past sixty? Why not? The needs of the psyche cannot easily be categorized. Certainly I was overdressed in my other pair of French trousers and an elegant shirt I had bought earlier that day from Brooks Brothers—with sleeves rolled up, naturally. The fan whirred silently in the corner of the room. I decided not to wear a tie, but I had shined my black shoes again. In truth, the discrepancy gave me pleasure. I felt like a million dollars, so to speak.

Kristin placed the contents of the bag on the table—all cleaning products. I watched her carefully refold the bag along its creases and put it in the cabinet under the sink. How did she know that is where I kept bags and miscellaneous items? Was there anything about me she didn't know yet? She held up a steel scrubbing brush and a bottle of PineSol for me to admire. Her face was suffused with that angelic look again. Still without a word between us, she started to clean the kitchen, scrubbing not only the stove, the sink, the floor, but the walls as well. I looked into the kitchen, watching her every move. She was efficient and vigorous. When she was on her hands and knees scrubbing the floor, I began thinking of the young German women who must have entered Auschwitz after the surrender to scrub it clean. Did they know a thing or two of what went on there? Just what were they thinking as they scrubbed, these *fräulein?* They must have used powerful disinfectant with just this pungent institutional aroma. How long was I transfixed, as Kristin labored, by a vision of my barracks now emptied and silent— except for a German woman who sweats to scrape away the top layer of its history? When she stretched forward on her hands and knees, the bottom of her sweatshirt lifted and the top of her tight jeans was pulled down, allowing me to see into the crack between her buttocks. Cold lust filled my being.

"If you want to continue to clean my rooms, Miss Dietrich," I said without planning it, "strip first and then clean." I spoke in my Lewis Schorr German accent. A cloud passed over her face. Her body quivered with rage.

"Don't ever talk that way to me." Her words were measured. Her voice was restrained. "Speak English your own way—or speak Yiddish—and I'll do anything you ask of me." She waited. I kept my silence. Slowly she undressed and tossed her clothes rudely into a pile at the entrance to the toilet. She looked like a sulking washerwoman gathering the last pieces of her young mistress's hastily strewn riding suit and underthings. For a moment her face looked coarse and thickened (like her mother's?), though a moment before when she pulled the sweatshirt up over her face the sudden sight of her springing breasts had jolted my loins. Then she started scrubbing the main room.

"Tomorrow I will do your laundry. Just keep writing your article on resistance in Vilna." She certainly had done her homework. She told me later that her first week back she had gone to the Institute and read all my articles available in English. The switchboard girl told her that I was presently in-

volved in a large project on resistance in Vilna. How come I
hadn't seen her at the Institute? Even that had a logical answer. She had asked where I was and Perl told her that I
worked in the main branch every Monday, Tuesday, and
Wednesday between 12:30 and 4:30. So now she knew even
my library schedule. Of course, I could do no work the whole
time. For hours I feasted my eyes, as they say, on this naked
German beauty scrubbing my bedroom and sitting room,
and my toilet. She worked in silence, fully concentrated on
the chores before her. I watched in silence, studying every
muscle of her body—the way her calves and thighs tightened
when she squatted, for example, the way her breasts lifted
slightly and quivered a moment when she flexed the muscles
of her arms to wring out a sponge, the way her buttocks
hardened and became slightly concave when she stretched
her spine, reaching to scrub the higher parts of the wall.
Once when I was looking at her breasts her nipples bunched
up and became pointed—how did she know where I was
looking? I could see right into her anus when she bent down
to wash under the toilet. She had a birthmark just to the left
of her tiny orifice that I resolved to kiss before the night was
over. I have one myself right in the crevice between my scrotum and my left thigh that Kristin had licked tenderly the
night before. I watched even when she urinated—she knew
my wishes and never closed the door to the toilet. I resisted
my urge to bound over to her and lick the drops before she
wiped herself. I felt twenty years younger. When she was
done cleaning she led me around the apartment by the
hand, proudly showing me her accomplishments. Everything
sparkled, as they say—the toilet water was now blue like
her eyes.

XLV

I am not a man without desire. I can summon up from myself—even now, in this deathly room—enough desire for many years yet of life, even for many different lives. Why have I decided that this will be my final Sabbath? My father went to his death a man with no desire left. If he had lived long enough to have got caught in the Nazis' net around Vilna, he would have taken his remaining steps in Maidanek or in Auschwitz, a walking dead man, one of the Mussulmen, as we called them in the camp. He was fortunate to have died in 1939, just a few months after our mother ended her life. He felt responsible for her condition. To my mind, Father was not responsible—Mother's Hassidim were. I never understood, though, why he agreed to send her back to Smargon, to them—not once but twice.

It is true that the first time when she returned to us she seemed better, a little. Of course, that she had abandoned her two children and her good-for-nothing husband for close to a year, albeit on her father's insistence, to grow chaste again and healthy among her own kind, became yet another sin they would not forgive her for. Poor Mother could not win, and her obscure sorrow simply retreated more deeply into her heart. Her returning health was no more than a mirage she created with which to buy a little more time—to pursue her mortality privately in her room, so to speak. Though Father slept there with her, the room in recent years had become Mother's tiny kingdom, where she spent as much time as she could manage to steal from her housework. Father tiptoed into it at night and slipped out in the early morning like a ghost. In the afternoons, when I often went into her chamber to visit her for a few moments, immediately I could feel how Mother had spread her resignation throughout its confines. I could picture Father edging along the wall in order to reach the bed. I could picture them lying in silence, back to back. Did Father immediately beg her pardon if the skin of Mother's back even grazed his as she tossed in her continuous half-sleep? Did he teach himself to lie there without moving a single muscle—not even to slap a mosquito humming behind his ear? For the sake of peace he submitted to her madness. He pretended with her that the mirage she projected was reality. Deeper in his mind I think he dwelled not next to Mother but with the young wife his memory had preserved.

The first time she went to stay with her father, Malkele and I were convinced that he would cut off her long black hair and she would return to us wearing a wig. Father told us not to be silly. Mother, he said, was an enlightened woman, a Yiddishist and a socialist like himself. She had once, he loved to remind us, spoken eloquently about the rights of women before hundreds of comrades. "A Woman"—he quoted her formulation of a then-popular concept among socialist women—"is not a cup of tea to simply sweeten and drink down and leave emptied and bereft on the kitchen table." His eyes at the same time burned and glazed over with tears when he spoke thus of Mother, his voice rising as though he himself were the young Basia at the lectern. Certainly it was not our almost entirely emptied mother that shone in his eyes. About her hair he was right. When she returned nearly eleven months later, we were delighted to see she still had her head of thick coal-black hair. Why do I use such phrases as "close to a year" and "nearly eleven months later" when I know precisely how long she was gone from us that first time—from the late morning of May 8, 1934, a Thursday, to the early evening of March 12, 1935, again a Thursday, three hundred and seven days and six hours, to be exact? Even with his high-minded proclamations about socialist women, Father was as relieved as we were.

XLVI

Both mother and daughter had wondrous hair. Mother's was coal-black and Malkele's was also black, but highlighted with red. For a short time after Mother returned, Malkele brushed her hair every morning. One morning Malkele went into Mother's room (without knocking, naturally) and left the door open. I stood quietly in the doorway and watched them—beyond Mother's line of sight, or so I thought. Except for their Sabbath duet, it was the first time in many years I had heard the two of them singing together. Mother was still a beautiful woman then—though her large brown eyes looked more fully open than they should have been. With voices of angels they sang of the joys of childhood in the summertime.

"You are so busy watching your sister brush my hair, you never take care of your own." Mother suddenly interrupted their singing to chastise me. She spoke with more intensity than the situation required. "Malkele, how could you allow your brother's hair to become so dirty? Just look at it. His lovely black curls are in knots." Malkele blanched at the anger in Mother's voice. I could see her struggling with her own rising anger.

"You are right, Mama. We should wash his hair right now." Miraculously, Mother responded almost joyously.

"Yes! Yes! Right now! Malkele, go heat up some water. We will make him shine. Leybkele, off with your shirt." What choice did I have but to submit?

The two of them washed my hair in a basin in the

kitchen—curl by curl, fondling each curl with tenderness. Then they combed, first in one direction then in another direction. They laughed and laughed—for a moment I thought it was Rivka who washed my hair with Malkele. They were deeply engrossed in their work. I pretended anger, wincing and frowning. In truth, I was angry—and worried. Mother had completely forgotten about school. Malkele and I were already too late for our morning sessions. Mother's joy was exaggerated, even strained—though she didn't know it. Malkele's joy was also exaggerated, on purpose. I must add that though the scene was overdone and even—as a harbinger— somewhat frightening, it was also, precisely because its exaggeration pointed to a soon-to-come end of all such moments, a precious and compelling morning among the three of us, lighthearted and even, you might say, happy. Malkele insisted afterwards that it was nerve-wracking and nothing else. Years later, in Warsaw, one night, we recalled that morning. Malkele admitted then that she too had found it intoxicating and complex.

More and more, however, Mother and Malkele began to ignore each other—except, of course, when they lit the candles. It was I who had taken care of Malkele when Mother was away—and when she returned she simply let this state of affairs continue. It was I, not Mother, who made sure Malkele was ready for school each morning. I made sure she practiced the piano and did her homework. Mother made the beds, swept the room, cooked the meals after a fashion—but mainly she had simply retired to her bedroom. Even during our dinners, while she listened intently, as though she was trying to memorize everything she heard to take back to her room and consider in her dreamy privacy, she kept almost silent. Except when she laughed. Malkele and Father (when he was home) always cleared the table and cleaned the kitchen together until it sparkled, as they say. It was their time—I kept away from them.

We were a family unlike any other in the neighborhood, but nobody knew it. The four of us were bound together with bands of fierce discretion and loyalty. What Rivka understood about us she never told me. Even when we embraced years later in New York, nothing she said revealed she knew just how totally I was both father and mother to Malkele when they were schoolgirls together. What Ben understood of my family he took to his grave with him—unless he spoke to Inge about it. Had they, as they lay together in bed some night, analyzed my relationship with my sister and blamed it for my erratic behavior as a husband and a father? About Warsaw Ben knew nothing except that Malkele was beaten to death. If I had been able to tell Inge what I have never told anyone, would she have deserted me right then and there? Taken her infant son and fled from the *Ostjude?* Perhaps we would still be together.

In the three years before she left us again Father reacted to his wife by constantly hanging his head and serving her hand and foot, as they say—though he was home less and less often. The only time I saw Malkele become enraged at him was once at dinner: he started to cut the piece of meat on Mother's plate into small pieces—just as he had years earlier for Malkele and before that for me. He did it without thinking. I remember he was in the midst of telling us about attacks on Jewish students at Stefan Batori University—I was particularly interested since I planned to attend the following year. "Were they other students or hooligans?" I asked. "They are one and the same," he replied, and simply reached across our small table and started cutting. Mother looked up at him, amusement crossing her face. It made me happy to see her so lighthearted for a moment. Perhaps it

was for me simply a diversion from the grim news. Malkele
reddened with anger.

"Stop it, stop it. How dare you do that, you fool."

The results were electrifying. Mother snatched the knife
and fork from his hands, leaving him nothing to cut his own
meat with. He slouched down in his chair looking stunned
and, I could see, fighting back tears. With a newly found
boldness Mother reached across with Father's knife and fork
and cut Malkele's meat. Malkele looked mortified, as though
she were seeing in her mother a complete maniac. Personally
I think Mother was exercising a subtle sense of humor. To
express my appreciation I reached across and began to cut
Father's meat. Malkele, to her credit, immediately changed
moods and also reached across and finished cutting Mother's
meat. Except for Father, who continued to sulk for a few seconds, we all started to laugh, an infectious laughter. As hard
as he tried, he could not resist our sudden mirthfulness. He
reached across, picked up Mother's knife and fork, and cut
my meat. He started to laugh—a high-pitched, nervous
giggle I had never heard before. In recent years I have discovered that very same laugh in myself, a sudden laugh of
short duration that comes out of me when I am alone—was
that Father's private giggle we were hearing? Soon the four
of us were snorting with laughter. We continued for an un-
naturally long time—we were terrified of the silence that
must follow. Though we never discussed it, Malkele and I
knew that Father had begun sleeping on the cot he had
placed crosswise at the foot of Mother's iron bed.

A few times my reflection intruded suddenly before my
eyes as I stood looking into the street earlier. My face appeared scornful, though in my heart there was a degree of
tenderness just then toward the girl in the street. The contrast startled me. Was that how I looked to other people?
When did this scorn implant itself so in my face? Was that

how people would remember me? I was overcome with silence, as though I were outside, gazing in, at Leon Solomon, as he stood, in a purple bathrobe, alone, in an alien hotel room, gazing out, at the darkness, on this, his final Sabbath evening—clearly a man who cannot say he has no regrets—as they say.

XLVII

I regret all. I regret the passing of each moment, even the most unbearable ones. I regret that I have not lived fully. I regret that I have lived at all. I even regret that I am writing these words. I regret that I have not the will to travel to Paraguay and smoke out Mengele and truly execute him. I regret, bitterly, that he will continue to live after I am gone, a free man back among his children and grandchildren. I regret that I did not rush down to the girl on the corner before she plunged into the darkness of Twenty-eighth Street. I regret that I never saw again the Vilna prostitute who shamed me—and saved me, on the train between Bialystok and Grodno in 1939. I regret that I ever called Fulani and debased myself over the airwaves—a caricature of a German Jew. I regret that I will not call her tonight, one last time. (Maybe I still will.) I regret that I did not perish in Auschwitz, a holy Mussulman. I regret that I have treated Emmanuel as Uncle Itzrak would have. I regret that I did not build a dovecote on the roof of my apartment building in memory of Samuel. I regret that Poopikle sits abandoned in my briefcase. (There is still time to do something with Poopikle.) I regret that I have abandoned Inge. I regret that I will not ever see her again. I regret that I have forbidden Kristin ever to talk to me again. I regret that I will not go to her at the last moment. I regret sixteen times over that I did not hurl myself past the armed guards and hold my dying sister in my arms. For a moment. I regret even that soon I will never see this desolate room again. I will never see the two brass spigots near the sink on the opposite wall. I will never see the sink. I will never see again the two mirrors that brought light miraculously from the outside world to me. I will never gaze from this window again. I will never again see the iron bed that I will lie in soon, my face to the wall. I will never again smell this particular mixture of urine, sweat, and decay. I will never again see Vilna. I regret that in less than twenty-four hours I will no longer be here to feel regret. Most of all, I regret that I will not have recovered my sister's papers.

Enough. Too many regrets add up to less than nothing.

XLVIII

The second time she went to Smargon, in March of 1938, I knew that Mother would never return to us. Father could not understand my dread, no matter how often I spoke to him. Perhaps he was relieved to get her off his hands, as they say. He would have listened to Malkele, but she refused even to think about it. She had started to ignore Mother more fiercely than ever before, after the fiasco with Samuel—she would not stop, no matter how high the stakes were rising.

When Uncle Itzrak appeared to claim his sister, I had a vicious row with him. I was frantic because I saw what Father and Malkele would not look at. I demanded to speak privately with him. Begrudgingly he accompanied me to the edge of the courtyard. The afternoon was gray. Harsh air bit us through our shirts. I told him that Mother needed a doctor—a psychiatrist, I said. He laughed with contempt when I spoke that word. I could see the laughter turn to steam in the air. He told me it wasn't any of my business. I moved up

nose-to-nose with him, or more accurately, I shoved my nose
practically into his beard, and whispered as calmly and fero-
ciously as I knew how that if anything terrible should happen
to my mother while she was with them I would get a gun,
travel to Smargon, and shoot him through the head. He
smiled smugly into my eyes until I added that I would shoot
his falsely pious father as well. He cuffed me across the face
with the back of his hand—my ear rang bitterly. When I
raised a hand to strike him back, he snatched my closed fist
with his hand and began squeezing. I was not then accus-
tomed to such excruciating pain, and tears came to my eyes.
I thought he had crushed my fingers. Samuel, I thought,
would have broken his grip and beaten him as he deserved. I
didn't even use my free hand—I was temporarily paralyzed.
Throughout this small ordeal he smiled at me contentedly,
even when I spat in his face. Three years later the Nazis murdered him for me—and his parents as well. A single nephew
escaped. He lives now in Sydney, Australia. I hope Uncle
Itzrak was able to crush a few Nazi bones before they humiliated and shot him down at the edge of a mass grave not far
from the Vilna ghetto—the Vilna he hated—where most
Jews of the province had been forced to gather.

Mother was not yet forty-one years old when she drowned.
She was buried in Smargon among her people. The three of
us traveled there for the funeral. Father said hello and goodbye to her family. Malkele and I said not a single word. They
were as silent as we were. If I had brought a gun with me,
perhaps I would have shot Uncle Itzrak and Grandfather. I
thought I saw Itzrak wink at me once while their holy rebbe
spoke gravely about Mother—in his wisdom he made of her
an example, almost, of how girls from pious homes can go
wrong if they are allowed to attend secular schools too long.
My grandparents seemed more upset at this public rebuke
by their rebbe than they were at the loss of their youngest

daughter. Is it really possible Itzrak winked at me—or did I once imagine it and so embed it in my memory for all time? Occasionally the scene plays itself through my mind—but I can never be sure. To this day, when I see again that rapid and elusive twitch of his cheek, a knife twists in my stomach. Malkele glared the entire time. Father cried softly, and on two occasions that I noticed, he smiled weakly at his in-laws. The memory of that small movement of his trembling lips also leaves me sour and weak. Malkele appeared to have lost all interest in Father as well. We left right after the burial. Certainly none of us desired to sit shiva with them—nor did they invite us to join them. How could Father have allowed his wife to be buried with her hostile family in a distant town, as though she had never married? As though she were not our mother?

Father died seven months after Mother. We couldn't bury him with her. As it turned out, it made little difference where they were buried—or even, for that matter, whether they were buried at all. Our days were numbered—even the days of our cemeteries. It would have been better if we had cremated them. We closed the apartment in Vilna, selling almost everything, including Malkele's piano—though I used the money to buy her another one in Warsaw. Ben helped us pack and move. Rivka, now a married woman of seventeen, had come for a day during the shiva. Ben was already there. It felt almost like old times. I sat on my stool with a book and watched the three old school friends talking—even telling a joke now and then. Malkele was not as grief-stricken as I had imagined she would be. Had the pain in her bones given her a perspective I had not yet achieved? The two girls even began teasing Ben in the old way, bringing a happy flush to his face. Samuel, now a husband and father, lived a few streets away. He still came to his roof each day to feed and exercise the pigeons. I could tell he was careful to come at times when

Malkele wouldn't see him. When his mother told me a little about him at the funeral, she was careful to take me aside. Was Malkele aware of his presence on the roof across the courtyard in the late afternoon? She betrayed no emotion. I saw him once during the week of sitting shiva. He was standing in the courtyard looking right up at our windows. Impulsively I shook my head at him and he retreated to his parents' building. I half expected to see a pigeon fly to our window. Did I know then that I would never see him again? I did know I must go say goodbye to him on his roof.

"Where are you going?" Malkele immediately broke her silence when I stood up and put on my jacket.

"Out—just out for a walk." I hesitated.

"Say goodbye for me as well." Malkele spoke in a whisper.

"I'll return in a few minutes."

Ben was in the apartment at the time. Except for the afternoon Rivka came by, Ben and Malkele sat for hours on the same sofa, in silence—like two horses that ignore each other but always stand close in the pasture. I could see him turn away when Malkele spoke up. This time he didn't leave. This time I left the two of them alone in the apartment. I am sure that if Malkele had wanted him, she could have gotten Ben back that afternoon, crippled as she already was.

"I was waiting for you." Samuel looked older, smaller. He was not stripped to the waist.

"How are the pigeons?" That was all I could manage to begin with.

"The carrier pigeon was killed."

"Killed?"

"I killed him."

"You killed him?" I felt like an echo. A numbness had seized my brain.

"Yes, to put him out of his pain. I had trained him to fly to the Jewish Students' Union. He was very useful to us. I would walk around the city and whenever I saw some trouble brewing I would send a message for help. One day some 'Endeks' caught him. They pulled off his wings, put a German swastika in the can, and threw him through the window of the union. Fine patriots, these junior Nazis. That night I hid on the street of one of the worst. I beat him nearly to death. He'll never be good for anything again, except eating and belching. Miriam and I had to leave Vilna for a time."

"Where are she and your son now?"

"In a port on the outskirts of Gdansk. We have been training to be sailors. Soon we leave for Palestine. I've returned to close our apartment and to say goodbye to my mother and father. I don't think I will ever see them again. The Germans will come. If not this year, then next year. But they will come, you know. And the Poles will collapse in a matter of days— they are all fifth columnists and cowards—and the Jews will be trapped."

Samuel was a perceptive man.

"Malkele is moving to Warsaw to live with me. She asked me to say goodbye to you." My voice sounded exceedingly formal, as though we were strangers.

"Did she really ask, or are you just saying this to me?"

"She said it in a whisper, but she did say as I was leaving the house, 'Say goodbye for me as well.' Those were her exact words."

"Leybele, I have missed you."

I said nothing but my eyes glazed.

"And Malkele. I loved Malkele deeply," he continued, looking stricken. "I am sorry for all her pain, and yours."

"Tell me about your son."

"Melech—we named him after Miriam's father—is almost two years old now, and healthy and strong. He will grow up in Palestine, a pioneer. We are very excited about the future. Leybele, your Communists will betray you in Poland, they are as poisoned by anti-Semitism as the rest of this land." Samuel was suddenly animated. "There is still time for you to arrange to come with us."

"Let us not talk of that now," I said gently.

He came over to me and I reached out my hand to shake his. He lifted me right off my feet and embraced me. He was as strong and tall as always.

"Goodbye, my young friend. You are smart and healthy. Someday we will see each other again."

"Goodbye, Samuel."

When he said I was healthy, he must have already known Malkele was doomed. None of them ever got out. Their project collapsed. He was destined to see his parents again. As far as I could find out, Miriam and Melech perished in the Vilna ghetto, and Samuel disappeared into the Rudnicki Forest. It is likely that he was killed in action, as he would have said. I found no trace of him after the war. His name appears in the lists of the martyred at Yad va-Shem. Israel will never know how much it lost in Samuel. I have always assumed he killed his share of Gestapo monsters before they cut him down.

After Mother's death I knew that I had to leave my father's house—and my sister's grip. It was for her sake as well as for my own, I told myself, when I accepted an opportunity to study and work as an assistant at the Jewish History Institute in the city of Warsaw. With a little time, I could procure a position for her at the Institute as an ethnomusicologist. She could then come to live in Warsaw—"the cultural center of Jewish Poland." I repeated this plan so many times and with so much enthusiasm that we both started to believe in it. It was under very different circumstances that I brought her to Warsaw less than a year later. About Father we said nothing to each other—and I didn't allow myself to scrutinize too closely his easy agreement to all my plans. Did I desert my father? Certainly in my heart I thought of him as Malkele's responsibility—I must admit that I blinded myself to her growing indifference to his day-to-day unhappiness.

In this time the Nazis were already carefully planning our fate, but we knew nothing about that. And what could we have done about the inklings we did have? The growing fascist movement in Poland we felt confident we could keep at bay—though they managed to make life almost impossible for Jewish students my one year at Stefan Batori University. The Nazis were another story, but we had daily lives to live— and they were removed from us, in another nation after all. I have written in detail about those years. My goal has been to lay to rest the ultimate blood libel that like ostriches we ignored the obvious, that like sheep we walked, one behind the other, to our collective slaughter. With more than a thousand years of Christian poison abundantly flowing in the bloodstream of Central Europe, in its intellectuals as well as in its peasants and priests, the odds we faced were more than impossible. Even so, after the apocalypse was played out, a remnant of us emerged with our values and our nervous systems intact, almost. How many of them emerged intact?

My work has dealt always with particulars. Who has refuted convincingly even a single detail of my numerous studies? Certainly now is not the time to start being sentimental and careless.

Ever since Rivka had started preparing for her inevitable marriage to her cousin by becoming overly formal with me; or, to be more precise, ever since I had stopped bathing Malkele when she was thirteen, I had not had even a touch of intimate contact with a female. How grateful I would have been if Esther had indeed offered herself to me, as years later she whispered in my ear Samuel had urged her to—though it is likely I would have repulsed her advances, hiding my shame beneath a youthful haughtiness. I left Vilna starved

for the flesh of a woman. How could I know then that I would
be forced to wait years yet, until I was twenty-eight years old,
for Inge, whose womanliness had started to blossom one
spring afternoon in Bergen-Belsen—in a woman's barracks,
where she lay ingeniously hidden, near death from typhus?
Is this how my mind has decided to formulate the chronology
of my sexual life? Do I continue to consider that short period
of intimacy with Malkele in Warsaw, though I have already
confessed to it in these very pages, still too intimate to list,
even privately—a shameful yet sacred period that exists in
an altogether different realm of my consciousness?

A miracle—the women who nursed Inge congratulated
her. The first drops of menstrual blood in their barracks in
an eternity of months, they teased her. A sure sign that one
day she would marry a handsome Jew and give birth to six
healthy children, they cheered her. The dying women kept
alive the dying girl. What other commentary can be made?
Inge recovered—the SS never discovered her secret disease.
But she had yet to endure many months in the camp—and
two weeks free of charge, as a final gift from the defeated
Nazis, in the airless black confines of a sealed freight car
being pulled aimlessly through the countryside. "There was
no way"—she spoke so softly I almost could not hear her,
though her lips were at my ear—"even to push out the
corpses." That journey of terror is now part of the historical
record—a recognized historical fact. What is part of my historical record—and a thing I will take to my grave without
ever having found a suitable repository to file it away in—
was the experience of first hearing about those two weeks
reported softly from the lips of Inge, late in the night we
made love, each for the first time—when together we started
her second menstrual flow—in Paris in 1947, April the
twenty-second, sometime after midnight, the beginning of
her seventeenth birthday.

The fingertips of my right hand are tingling right now from their gentle exploration thirty-eight years ago of the length of each fragile rib of the right side of her thin body as she whispered in my ear. The shiver brought to my body by the warmth and the faint pressure of her breast, as I lay on my back absorbing each word she spoke in her heartbreaking German, is radiating again from the third rib on my right side to each cell of my mortal body. How sweet—why am I tasting it again so fully at this impossible moment?—was the walk we took through the pre-dawn streets near the Centre de Documentation Juive, in Maurice Ravel's city of mists, my princess and I, back to the Luncharsky apartment.

XLIX

Why heartbreaking? Do you wonder why I refer so to Inge's German? German as Jews spoke it is a doomed tongue, a language without a piece of land around it—just a few apartments on the Upper West Side, and in Tel Aviv, in Jerusalem. Jewish German was rich and complex. It was Freudian, Marxist, Kafkaesque, it was the language in which Hannah Arendt (and Inge as well) listened to the Ninth Symphony of Gustav Mahler on a Friday night. There is no new generation of writers hungry to nourish it. Inge and her pathetic circle are among its final practitioners. They believe themselves German when they speak it. They are something much rarer and more precious than that—they are Jewish Germans. As Lewis Schorr said on the air one night to Fulani, "When we are gone, Germany will have accomplished the Final Solution of its language problem—Heine and even Goethe, except for his Christian shell, will be lost to them for all eternity. They will bequeath to their children a language of barbarians—a tongue with no redemption." I would have gone on, carried away by Schorr's tendency to feel sorry for himself and to pontificate, had not Fulani wisely translated my point.

"Kind of like American without the blues." At that specific moment I could have kissed her—not her feet or her panties but her lips, tenderly, like a compatriot. Instead I answered in my most exact Lewis Schorr style, "Precisely, my dear girl."

L

Five months after I left Vilna I returned for my father's funeral. I will always remember the train ride from Warsaw through Bialystok, then overnight to Grodno and finally home. After the lights in the compartment were turned off, I sat watching the moonlit Polish countryside waver past me, my face materializing occasionally in the glass. In recent years, and gazing into this rainy street earlier was no exception, whenever I have looked from a window at night and confronted my own face, I have found myself thinking of that last trip home. I remember how I looked at my ghostly reflection, searching for my poor father, and how, instead, I caught snatches of my mother—her slanted eyes, her high cheekbones, and, most important, an expression of sorrow as obscure as her ancestry interwoven with an unexplained excitement. Would I suffer her fate?

Finally, in that compartment filled with strangers, while I was being rushed home to my father's funeral, my mother came into my mind, as I had not permitted her to since her death seven months earlier. I saw again the womanly fever in her face when she talked to me of my future. In the afternoons, while Malkele practiced or spent an hour or two with Rivka, I would visit her for a few minutes in her bedroom. In those days it was always dim in there. All four windows were shut. Over three the shades were drawn—as yellowed as the aged ivory wallpaper. Mother sat looking through the fourth, like a child. I would push a chair over to her side, but a little behind, and gaze out with her. Were we seeing the same thing? The sudden upward spiraling of Samuel's flock escaping from its coop for a few minutes of afternoon freedom always startled her. Though her eyes seemed more intent on following the downward path of a last feather, certainly it was no coincidence that at the precise moment the birds began their flight, while I sat by her side wondering whether Esther was on the roof with Samuel, their hearts palpitating as one, Mother would begin to talk to me about her girlhood in Smargon.

Her six brothers had attended cheyder with a prominent disciple of the rebbe. Because she was a girl she was sent to the free state-run school, where she learned about the world among freethinkers and gentiles. These Hassidim didn't believe in wasting money educating girls. Everything she learned her father criticized her for knowing (there were even occasions when he whipped her): the geography of Europe, for example, or the stories of Chekhov. Many of the gentile students and a number of teachers were anti-Semites. At school she was hated for being Jewish, and at home for not being Jewish enough. The other Jewish girls who went to the school adjusted to this state of affairs by losing all interest in what they were learning, or by becoming experts at feigning indifference to their studies when they were at home. Mother loved learning about the world and she was too ingenuous to feign indifference. She began to dream of becoming a teacher.

A young gentile woman who taught literature encouraged her in this aspiration. Certain days, when they talked, she walked Mother partway home. She held her hand as they talked. This was not unusual for girls, but for a woman teacher to hold the hand of a girl pupil was certainly irregular. One day her father saw them. Without a word, he ran up to them and cuffed the teacher across the face—Grandfather feared no one—and dragged Mother home. For days she cried hysterically. She never returned to the school. When she was sixteen she left to go live with a second cousin in Vilna. She received a job in a vocational school as a teacher's apprentice. She learned how to create evening dresses for wealthy women who patronized the school. By the time she was eighteen she had become a sewing instructor. Without any outside influence she became a member of a Marxist party. In her own way Mother was as drastic as her father and five brothers. Was it, I wonder, a concession in her own way to her family that she joined the Jewish Labor Bund rather than the Bolsheviks? She met Father at a Bundist social evening. His father, also a religious man, blessed their marriage, but no one from her family attended the wedding and she had no dowry—her father got off cheaply, so to speak. Always the flight of the pigeons over the courtyard inspired Mother to speak.

"How could you have returned to them for almost a year?" I quietly demanded one afternoon.

"Where else could I go?" She spoke after a long hesitation.

"Why didn't you stay here with us?"

"I left for your father's sake." She spoke slowly, with deliberation. She looked bereft in the gathering twilight.

"Why?" I continued stubbornly, but with diminished confidence.

"Your father has disappointed me." My face became hot when she uttered these words. "I cannot forgive him." Somehow Malkele, though still a child, understood that Mother harbored such strong grievances toward Father, and could not forgive her for that. So she adopted Father—he was now her little boy. She told me later, in Warsaw, that in the months between their deaths Father spoke a little to her about Mother. He confessed that one night in the weeks preceding her first leave-taking Mother had almost murdered him. He woke up abruptly to see her standing over him in her nightgown with a hammer in her hand, poised to strike. What woke him up he never knew. For minutes, he told Malkele, for an eternity, as they say, they looked at each other. Then she turned and walked from the room. After that, for many weeks he was afraid to go to sleep at night. He also told Malkele that he feared for our lives as well. He explained it as a change of life more difficult than most. But Mother was then still in her mid-thirties.

A single shaft of light from the setting sun appeared on her face.

"In what way has he disappointed you?" I shivered when I asked. This was not a question a son should ask his mother about his still-living father. Mother turned in her chair and sat looking at me a long time without speaking. Her eyes narrowed and focused on a spot inside my brain, probing, sizing me up as though I weren't an entirely separate individual but one whose ultimate fate was in her hands at that moment. I fidgeted. The pigeons raked her face with bands of darkness as they swept past, returning to their coop. Were Samuel and Esther finished, or was he still within her mysterious body, sucked in by her powerful wetness as the pigeons had sucked in much of the remaining light?

"Leyb." I trembled when she uttered my name without the comforting diminutive. Her voice was intimate and husky, not the voice she ever used with her children—yet dizzyingly familiar, from another time that eluded me. Was it the voice I heard while within her womb, her first child, when she embraced my father among the enormous pillows on the thick mattress on the iron bed that sat now in sorrow behind us? The ivory wallpaper was fresh then. The spidery mouldings gleamed. A white cradle woven of cane perched in a corner awaiting my arrival. My father hid, greedily content, between the swollen breasts of his pregnant bride. "Whatever you become, whether a revolutionary or a schoolteacher, become it entirely." She spoke now in this new voice, without hesitation. "Your father is a man of little conviction. He forced me with his weakness to abandon my true work. I am now no different from my own mother. In his way your father is no different from my father. Do you understand me?"

She leaned close to my face and placed her hand on my wrist. The drop of light that still managed to enter was now behind her head lighting the loose strands of her thick hair. I felt disturbingly aroused. I wanted to answer, but only a squeak came from my mouth. I nodded to her. I don't think she believed that I understood. She smiled as she pulled her head back and nodded in imitation of my nodding.

Samuel's pigeons had returned to the coop. Had Esther dressed and disappeared, carrying off Samuel's fluid in her body? Was Samuel dozing on the straw mattress they had fashioned, near his satisfied pigeons, naked and curled up beneath the blanket Esther had put over him—his forehead warmed by her maternal goodbye kiss. I had watched them more than once. I knew their customs.

I sat there beside my mother, shaken by the confrontation. I had never seen such decisiveness in her face before, nor did I ever see it there again. When she threw herself into the river, though, I imagine she lunged forward with enormous conviction—more than I will ever locate in myself. We watched a stranger wearing a black fisherman's cap enter the courtyard. "See," my mother hissed. Precisely at that moment Father peered up at the darkened window and lifted his new cap gallantly to his bride. I sat to the side of my

mother and a little behind her with a heart that weighed a
thousand pounds. "I was not yet sixteen," I can remember
whispering explosively at the cold glass as I gazed, my nose
against the window of the train rushing me home to my father's funeral and to my ill-starred sister. Someone in the
compartment stirred for a moment.

"I love you, Leybkele," my mother said as she continued
watching through the window. Her voice was normal again,
girlish, maternal, and defeated. "I have not been myself
lately. Your father works harder than a man should to provide
for us."

LI

Later in that journey home I had plenty to distract me.
There were many fascists riding the trains in those days. A
Jew had to choose his compartment with care. It turned out
that my choice was not fortunate. In the middle of the night,
somewhere between Bialystok and Grodno, while I was in
the toilet, the train slowed to a halt at an isolated rural station, so gently that the sensation almost escaped me. Except
for the continuing sighs of the brakes holding the train in
place in the winter air, all was abruptly suspended, still. Was
I dreaming? I hesitated to flush the toilet. Chills passed
through my body. Was I the only flesh-and-blood passenger
in a train of ghosts? When I looked out I could see nothing,
not one light, not a star, not a snowflake, not even the
moon—only an inkling of steam drifting past the tiny
window.

At that moment I finally encountered my father—traveling
far into the peasant villages of White Russia, carrying his
sewing machine and his leather satchel. As a small boy I
carefully peeled thin layers that flaked from that satchel the

mornings after he returned to us. For a few days he would stay in a certain village, and for a few days longer in a neighboring village, with hardly another Jew less than a day's journey away. All day he pumped his leg up and down on the treadle like a beast of burden, and delicately fitted garments to the lumpen shapes of strangers who loved him not, as they say. Back home in Vilna his wife crawled further into melancholy and revulsion. His lustful son was now superior and puffed up with contempt, like a peacock. His darling daughter—he had worked double time, happily, to pay for her piano—ignored her music and sat transfixed by the twisted progress of her doomed fingers, her obsession with Samuel refusing to pale, and grew remote. In the long evenings, while they shared their meal with him, he spoke their peasant tongue and swapped songs with them. He always returned to us in good cheer, bearing small gifts and new songs. How had he kept his disposition so sweet? Had he ever tumbled in the hay, so to speak, with a starved widow or a strong-limbed daughter? He was still a young man: now I could be his father. But he was a careful man—not merely cautious, as Mother saw him—but careful, refined, delicate. He retained his belief in human equality. And with each gesture of his hands and his heart he embodied the conviction that the Jewish people would live forever.

In that isolated water closet somewhere between Bialystok and Grodno, gazing out into nothing, I began, finally, to sob for my dead father. The train was speeding with abandon again through the Polish countryside when I flushed the toilet and lurched back through the car to my compartment.

I was already inside the compartment when I spotted them, the two young men with golden hair sitting opposite my seat. Before I even pivoted to sit down I felt their eyes dancing up and down the length of my body. Was it too late to step backwards out into the corridor again? I was already

sitting, caught like a fly, so to speak. I held my posture
straight and immediately started looking through the window—though I kept my ears cocked. My eyes burned. It was
only then, through its reflection that reached out along the
glass, that I realized there was a light burning in the compartment—in the middle of the night. It was a soft golden
flickering light. These two had lit a kerosene lantern and
hung it from a hook over the window above their heads. I
could see nothing in the glass but the swaying of this eerie
light. Was it possible the others in the compartment had
simply pretended to sleep through their dramatic entrance?
Why had they chosen this compartment? They weren't lured
there by me, I comforted myself. I was not then an expert at
using my eyes as a weapon, and I couldn't prevent myself
from rapidly glancing at them a number of times. One, I noticed unhappily, had a carefully cultivated scar the length of
his left cheek—in the German university student style. The
other was an immense man. His arms were thicker than my
legs. Their Polish marked them as aristocrats, particularly
the scarred one. I was, like so many Jews in those days, less
terrified of aristocrats. Weren't they, after all, men of culture?
Though certainly arrogant, weren't they also refined men
who behaved properly in public places, regardless of their
political beliefs? Were they fascists? Were they returning to
Stefan Batori University from a rural gathering of Poland's
finest youth—as they called themselves? Certainly they
couldn't be hooligans. They looked familiar. Hadn't I seen
them the year before, when I was a student at the university?
Would they recognize me? In spite of the treatment we had
encountered from these aristocrats at the university, my mis-
conceptions still offered some small comfort. To this day, in
the face of all evidence, a number of my colleagues would
still react exactly this way. Perhaps, given the right degree of
terror, I still would too. The Nazis used that to fatal advan-

tage—so many of their officers were men who pretended to education and class, appealing to a Jewish sense of refinement. Was my father's refinement and love of culture deadly to more than my mother?

There had been four other people besides me in the small compartment when the train pulled out of Warsaw that afternoon, all gentiles. Could one have been passing as a gentile? A middle-aged couple sat diagonally opposite me, near the sliding door. They ate dourly from a large box of Dutch chocolates, never once offering one, even to the beautiful woman. Opposite them sat an elderly gentleman, dressed immaculately in a navy-blue suit and shoes that shone like the ebony keys of Malkele's piano. When he glanced down I was sure he could see the reflection of his narrow white face. His lips were thin and almost blue. His nose was prominent—almost Jewish, but sharper. He wore tinted glasses that hid his eyes, even when he read. His tie of blue Italian silk was matched by his sharply tucked-in handkerchief. A retired businessman? More likely a professor emeritus, as they say. An elegant black overcoat with a velvet collar sat exquisitely folded beside him. Sitting between us was a very beautiful woman in her early twenties, perhaps even my age. Even now, with all that happened a few hours later, after the pair of golden-haired youths materialized from the rural blackness, I cannot think of her sitting there in the early evening light except in sepia. She was dressed tastefully in a gray suit with a pale-lemon blouse and a delicate pin of black opal holding the collar close to her throat. A luminous neck. Silk stockings showed beneath her fashionably short skirt. She kept her black hair very short and highlighted with tiny gold earrings. She sat looking straight out into the cosmos, so to speak. Her large brown eyes were misted yet remote. She was the reason I had chosen that compartment. In those days, at the sight of a beautiful woman, especially if she was Polish, discretion fled from me like a parakeet from a cage. When I had sat down brazenly beside her, even my preoccupation with the death of my father and the predicament of my ill-starred sister had temporarily fluttered away. Only later, when the compartment was darkened and I started to gaze through the window into the immense emptiness, was I able to recapture my moral nature for a few hours—until I returned from my trip to the toilet between Bialystok and Grodno.

LII

The couple's voices had been the only ones we heard. No one else spoke from the time we left Warsaw before sundown until the fascists joined our small party. The few times I glanced over at their gluttonous faces, the couple had immediately stopped chattering and sat frozen in place. Were they afraid of me? Perhaps they thought even a weak smile would obligate them to offer me a chocolate. The retired gentleman held his nose in a book the entire time the lights in the compartment remained lit. Did he later take advantage of the lantern glow to resume reading? Though I tried a few times, I failed to catch a clear glimpse of the title, or even the language of his volume. I regret that small failure. It might have provided a clue concerning the question I have had about his identity.

The girl I did manage to peek at—I had not the nerve then, in 1939, to look directly at her, even to smile. I wanted to say, "My father has just died." Was that a good way to awaken her sympathy? Perhaps I simply needed to tell another person. I had departed immediately when Malkele's telegram arrived—"Father died suddenly. Please please hurry home. Poopikle." Malkele was not playing a grisly game with me by signing her name so. In a most intimate way she was begging me to rescue her from the belly of a monster. I left a note for my landlady and slid another under the door of the Institute, but I had spoken to no one.

"Excuse me, my dear woman, but my father died this morning." Over and over I invented sentences with wild variations of tone to tell her of my loss—somber, bouncy, tearful, matter-of-fact. "I hope you are traveling for a happier occasion than I am. My father has just died." "I didn't mean to stare, but my father is dead and you have such a sympathetic face." What could she have replied? "Oh you poor boy!" Her moist eyes would have shone forth. I could almost taste the smooth sound of her silk stockings when I imagined her uncrossing her legs to lean close and impulsively reach a delicate arm toward me and put her warm hand on mine. The top of my hand tingled from the thought. We never talked, but my greedy eyes continued to snatch glimpses of that exposed narrow band of silken mystery above the knee of her crossed leg. Once, for a second, she shifted and I saw a touch of inner thigh above the stocking line of the supporting leg, even the clasp of her flesh-colored garter belt. Had she been pestered by my nervous homage as she sat among us, yet fully above us, as we sped north toward the coming darkness?

The two fascists chose the compartment for the same reason I had. I should have anticipated that. Had they thrust their lantern into a number of compartments searching for a beautiful woman to impress—or a Jew to torment? How fortunate they were when they were lured in by the girl's haunting charms. They weren't counting on me—unless they could smell my presence even when I was out. A combination of their two chief desires—the psychosexual possibilities were now irresistible (to borrow terminology from my son's Holocaust advisor).

LIII

I was not five minutes under the spell of that swaying fascist light before their whispered conversation became loud and dramatically punctuated.

"Suddenly there is a Jewish stink in this compartment." The scarred one spoke first. His scar stretched and contorted when he spoke. When Kristin and I first made love—more precisely, the moment I was first on top of Kristin, peering down into her eyes—I saw again the man's chiseled face, including the scar. Not exactly his face. On Kristin's soft feminine complexion I saw his features and his scar. I had to blink more than once before the scar disappeared. I became impotent for a few minutes, but Kristin, of course, knew just what to do. Still, I remained convinced that she looked just like him. Could he have been her father? Over and over those few days I questioned her. She hated each question more than the previous one. Still, she answered as though compelled. Yes, her father was a university student in 1939. Yes, he was an extraordinarily handsome man with blond hair. Yes, yes, she looked like him. Yes, her father drew playful cartoons to entertain her with. Yes, there was an old friend of her father's who was large and stupid—a brutish man, she volunteered, a disgusting man who frightened her. Why had she shuddered for a moment at the memory of her father's friend? Had he molested her, this Nazi who survived the war so comfortably? I continued my inquisition without pursuing this side issue. No, his name was not Zbigniew. Her father was a German, not a Pole. Of course, I knew this— but the resemblance was uncanny, as they say. And yes, Kristin's father did have a scar running down his left cheek. Kristin too had a scar on her face—but not running the length of her cheek. Her tiny scar was lodged over her right eye—just

like Malkele's. Yet it is this man Zbigniew's face and not
Kristin's that I am seeing before me now as I concentrate on
her. Will his face accompany me to the grave?

"Where could the vile smell be coming from?" his sidekick
asked on cue. His face I have not so clearly in my mind—
only that he looked stupid and massive, though he spoke in
the accents of a gentleman. The four others in the car had
grown more than silent. I could no longer hear even their
breathing.

"Why, my dear Pavel, use your nose and tell me." Soon, a
few months after I returned to Warsaw, I would have the
same Christian name as this lackey.

"Why, my nose tells my eyes to look straight ahead."

"Why, my dear Pavel, you certainly have an educated nose,
swift and efficient."

"To sniff out a Jew a gentleman does not need an educated
nose."

What would Samuel have done? I had not pictured him so
clearly for months. Before my eyes he walked over and
planted himself right above these two cowards and peered
down at them with a smile on his face. Just as they moved to
stand up, Samuel went swiftly into action. He pushed them
back roughly, grabbed them by their hair and scalps and
knocked their heads together once, twice, three times—so
hard we all heard the sickening thuds. Pavel passed out and
his chief cowered in the back of his seat, blood dripping from
his mouth. Samuel spun around, bowed to the beautiful girl
and winked affectionately at me. As he left the compartment
he helped himself to a Dutch chocolate from the couple's
large box, and politely lifted the gentleman's book and read
its title. Except for my heart, which raced, and the uncon-
trollable movement of my eyes, I simply sat silently, with my
nose breathing against the cold glass.

"Jews should not be permitted to share compartments with

patriots," the one called Pavel continued, his voice rising to a higher pitch.

"They shouldn't be permitted at all on our trains, my dear Pavel." The scarred man spoke in a tone that managed to sound both amused and authoritative. "What do they need to travel for? Wherever they go they make trouble."

"And profit on the side." Pavel's laugh sounded as though it came through his nose. How expert they both were at making their Polish sound like German I wouldn't know until I became acquainted with the Gestapo less than a year later.

The scarred one, the one called Zbigniew, took a pen from his pocket and began sketching—he made it obvious whom he was sketching. He held the lantern out two or three times so that it cast its terrible glow over my face. I continued looking intently at the window, trying to see past the various reflections into the emptiness—though again I could not prevent my eyes from darting to the sides of their sockets and focusing on the exact spot in the glass where I saw him under the warm glow of his lantern, calmly sketching his prey. Once our eyes met in the glass and he winked at me gaily.

That was the first time I saw a Mont Blanc fountain pen. It immediately caught my eye. It was a remarkably thick pen with gold trim. When he made exaggerated flourishes with his hand as he sketched, I could see its gold point gleaming. I am writing these words with such a pen. It was a gift from Inge thirty years ago. I was so shocked by her bad taste that I nearly flung it from the window of our apartment. She was extremely upset, but I would not let her return it. Since then I have written most of my articles with it. I have grown rather attached to it. Such a pen was clutched by the manicured fingers of a Gestapo officer as he signed extermination lists. More than once this image has come to me as I walked between the shelves holding our precious collections in the storerooms of the Institute—with my Mont Blanc clipped

snugly and secretly in my shirt pocket beneath my jacket.
How often has this pen danced lasciviously in its dark hiding
place before the Memorial Books of my martyred people? It
has been sentimental of me, and distasteful on a number of
counts, to continue to use this pen—three times rebuilt in a
factory in New Jersey—to write the first drafts of my articles
for these thirty years. If I used green ink, the picture would
be complete. Could it be some impotent sense of revenge
that has kept me at it—even now?

The scarred one displayed his drawing and laughed—his
scar insolently danced. His immense goon, Pavel, held the
lantern so that the light flickered against the paper.

"Miss," he bellowed, "is this not a wonderful likeness?
Isn't my friend Zbigniew a first-class artist?" I caught the
reflection of the drawing in the glass. It was a caricature of
the kind popular in the anti-Semitic press in 1939. Both the
nose and the now scraggly chin were elongated so that they
met.

I felt everyone's eyes looking at the back of my head.

"They need to see his face to make a proper comparison,"
Zbigniew laughed. I thought of his scar and shivered. I kept
my face firmly pressed to the window until suddenly—so
quickly I didn't feel it—Pavel had gripped the top of my head
with his massive hand and twisted it slowly, so that my face
was exposed to everyone's scrutiny. With his other hand he
held the lantern to the side of my face. First I saw the couple
diagonally across from me. Their eyes were open. Their
expressions were blank. Then he pulled me forward as he
twisted, so that my eyes next met the eyes of the fashionable
gentleman, who turned away. Then he pushed me back and
twisted a little more until I was looking directly into the eyes
of the beautiful girl. She smiled at me. What was the meaning of her smile? Was she enjoying the sight or was she
simply nervous? Could she have been sympathetic? My mind

buzzed in confusion. Pavel smelled of whiskey. Why did I not lift my hands to stop him? After all, both of his hands were occupied. Was I stunned by the death of my father? Was I a coward? Was I already practicing techniques of survival?

"What do you think, Miss, is it a proper likeness?" the scarred one, Zbigniew, asked her in a deferential tone. Her face was not more than two feet from mine. Both of us were lit by the glow of Pavel's lantern. Without ceasing to smile she looked first at me, then, following the movement of the lantern, she looked at the caricature. Her lips emitted a short giggle, almost a squeak—of acquiescence, of approval. That was all they needed. The one, Zbigniew, bounded across to her side and sat down right on the gentleman's coat and pressed her closer to me with his body—all the while chatting gaily. Was she totally corrupt, this young aristocrat? Or was she as petrified as I was?

"Mademoiselle!" The elderly gentleman spoke roughly to the girl as he stood up. "This is disgusting," he hissed into the compartment. "Allow me." He held out his arm toward her. Pavel swung his light so that it glowed into the man's face.

"The gentleman is addressing you." The one called Zbigniew spoke with the intimacy of a husband, and practically nibbled her ear. He too must smell of whiskey, I thought. She looked down at the floor and said nothing.

"Disgusting," the man muttered, as he pulled his coat out from under Zbigniew's buttocks.

"Excusez-moi," Zbigniew happily mimicked the man's French and pressed his boot down on the gleaming shoe. The man actually clicked his heels after he freed his foot. He turned and walked from the compartment. What had disgusted him? Was it their behavior? Or mine? Or me? Was the girl petrified? Was she having a good time? It is even possible that she remained for my sake. With her there, they would certainly humiliate me, but they would not beat me. Everything she said and did during the following few minutes was enigmatic. Though I was soon to understand something of her motives, in my memory she remains an enigma to this day. The middle-aged couple had fallen asleep again. They were both snoring. Even when Pavel shone his light in their faces, their eyes remained closed—locked, so to speak. They continued snoring almost to the very end of the agony I now faced.

Why am I remembering this event in such detail now? The Nazi occupation of Warsaw turned it into a trifle. I simply stopped thinking about it. One night, though, in our apartment among the Aryans, I described a version of my humiliation to Malkele. She reacted with cold fury. Late into the night she whispered to me of murder. We should plot to murder a few Polish fascists—particularly university graduates with scars on their left cheeks. Not young blond Gestapo officers—that would be too dangerous. Killing Polish fascists might even prove popular. So many of them were now collaborators. She invented intricate strategies. If she had not been crippled by rheumatoid arthritis, Malkele probably would have become an anti-Nazi terrorist. Certainly she had fewer scruples than I had then.

"Now open your fly and permit m'lady a glimpse of your gorgeous Jewish cock." The one called Zbigniew spoke with the authority of a landowner addressing a peasant. He made even vulgarities sound exact and correct. I ignored him. I tried to twist my face back to the window, but Pavel's grip was so powerful I could not turn even an inch. He began to squeeze the sides of my head with his thick fingers.

"It is quite rude of you to keep a lady waiting." Zbigniew's voice was low and compelling. Still I ignored him. Pavel's pressure on my head increased—I felt his thumb was about to push through my temple right into my brain. I didn't want to look at the woman whose smiling face was so close to mine. Zbigniew's chin rested on the top of her shoulder so that they were cheek to cheek. I was too afraid to spit in their faces. I forced myself to keep my eyes tightly shut.

"Pavel, a little pressure, please, with your knee. It will prove more entertaining than crushing his thick skull."

"I can't just sit here and wait for him to give us this treat." There was seductive sweetness in the girl's voice, so startling I opened my eyes just in time to see her reach across my pants and begin unbuttoning my fly. How could she say and do such things and yet sound just like an angel? Was she under the spell of the one called Zbigniew? He held her ear-lobe between his lips. The earring glittered like a gold tooth. Perhaps she acted to save me from Pavel's brutality. I felt her fingers spread the flaps of my fly and reach in. Then I felt her fingers spread the flaps of my shorts and gently grip my penis. I wanted to cry out at the horror. Across the compartment the couple snored. This was the first time in my life a woman had touched me so.

"I had trouble locating the poor thing—here it is, shorter than my thumb." She was right. It was soft and tiny. As I was to learn vividly in Auschwitz, terror has the effect of making a man's penis almost disappear. Just enough remains to urinate from. This was the first time I experienced that diminution. I thought my humiliation was complete. All resolve to resist fled from me like a dog with its tail between its hind legs. I felt her pulling the tip firmly but still gently.

"Here it is."

"Fish bait," Pavel bellowed.

"A lovely specimen, Pavel. I think you too should consider circumcision."

To my horror I felt a slight swelling against her fingers. My humiliation was not yet complete.

"Look," Zbigniew said, "the little worm is growing."

"All Jewish pigs lust for Polish maidens," Pavel snapped in his stormtrooper tone. Immediately he took his hand from my head and pinched her fingers that held my penis. Excruciating pain radiated throughout my body.

"This is not for a man to do. I can manage myself. Please let go." The girl spoke with an authority equal to Zbigniew's.

"Yes, Pavel, release them. We must observe this interesting phenomenon. Even in extreme circumstances the Jew cannot control his lust for a Polish woman. Hold the lantern close to them." Pavel obeyed his master like a bulldog.

She continued kneading my penis with her hand, but it had retreated. I felt the one called Zbigniew would punish her if she didn't succeed in arousing me again. I watched his fingers reach around her neck and undo the black opal pin. He tossed it to Pavel, who bit down on it as though it were a gold coin before putting it in his pocket. Then he placed his hand on her breast and began unbuttoning her pale-lemon blouse. My eyes were glued to his fingers as he loosened each button. I looked up at his face and he winked at me. The scar shimmered. Pavel pressed the hard bulge of his groin against my cheek. She wore a white lace camisole tied on top with a yellow ribbon. Zbigniew deftly undid the ribbon and slowly reached in and exposed one of her small breasts. His fingers caressed her nipple in unison with her movements as she turned the tip of my penis between her fingers. My penis began to swell again. He leaned closer, forcing her body close to my face. He held the bottom of her breast in his palm and began rubbing her nipple against my lips. I turned my head away. Pavel gripped it again and twisted it toward her nipple. The girl laughed. I have often thought about that laugh in recent years—but I have never understood it. It held confidence, yet it held terror as well. Why hadn't she left when she could have? Was she a saint or was she simply depraved? I could smell the sweetness of her flesh mingled with the schnapps on Zbigniew's breath.

"There, there," he crooned at me, "enjoy this wonderful opportunity we have given you, little Jewboy." There was a hand on top of my head, caressing it. Whose was it? Even now I wince at the thought that it had to have been the cruel hand of Zbigniew—it was like the touch of the "Angel of Death" lovingly selecting a new specimen. The pressure was certainly more delicate than Pavel's, who now kept his paw on the back of my neck so that I could not jerk my head away from her nipple, which brushed my lips like the tongue of a serpent. The bulge in his pants he pressed to my ear. I held my lips tightly together; it was as though they were trying to force bitter medicine into my mouth. The sweet smells were nauseating me. I had difficulty breathing. My treacherous penis was responding, oblivious of everything except the hypnotic female fingers playing with it. I struggled to keep from ejaculating. I made myself picture my father lying dead in a box. I made myself think of my small lending library in Vilna where I read *War and Peace* in Yiddish translation. A drawing of an elephant in deadly battle, an enormous serpent wrapped around its body. Mr. Gordon's drawing. I made myself think of the serpent's fangs. If I permitted her nipple to part my lips, I was lost. My tongue would betray me—just like my cock.

"Yes, yes," Zbigniew went on and on. I can hear it right now as I sit in this room—his unctuous and sinister coaxing. "A Polish virgin, a countess, is throwing herself at you. Your puny little heart is heaving. Your scrawny little cock feels huge—just like a man's. You are a powerful Polack, just like Pavel. She wants you. More, more, she pleads, more, my master. Take her, you twisted little worm. For this moment were you brought here. Nothing but darkness awaits you."

For forty-six years his exact words have lain dormant, like a cluster of viruses in a corner of my consciousness. How many eruptions have they brought forth on the covering of my soul?

I struggled to keep from crying. My shame was consuming me. With his words, and with Pavel's muscles and the woman's body, this fascist was raping me—and the woman as well. I was helpless before them, and I could not even control my urges. Why must I confess this shame?

But haven't I devoted my life to restoring the complete picture? Can I destroy any evidence without betraying my calling?

"Countess." Zbigniew's voice was suddenly brazen and devoid of encouragement. "You have succeeded beyond my expectations. His worm has grown as thick as your thumb. Open Pavel's pants and compare it with a Polish cock." Her fingers stopped caressing me without letting go while she unbuttoned Pavel's fly with her other hand. I felt myself growing soft. Before she could reach in, Pavel's penis pushed through his unbuttoned fly like a rapacious shark being born.

I had never imagined a penis so monstrous. It was thicker than her wrist. Under the glow of the lantern it was so red it looked drunk. Strangest of all, it came to a hideous point. I imagined a series of razor-like teeth emerging from under the crimson flap. It twitched between our two faces.

"You know what to do, my Countess." Zbigniew nudged her head forward.

The woman opened her lips and took Pavel's uncircumcised monstrosity into her mouth. From the corners of her eyes she kept looking at me. For a split second the future opened before me in her doomed face, but I didn't know it until later. Pavel held the back of my neck with a grip of iron, so to speak. I could not turn away. What was she declaring to me with her eyes? A solidarity of sorts? Zbigniew had leaned back and begun sketching again. As she moved her mouth playfully on Pavel's cock she slipped my softened penis back into my pants, and with a careful gesture even into my shorts. Slowly she buttoned my fly. How did she know that this act was blocked from Zbigniew's sharp eyes by her own act of humiliation? Again, she may have rescued me from a more terrible fate. I must admit that in part I was disappointed at losing her attention—so powerfully had their fascist depravity demeaned my starving heart. If Zbigniew had encouraged me, would I have thrown myself even on the wife who pretended to snore across the small compartment and raped her before the closed eyes of her pathetic husband? I kept closing my eyes so as not to have to watch her tongue licking the head of that unclean monstrosity. But I could not keep them closed.

"Would you mind terribly, my dear fellow, putting your face at the center of this tableau and joining m'lady at her exciting activity? For the sake of art, mind you."

Pavel immediately forced my lips down to his penis. The woman's eyes were looking directly at my own. Pavel squeezed the back of my neck so hard I felt paralyzed for a moment. Her fingers were at my lips trying to coax them apart. Pavel squeezed harder. My mouth was forced open like that of a fish.

"Very good—a marvelous still life."

I ached to bite down fiercely—to make Pavel shriek in agony. Perhaps she too would bite down. While Pavel writhed I could leap across and strike at Zbigniew's ugly scar-face. Throughout this ordeal my hands were free. Why had I not lifted them even once? Was I simply a coward? I had not been so passive before, nor was I ever so passive again. Was I protecting the girl? Was that what her eyes were asking of me? Was I allowing her to guide us safely through the danger? Zbigniew was now speaking: "Perhaps I will present this to Poopikle at your father's funeral. She will simply adore it. They will think how worldly our Leon has become."

How did he know about Poopikle? How did he know my father had just died? How did he know my name? Had he recognized me from my one year at Stefan Batori? How could such a thing be? I had not been active. He was at least two years older than I—a leader among the fascists. Tears of helplessness came into my eyes. I felt her fingers on my cheek. No, she shook her head slightly, no, do not cry. I realized suddenly that he had taken the telegram from my bag. At that very moment Pavel jerked his penis from her mouth and ejaculated in my face, then lurched backward and fell into the opposite seat with such force that the couple jumped up and ran from the compartment. The lantern dangled from his hand. Semen continued to seep from his spent penis. It smelled like chemical bleach on my face and my cheek felt seared.

"Pavel, before you become too content, see to it that these two leave our compartment."

Pavel again clutched the backs of our necks with his massive hands.

"And don't forget to pay the slut. It certainly won't do for her to malign the honesty of Polish manhood with her Jewish tongue."

The woman clutched the few bills Pavel gave her. "The pin," she demanded, staring into his flabby face. Zbigniew nodded. Grown docile as a beast before its master, Pavel handed her the pin. Then she pushed him away. I watched her straighten her camisole and button her pale-lemon blouse, highlighting it again with the black opal. She moved slowly, with deliberation. I felt incapable of moving at all. I watched her put on her coat. Then she straightened her hair. She acted as though these two monsters were not in the compartment with us. She carefully put on lipstick. The whole time the one with the scar sketched her. Finally she looked at me. God knows what she saw in my face.

"Wipe your face," she commanded as she handed me a handkerchief from her bag. Then she handed me my coat, which I put on as though in a dream.

"Take your bag and come with me. We don't belong here with these two swine." Pavel seemed already asleep, his mouth open, still clutching the lantern. Fluid still seeped from his naked monstrosity. The other one ignored us. He sat sketching this new sight. Was he planning to humiliate his comrade? I had not the will to leave.

The woman took my hand and led me from the compartment.

Throughout the ordeal I had taken her for someone else. I felt cheated bitterly that this beautiful woman who caressed me was not a Polish aristocrat but simply a Jewish prostitute from Vilna. I could have bought her services more cheaply on Polutsker Street. Zbigniew, even Pavel, knew what she was. How had they seen so easily into my lustful heart? I cringed with rage and shame.

"Whore," I hissed at her in Yiddish.

"You fool," she hissed back in Polish.

I took some bills from my pocket—more than Pavel had given her—and flung them at her feet. I turned away and walked a few steps to the end of the car. I turned in time to see her picking up the bills. Her eyes looked up at mine.

"Don't go. You better stay with me until we reach Vilna." Vilna she pronounced in Yiddish. My confusion and shame were too great to permit me to acknowledge her. I pulled open the heavy door and stood bent and shaking between the cars until I vomited. When I returned to the car she was gone. I didn't search for her. But I have remained grateful that she called me fool rather than coward.

Night

LIV

I had to banish Kristin. Her surrender of body and mind to my every desire would soon have robbed me of my work. Could rescuing the daughter of a Gestapo officer have been my proper work?

The third night, long after Kristin had fallen asleep, I lay awake on the black bed, carefully listening. Each breath from her body, intermingled with a psychotic yelping from late-night upper Broadway, brought forth from my heart a protective tenderness almost as rich as what I had felt, awake, beside Malkele as she slept in Nazi-occupied Warsaw. Still, I was attacked by doubt—no, more than doubt. I was gripped with a growing disgust that I could not control. She slept on her side with both arms stretched toward me. I held myself just out of her reach.

Finally a dim light filled my window. Momentarily it looked solid—a screen with a silhouette projected on it of a milk box blossoming with petunias sitting on a Manhattan fire escape in the early morning. But there couldn't be any petunias. We had not even planted the seeds yet. Soon the light passed through the glass, the screen dissolved. The box was empty. A sinister presence that had drawn my gaze with nervous regularity throughout the night turned out, now, to be simply a Chinese lantern that Kristin had hung from the ceiling the previous evening. I lifted my head slightly and began scrutinizing her hands, which lay, one up, the other down, on the edge of my pillow. The skin was smooth, silken, but her fingers were surprisingly thick, particularly her thumbs. Clearly they were the hands of a woman destined to grow stout in her middle years, the hands of a *hausfrau* like her mother.

I knew on that Monday at dawn, after three nights of love that had sweetened my soul a drop, so to speak, when I finally started to fall asleep in the unnerving glare, that I had to act quickly or be lost eternally.

A short time later I awoke languorously to Kristin's tongue on my nipple and the aroma of fresh coffee. Not once had I brewed coffee in that apartment. She must have carried in the coffee and the coffeepot the night before.

"Leybele," Kristin crooned. "You have to get ready for work, it's almost eight o'clock." Did she pretend she was my wife?

My growing irritation was tinged with a kernel of desire a moment later when I allowed her to lead me to the toilet by pulling on my half-aroused penis. I permitted her to aim the stream and shake my member when I was finished. Shame heated my face when the paltry stream took so long to cease finally. The whole time Kristin hummed and cooed in my ear. Was I a child? I was almost disappointed when she left me to brush my teeth and move my bowels by myself. She knew that underneath my irritation I was delighted when she began to help me dress in clothing she had picked out beforehand. Perhaps she blamed my irritation on Monday morning and was simply trying to cheer me up.

"Irish oatmeal and freshly squeezed O.J.," she sang. "Fiber for healthy bowels and vitamin C so you won't catch cold." She was out to make me over. I winced even before I figured out what "O.J." was. Had she also carried in a juice squeezer and oranges the night before? How little I had noticed. What had she carried out?

I sat dressed like a gentleman and ate the most nutritious breakfast since the early days after Inge and I married. There was a dainty dish with a stick of sweet butter on it, and a small pitcher of milk. The cup and saucer were of white china; the bowl matched. Had she brought these things back from Freiburg, from her father's house? Hirsch would have enjoyed every aspect of this breakfast. Would she soon paint my floors white? Would the white cat be joining us on our black satin bed? Kristin sat across from me beaming while I ate, without a stitch of clothing on. Her happiness, and the way her nipples bunched when I looked at her youthful breasts, made me dismiss my doubts, for a moment. The whole day that picture played before my eyes: Kristin sitting naked across the breakfast table, her nipples continuously ready to receive my lips, her face shining, watching her man eat his breakfast before going off to his office. I did no work. I needed to manufacture the strength to drive her away.

Writing about the incident on the night train left me exhausted. I lay down on the mattress and napped for twenty minutes. When I awoke, I thought Kristin was next to me. Perhaps that is what woke me up.

Stitched into every moment of passion and tenderness those three nights had been the nagging question—was it all an elaborate joke she was playing on me? More likely, she was playing the joke on herself. In any case, no matter how sweet the nights had become, we could not continue. How could an aging Holocaust survivor and the ravishing daughter of a Gestapo officer perform such unspeakably intimate acts on one another without sinking? If I was sinking anyway, let it be unattached to this German.

I did no work that day. I pulled down the window shade

and sat in my darkened cell, tasting over and over highlights
from the weekend. I didn't even go to the Library, though I
had reserved an invaluable volume. Three times the phone
rang. Were they ringing to connect Kristin? I counted each
ring, but I didn't lift the phone to my ear. Would Perl think I
had collapsed from a heart attack and notify the Director?
Soon they would unlock my door and discover me sitting at
my desk in a trance. The bulge in my pants would prevent
me from rising to keep them from standing over me while
they asked their stupid questions. Luckily, no one came by.
Was I simply deluded to think they would be interested?
Could Kristin feel what I was going through? If I had suffered a heart attack, I would have lain there for three days.
Oscar would have been shocked, even uncomfortable, to find
himself in the same room with my remains when he came
to empty my basket that Thursday. No. Kristin would have
come just in time to snatch me from the jaws of death. Not
since Malkele lived had I been so confident about another
person. Inge, even in our good days, would have been too
cautious and dignified to call, even when I didn't come home
a night or two.

Twice, unseen by the others, like a thief I slipped out of
the room to go urinate. I could almost not bear to touch my
member. That coming night, I repeated over and over, as
though to brainwash myself, I would send her away.

But why have I skipped the third night, the most intimate
of the three? I should leave out nothing. There will be no
time later for the whole truth.

Outside, the half-naked girls have reassembled. Their
whispering, punctuated from time to time by short bursts of
knowing laughter, jolts me back to the apartment on Wiwulski Street. How, you are probably shaking your heads in dis-
approval, does my mind leap from these streetwalkers on
Lexington Avenue to my childhood home in Vilna? Such

conjunctions are, of course, miraculous. They constitute a
kind of fourth dimension that makes the study of history
possible.

One time, in the year I first stopped bathing her, that was
1935, when she was already not much younger than those
dark teenagers outside, Malkele had Rivka and two other
school friends stay over. Her small bedroom connected by
French doors to the parlor where I lay restlessly on my
daybed near the piano. A pajama party they called it. Late
into the night I listened to their intense whispers and girlish
laughter. From a clear word here and there, I began weaving
a scene of another pajama party with the prettiest girls from
my class marveling and joking about my manly powers and
biting wit.

"There is only one thing they want from us, and don't you
forget it." From where in Malkele did these bitter words of
advice come that so shocked me that the fantasy instantly
fled from my overheated consciousness? Momentarily, my
thirteen-year-old sister was possessed of the husky voice of
an embittered femme fatale—a voice I did not hear again
until I encountered the young woman who called me fool,
rather than coward, on the night express from Warsaw to
Vilna, as I sped home, to my father's funeral, in the spring of
1939. I would hear it years later from Inge and just recently
from Kristin. It was destined, in Warsaw, to become Malkele's nightly voice echoing inside my head.

"Malkele, what's the matter? Why are you talking like
that?" Rivka's girlish voice trembled with fright.

"Nothing. Nothing." Malkele sounded embarrassed but
herself again—the dreadful future she had conjured up for
her girlfriends receded. "I was only pretending. I didn't mean
anything. I remembered two women talking in the street,
that's all." She sounded desperate to restore their earlier lev-
ity. That moment had frightened her girlfriends and left

them mirthless and perplexed. I was relieved for Malkele's sake when she succeeded in charming them once more.

They weren't the only ones so upset. I felt that her words were directed at me. Did she know I was listening? Certainly she spoke loud enough for me to hear. Why would my little sister be so suspicious of me? Had she seen the lust in my heart? Suddenly I was afraid to face her.

"Let's go to the parlor and play songs." Her voice was gay and commanding. I lay very still, fighting an urge to flee the apartment.

"But your brother."

"He won't mind. I'll play his favorite piece. Besides, Rivka can keep him busy." Malkele squealed with excitement.

"Shh, he'll hear you." Rivka practically shouted.

"We can pull off his blanket and tickle him." Malkele's voice rose in volume and pitch.

"He will never forgive us." Rivka sounded close to tears.

"You really think so?" Malkele lowered her voice dramatically.

"And besides, we'll wake up your mother," one of the other girls added. Father was then away on one of his trips.

"There is nothing in the world I could do that Leybkele wouldn't forgive me for," Malkele bragged. "And as for my mother, she sleeps through everything." Momentarily her voice was bitter again.

They didn't come into the parlor. Soon they were chattering about other things. My anticipation and my anger took a few minutes to dissolve. I was prepared to yell at her and even to smack her across her behind if she brought her girlfriends to my bed. Rivka was the only one of the four to live beyond her teenage years.

Are the ones outside the same three as before, back for a second tour of duty tonight? Their chatter sounds so care-

free. Is the hesitant one with the limp among them? Perhaps
she has already faced the wrath of her pimp. She's better off
risking a customer. This time she won't withdraw into the
shadows. There is another chance for me. Among those
cruising down Lexington Avenue may be the same buyers,
not yet fully sated. If one of these men, his eyes clouded by
lust, picks the same girl as before, will they recognize one
another in the act of love? Will that draw them closer? Will
they recoil? Will it make no difference at all? Perhaps the
girls have rooms in this hotel.

LV

She arrived the third night dressed conservatively in a gray
suit—she could have been visiting her therapist or her gynecologist. (Are there therapists who specialize in the daughters
of SS men?) She took a gleaming instrument and a bottle of
rubbing alcohol from her handbag.

"This is a speculum. It will enable you to look inside me,
Doctor Solomon. Sterilize it, please, while I prepare your
table." She was all business.

I must admit that I blushed at her tone. She remembered
a desire I had expressed half-playfully the previous night.
Before we fell asleep that second night, before she fell asleep,
that is—not once did I fall asleep before dawn those three
nights—I confessed that I had never fully gazed into a woman's body, even in the good years with Inge.

"Do you want to look into me?" She was immediately alert
and interested—something new in our rapidly growing repertoire of intimacies.

"Yes."

"A precise examination, like that given by a gynecologist?"

"That and more." I immediately matched her mock-professional tone, though I managed to stop short of shifting to my Professor Lewis Schorr German intonation.

"More? A gynecologist must remain businesslike and remote."

"More in the way a specialist would perform more than a routine exploration." I was so taken with this game of doctor she had introduced, I practically rubbed my hands together when I uttered the word "exploration."

"With a few small changes your desk would make a first-class examining table—oh, Leybkele, feel how wet I am." Her sudden dramatic shifts of emotion and language never failed to captivate me. The picture of Kristin lying naked on my table, waiting for me to take possession of her, had rejuvenated both of us. Our kisses dissolved the playful tone.

"You become hard as often as a boy," she whispered in my ear, half in English, half in Yiddish.

Kristin climbed on top and received me for the third time. I didn't quite have the strength of a boy. I stayed hard but I didn't ejaculate again. My chest began to hurt, but I didn't stop. The sweat from her body enslaved and soothed me. I would have been happy to die. The pain eased and disappeared.

Her surrender made it possible for me finally to banish her. If she had held herself back, aloof, arrogant, I would have been hers—and I might not be here now. My obsession with her might easily have grown out of control. She has just the correct degree of German arrogance to make her abundant sexiness steamy and dangerous—à la Marlene Dietrich. I would have become her slave. A ridiculous figure like the schoolmaster Emil Jannings, lost in a sensual fog, his white shirt stained, his collar curled upward, I would have crowed like a rooster in theaters all over Central Europe for Kristin Dietrich, world-renowned chanteuse and femme fatale. On our Eastern tour, in Vilnius, as they now refer to it, I would crow and crow while Kristin carried on backstage with a handsome youth from Stefan Batori University.

I spy them through the wings. Her bare shoulders tremble with abandon. He, with a scar on his left cheek, her double, her Zbigniew, still young, still confident, brazenly embraces my Kristin before my eyes. The audience, big beefy Endeks and Jew-baiters, hoots and howls—somehow they are in on the joke—while I crow, crow, crow, crow, flap my vestigial wings pathetically, my heart brimming and swelling impotently.

This abasement would not only have kept me from turning into a Nazi; I would also not be here tonight. The death of libraries in my life would have meant nothing. The arrest would have meant even less. Into what corner of my mind would my memory of Malkele have disappeared? Poopikle would be sitting on the night table by Kristin Dietrich's bed. He would look pampered and self-satisfied, this lobotomized survivor, with his mistress's pearls draped about him. As it was, he managed to spend a night, perhaps two, wrapped in the fragrance of her discarded panties.

When her handsome student ejaculates in Poopikle's face, Kristin throws him out so quickly he hardly has time to dress: she is very sentimental about the little mouse, a gift from her Jew. She carefully wipes his face with a soft cloth dampened with warm water and coos at him.

I would be damned to hell by my obsession with this Nordic beauty. But I would not be here in this hotel room tonight.

Kristin, however, needed me to become a Nazi. Her camp commandant. Her torturer in Gestapo headquarters in Warsaw. Such an abomination would have presented Hitler with another small posthumous triumph. And that's what gave me the strength to resist her powerful enchantments. Did she understand? Does she understand? It may have saved her as well. She would have succumbed even more quickly: survival is not etched in her genes as it is in mine. Let her find another Jew to surrender to, to beg pain and humiliation from. I know enough not to permit love to serve retribution. What does it say about my life that if Kristin hadn't needed to surrender herself to me so thoroughly I might have surrendered myself to her? Right now I could call her. Right now she is listening to Fulani, of course. She has probably called the program, in her new identity. Her line will be busy.

Are you wondering why I think of calling Kristin at this time? You might say I am fighting for my life. To the very end I will fight for my life. Even after I swallow the twenty-four phenobarbitals with a glass of bourbon I will be fighting for my life. That, too, is my specialty.

LVI

The sweetness of gazing into Kristin's body that third night was so remarkable that we almost transcended our historical predicament. I washed my hands and the stainless steel instrument, first with soap and warm water, then with the rubbing alcohol. I returned to her side with my sleeves rolled up and held the instrument in my upraised hands, like a surgeon, for her to inspect. She smiled indulgently. My desk was transformed into an examining table. The books were gone, the papers were gone, my Yiddish typewriter was gone. A white quilt lay spread on top. A small white towel was carefully placed on the lower end. On it lay a circular mirror, a flashlight the size of my Mont Blanc, and a magnifying glass. She was just about to fasten a board to each side of the same end of the desk. She must have fashioned these two identical boards earlier that day. Each was twelve inches high, already had two holes at the bottom for the screws, and was stained almost the same color as the desk. A swatch of white cloth was attached near the top of each one. Two eyes were sewn into the ends of the cloths, two hooks were nailed to each board just above the cloth—hooked, the cloths would become slings.

"Homemade stirrups," she sang in a low voice, proud of her handiwork. "The best I could manage." I felt myself growing hot with embarrassment.

"Yes, for your heels. Of course. Very good. Excellent." Kristin laughed at my discomfort.

"I have one errand to run before you begin your examination. Please leave the speculum on the towel here and be patient, my dearest Leybkele." By now I was stricken with lust.

"Certainly," I said gruffly, in my Lewis Schorr tone. Kristin blushed but held her tongue. Was she determined to outlast me at my own emotional game?

"Laundry," she whispered. "White things only."

She gathered all my white sheets and pillowcases, all the undershirts and Jockey briefs—not merely the dirty ones I had stuffed with the used sheets into a corner of the closet, but the clean ones as well—and my two or three white towels that had sat folded in a drawer for years. The towels were embroidered "Camp Boiberik." To Inge's great embarrassment, the one time she consented to take our week's vacation in this Yiddish resort, I had insisted, partly to spite her, on packing them into our suitcases when we checked out.

"Why are you taking the clean underwear?" I asked sweetly in Yiddish.

Would we be a big hit this season, as they say, if Camp Boiberik still existed, and I took Kristin there for a long weekend? Five hours we would sail up the Hudson on the Day Line to Poughkeepsie, where a station wagon would meet us for the drive into the countryside. On amateur night she could sing "I Am Ready for Love from Head to Foot." Her German would scrape sorrowfully in the ears of the audience. Would their souls tremble as mine did less than two years after the war when Inge and I listened to Marlene Dietrich in my small apartment in Paris?

"To wash and to whiten." She answered neutrally in English. "Please take off your clothes and give me the underclothes."

"From my body?" I teased in Yiddish, as a peace offering, so to speak.

"Yes, still warm from your sweet flesh," she almost sang. "I have something for you."

Kristin believed in thoroughness. As I stood before her naked, my practically fresh underpants and undershirt in her laundry bag, she handed me a box from Bloomingdale's. She looked proud and expectant as I opened it. I removed a most beautiful garment—a robe of purple silk.

"Is this for me?" My voice sounded meek and unfamiliar to my ear.

"Yes, my darling," she said proudly, "it is you exactly. Let me help you on with it."

That was the first gift I had received in many years. I am wearing it right now. A silk robe and a sweater of pure lamb's wool—impressive gifts, are they not?

Kristin playfully twisted the silken cord around my hardened penis and said, "Be patient until I return. Read your Baudelaire."

After Kristin left I looked into the underwear drawer. It was empty except for one item. The black panties sat there all alone, begging to be pulled through Fulani's coat again. This time I could send Kristin to perform that mission. If Oscar spied her in his basement room, he'd close his eyes in confusion. What if Fulani caught her?

I resisted an urge to hold the panties to my face. I closed the drawer and walked back into the other room to my desk. I hooked the homemade stirrups into place and put my hands through them. The soft cloth felt cool against my wrists. My mouth watered. I resisted an urge to put my mouth to the stainless steel instrument and lift it with my teeth like a dog. I would not spoil the purity of the coming encounter. I freed my hands and brought a pillow from the bed which I placed at the head of the desk. The black silk pillowcase looked mysterious and alien there on the white quilt and heightened my expectations. I forced myself to withdraw to my chair. I sat waiting with my sterile hands up in the air, like a surgeon.

Where did she get the money to buy me such an expensive gift? Perhaps, with Maria's sense of poetic justice, she stole a family heirloom on her last visit home. Was I already on her mind? Was this robe, then, reparation? What other gifts would I receive from her? Why had she said Baudelaire? Did she not understand French? Or was it a playful allusion? To what? *Les Fleurs du Mal?* Now I'll never know.

I am running out of paper. Soon I will have to write on the backs of the sheets—something I have not done since I wrote my first article in the D.P. camp thirty-nine years ago.

I had plenty of time to brood while I sat. Had I in some way embraced her Nazi father when I embraced Kristin? Perhaps I was stealing his precious daughter away from him. Each time I had entered her the previous two nights I thought not only of her father but of Malkele. How could that be? Like her father, Kristin was scarred, but her scar was tiny and over her eye, like Malkele's. What sort of connection is that? If I had thought of Inge rather than Malkele, I would not have been shocked. The two women had Germany in common. Of course, I know why I thought of Malkele. These were not the first times I had thought of her at such moments. The last time—before Kristin—that I had embraced a woman, Malkele was there. But with this Gestapo daughter—how could I so blemish my memory of Malkele? But why, at this late moment, do I defile Kristin by speaking this way of her?

LVII

It is not true that after I discovered her adultery I never again made love to Inge. One night in the third year, just days before I moved out permanently, I was lying on the daybed reading in the semi-darkness long after Emmanuel had gone to sleep. Inge opened the door to her bedroom and stood facing me. Her nakedness in the glow of her room so unnerved me that I did no more than look back at her, furtively taking in her womanliness, and avoiding her eyes like a guilty dog.

"Leon." The quiet in her voice dignified her nudity. "Please come to bed." Was she pretending that the bed was still mine as well as hers? Did she think we could so easily obliterate three years? What would Schwartz think of his seductress now? Was she about to complete the circle by asking to what were Chopin's Preludes preludes? I shivered with outrage. The word "slut" came as far as my lips, but my tongue turned to wood. It was impossible to call Inge such a false name to her face. In truth, I found this straightforward expression of desire, particularly in so modest a woman, too compelling to withstand.

I went to her door and let her take off my pajamas. She led me by the hand into her candle-lit room, where I had not been in three years. Had Schwartz introduced her to the pleasures of candlelight? She pulled me to her bed and held me in her arms and kissed my parched lips and took me slowly into her body. Something more than candlelight was different. It felt illicit to be inside her, dangerous, as though we were cheating. Then it felt indecent. What did Inge feel at that moment? Once again I could not take my mind from Schwartz possessing her in their candle-lit love nest. Like an animal I sweated and groaned on top of Inge—and it was he who went down into her thirsting body, it was he who sweated and groaned, who whispered his Yiddish love words into her famished ear. Ben and I had merged into one hungry young Jew from Vilna shuddering in the frail arms of his dying princess. Somewhere, in the candle-lit blackness that enveloped us, Inge had turned into Malkele—totally.

"Finally," we groaned hoarsely. "Finally," we repeated. Then Ben was gone and I was alone with my sister in her candle-lit bedroom on the Aryan side of occupied Warsaw. I was so shaken that I had to fight an urge to flee after him—to bring him back to the safety of the room? Perhaps Inge thought I referred to finally having my wife back. She never asked. It was Malkele, pure and simple, to whom I was groaning so hoarsely. Finally I was fulfilling my sacred duty to my sister. Inge knew more than she let on, as they say, but her responses were familiar—her body tightening in anticipation below me, her fingers clutching my wrists, then the sense of a trapped creature flying up from her chest as she came to orgasm—and despite the unendurable presence of my sister in the room, she managed to move me as she once had.

"Inge." Her name escaped from me before I could swallow it.

Afterwards, I lay with my arms held stiffly at my sides. Inge nestled her body against me contentedly. I could feel a number of isolated sensations: her moist breath on my shoulder, her soft breast across my arm, the point of her nipple brushing my rib cage, the scent of the Joie de Patou.

She took my hand and pressed it tightly between her legs. I could feel how resilient and muscular were her slender thighs. Had she already started bicycling each morning on Riverside Drive? She was no longer at all like Malkele. But didn't Ben, who had adored Malkele, adore this physically fit German woman as well? I wondered what she wanted from me, this other man's woman.

A war engulfed my heart. I wanted Inge—even as I lay there, withdrawn and agitated, my body was starting to respond a second time to the provocative fragrance of her flesh that so lightly touched me. Truthfully, I had never stopped loving her, this beautiful woman next to me in the bed, into whose body I had entered so many times. This fearful child who had blossomed into a woman right before my awestruck eyes. This wife with whom I had a son. This companion without whom I was nothing, a friendless wretch, an object of scorn, a joke. A rotten father. Yet I hated her, and not simply because of Ben. Not even because of her German habits. I confess that it was her very womanliness, her fullness, even her health, her contentment, that had so embittered me. To where had my malnourished fledgling flown off? To where my Malkele? To where my Inge? And what about the horror that had delivered us into each other's hands so miraculously, in Paris in 1947, with such an immense hunger for each other's life, with such grave responsibilities, as we worked to rescue our plundered collections?

Could I not have opened my heart to Inge that night? Not in order to hurt her. Not to drive her further away from me. But for a new chance. Surely she would have understood her unshatterable connection to my memory of my sister. Hadn't she once, in the early days, graciously permitted Malkele to live for a moment inside herself for me? Would she not see how Ben's presence in our bedroom had revived this ghost of

my sister? How could I tell her that her ability to get on with
life, her very health, had made a caricature of Malkele's return? But why, then, had she turned so thoroughly into Malkele earlier when I came into her?

Wasn't my predicament even more shameful? The two
women of my life belonged now not to me but to him. Would
I once again sit and watch with a book in my hands? No, it
was worse than that. It was the opposite of that. Inge might
fill Ben with her capacity to live by forgetting. She might
take him away from Malkele, as she had half taken me.
Would both of Malkele's still-living suitors belong now to
Inge? Malkele needed more than my historical interest in
her life. She needed my soul. What choice did I have but
to leave Inge to Ben and return totally to my sister? Ben had
not been worthy of her. I would now live without comforts. I
would live dangerously again, on the Aryan side, so as to
never lose sight of my sister, of my work. Poor Ben . . . what
chance did he have, between Malkele and me? Even when
we used to meet in midtown for lunch, he must have known
how much I needed to keep him in bondage to my dead sister. I never let him off the hook, as they say here. And now
he is buried. Thank God he found Inge. Poor Inge . . . to have
been loved by a husband who hated his very love of her.
Thank God she found Ben. Poor Emmanuel . . . to grow up
seeing that both he and his mother together were less in his
father's eyes than an aunt who was murdered before he was
born. Nothing can be hidden. Thank God he had Ben for a
few years.

I continued lying on my back long into the night watching
the unsteady pattern of candlelight that was made even more
unsteady by the threatening headlights occasionally sweeping in from the street. I found Inge's breathing even more
painful to hear than I had expected. I fought off an urge to

weep. She cleared her throat but continued to sleep when I
carefully dislodged my hand that had started to tingle from
the pressure of her moist thighs. It seemed essential that she
not wake up and find me in this weakened state. Would
things be different now if she had opened her eyes and we
had talked then, in bed, rather than later in the dining room?
I sat up in slow-motion and blew out the candle that had just
started to sputter. Now there was a grayness around me. On
the way out I stopped to pick up my pajamas from the floor.
I turned to look at her one more time, but I could hardly see
across the darkened room. I wondered whether she needed
to be covered. I was afraid to go back and see, so I turned
and tiptoed out and closed the door behind me. I never saw
the inside of that bedroom again.

It was nearly dawn when I lay down on the daybed for an
hour's sleep before I had to get up and out of the apartment.
In better times I had lingered with a cup of coffee and
thought about my work the coming day. Now each morning
I simply left by 6:30 to sit in a diner until I was awake enough
to take the subway downtown—I was ashamed that Emmanuel
might find me sleeping in the dining room. Did Ben wait
at the corner for me to leave so he could join them for breakfast with a bag of bagels and smoked salmon from Inge's
favorite appetizing store? Did Emmanuel still choose dry ce-
real each morning from his collection of individual-sized
packages? Better I should move out and leave them alone to
live the way they wanted to.

Again Inge opened the door to her bedroom, but this time
she was wearing a robe. I got up from the bed in embarrassment.

"Leon, I thought you could stay the night with me." Once
more her voice was calm and dignified. I sat down on the
edge of the bed before I spoke.

"I was not able to fall asleep," I said in Yiddish. Was I

protecting myself by answering her in my mother tongue? Was I pulling further away from this German Jewess?

"Perhaps you could get used to me again." Inge went on with no reaction to my choice of language. What was she hoping to accomplish?

"The bed is too small for three." My nasty Yiddish made her wince. It sprang out of me, against my will, so to speak.

"There has always been a third, hasn't there?" She spoke angrily, in German. She stood over me.

"So you added a fourth." Why was I continuing to provoke her?

"That's right"—she shouted, but in English again—"I added a fourth, but he is not a fourth, he is a first because he is all mine. You were never mine." Her face had grown pale.

"Ben Schwartz all yours?" I was screaming, but in a whisper because I did not want to wake the boy at this hour. The last thing I wanted were his eyes on me. I controlled myself by not standing up.

"Stop it! Stop it! Stop feeling so sorry for yourself. You were not the only one who lost a family. What about me? What about Ben? Can we go on grieving forever? We have a right to enjoy life a little, sometimes."

Did she really think that all I did was grieve? And only for my family? Had she never understood the meaning of my work as an historian of a slaughtered people? I was afraid she would wake the boy, so I put a finger over my lips to quiet her down.

"And I certainly can't live in your past!" She continued shouting, but a little lower. "And Emmanuel can't live in your past either. For years he has had nightmares about your family, about your sister, about your Auschwitz. What have you filled his head with? We need more than this—all this blackness, this scorn. I will not allow you to infect our son with your scorn and your nightmares."

"Nightmares? Do you think it is all in my head? These things happened." I knew I had just said a terrible thing to her. Her eyes widened.

"Do you think that you have to tell me that these things happened? Have you forgotten, you memory man, have you forgotten that I was there too?" I had never before seen Inge so livid.

"Remembering is my work." This I said quietly in English, as a gesture to her, but Inge was not interested.

"Well, it is not my work. And it is not Emmanuel's. No! I won't have it! If not for Ben Schwartz, Emmanuel would be a nervous wreck by now. Don't you know how he has needed you to be here, here, right here, in this world, here, for him?"

"But I thought you were part of my work."

"You thought I was your sister."

"Have you been seeing a therapist? Is Schwartz paying for it?" Now I too was livid.

"What of it?"

"What of it? You trade in your memory for a little self-knowledge. All you German Jews are the same. All you want is peace, happy families, respectability, interior decorating, Christian friends. . . ."

"Stop it, you fool!" She was screaming. "I am as Jewish as you are."

"Don't shout, you will wake up your precious son, your bar mitzvah boy. Why doesn't he know any Yiddish?"

"Because you never taught him any, you busy man, you! And what if he does wake up? He is sixteen years old, he hasn't been a bar mitzvah boy in three years."

Suddenly I felt drained. "Please," I begged, "I don't want him to see me like this, on this couch like a dog." For a moment Inge said nothing, but I could see her jaw trembling and tears sliding down her cheeks.

"Leon"—she spoke slowly—"I have always known your work was necessary."

I remained silent.

"Why did you come into the bedroom with me?" There was sweetness not accusation in her voice.

"Why did you entice me?" How could I have used that word at such a moment? Thank God my tone was gentle.

"Because I have never stopped loving you."

Why didn't I answer her that I had never stopped loving her? What madness held me back? I could taste the defeat in her voice. She stood over me where I sat, and her robe had fallen open. I wanted to reach up and gently tie her robe. I wanted so many things. Instead I said, "Good night," in a weak voice, and lay back on the daybed and turned my face to the wall so she wouldn't see what I felt. I was grateful that somehow Emmanuel had slept through all of this. Or had he? As I waited for her to retreat I kept hoping that she would touch my shoulder. I knew I wouldn't hear her steps. Her tread had always been very soft. Did she stand over me a long time waiting for me to turn toward her again? I'll never know. Perhaps she is still standing there, waiting.

Now that Ben is gone, doesn't Inge need me again? Doesn't Emmanuel still need a father—my young boy who clutched my hand and looked up at me expectantly, glowingly, as we walked in the park, through the tunnel that led to the water. We could yet sit at the table while Inge blessed the newborn Sabbath in her German style that is in its own way dignified and Jewish. Why have I been unable to entertain these new thoughts? Why am I turning away from them yet one more time? Has Malkele become finally no more than my executioner? Never will I let myself accuse her so. Never. Never. Never. Never. Better to be dead than to live by abandoning my murdered sister.

Stop! Enough of this. Sit still for a moment. Then go on with your work.

LVIII

Kristin returned one hour and fifty-two minutes after she left. She smiled tenderly when she found me sitting with my hands upraised.

"Just sit that way another moment, my sweet darling doctor, while I put this fragrant laundry away." Like a dog, I could hardly contain myself.

She came back in two minutes, still smiling, carrying Poopikle. My anger lasted only a split second. Why not Poopikle? He would be an appropriate witness.

"Why, thank you so much, Doctor, the pillow is a marvelous touch—so homey. I do so like your bedside manner." She spoke with the inflection of a Southern belle.

"Yes, Miss Dietrich. And if you don't mind"—I pointed at Poopikle—"my apprentice will observe these procedures." My German accent would have been perfect here, but again I resisted my urge—why sour Kristin at this moment? She craved to hear me speak with a more pronounced Yiddish accent, but I resisted that as well.

"Oh, Doctor, I'd be simply delighted."

"Please remove your garments and place yourself on the examination desk."

"You do mean this examination table, don't you, Doctor? I would find it disconcerting, to say the least, to dash down the hall to your inner office in a state of undress." Again I felt enticed by this inflection to break into my German accent—but why make trouble?

"Yes, yes, I mean the examination table, not my desk—this one, here." Did my voice betray my impatience?

"Just my outer garments, Doctor Solomon?" Kristin went on gaily.

"Everything, Miss Dietrich." I felt dominated—forced to continue this role of doctor with no personality.

Without another word Kristin began taking off her clothes. I watched her, just as on the first night, mesmerized by her emerging nakedness. My lust had not diminished at all. Suddenly I was delighted to be this nondescript Doctor Solomon. Each item she removed she folded and placed carefully on the chair, each time lifting Poopikle up and putting him back down on top. She wore a black brassiere-and-panties set. The brassiere, like the one she wore the first night, unsnapped in the front. Once again her breasts sprang forth so dramatically that my heart heaved within my chest. Once again, when she saw me gazing at them, her nipples bunched up and pointed forward. Once again, years of deprivation fell away like clothing and left me quivering. Once again, grateful, cold lust overtook my heart.

"Is this familiar?" It took me a second or two to understand that she was referring to the panties—an exact duplicate of Fulani's panties, and even, I thought, the same size. "Lily of France," she continued. "It took me half the afternoon to locate them."

"Do you always prepare yourself so alluringly for doctors' appointments?"

"It just depends on the doctor, Doctor." She still played the Southern lady.

"Just for Jewish doctors?" The moment I uttered it I regretted that small cruelty.

"Just for you, Doctor Solomon." She said this quietly, with no trace of a Southern accent. She removed the panties, placed them next to Poopikle on the chair, and lay down on the table. She held her long legs up so I could put the stirrups around her heels. Then she slid toward me so that her buttocks were near the end of the table, her knees angled back toward her shoulders, and her vagina fully exposed. I put the pillow under her head and stood timidly waiting for her instructions. "You must help me. I don't know what to do." I spoke in Yiddish because I felt suddenly very close to her— more than close—and ashamed of my earlier harshness. This woman was giving me everything.

Helpless beneath me, her feet in stirrups, her ten red toenails pointing up, she lifted her head from the pillow and looked into my eyes. I will never forget the sorrowful and luminous smile that met my gaze. Perhaps it came from the awkward angle she was forced to assume to look into my face, perhaps it was simply her helpless exposure beneath me, but instantly I felt her being rush forth into my heart. Kristin's luminous sorrow beckoned to me and freed me, temporarily, from all necessity to hate her. How could such a thing be? How can there be a truce? How can there be forgiveness? Not for such things as they did to us. Never. I was being tricked by my own unspeakable loneliness, by my own lust for her Teutonic body, for her wide-nippled breasts, for her long legs suspended in majestic helplessness, for her blonde hair that lay almost glowing about her head on my table, for the silken curls and moist lips of her cunt waiting to be parted by my grief-stricken fingers. Trick or no trick, my heart ran over, as they say, with desire and tenderness.

"Insert the speculum—you will know just how to do it, my dearest Leybele." Her words startled me, but this unbearable closeness I felt to her did not vanish.

I lightly kissed each of her ten toes.

"Why, Doctor, how original."

"Shah, bubele." I put a finger to my lips.

I did know just what to do. I parted the secret folds of her vagina with my left hand and slowly inserted the instrument. I slowly turned a small knob and before my eyes the walls

of her vagina parted. I peered into a darkness. I directed the
tiny spotlight into her body. I saw a small rose moon surrounded by pink walls. I held the magnifying glass before my
eyes and peered again. I saw the inside of a flower—a rose.
There was nothing Teutonic about the inside of her vagina.
It could have been Inge's womb I was looking at, or Malkele's, or my mother's.

"The wombs of all women are Jewish wombs," I whispered
into the room. The fragrance from her body flooded my consciousness. How could I have lived so many years separated
from a woman's body? I was drunk with tenderness.

"You are still the same little boy who thinks all mothers
are Jewish." Even the way Kristin pronounced the word
"Jewish" touched me at that moment. She was referring to
an article where I mentioned that as a small boy in Vilna I
believed that though there were gentile children and gentile
men all mothers were Jewish.

I peered and thirsted. Again she lifted up her transfixed
face—I held the mirror so she could see her womb reflected
there. Her face looked like a child's. Her womb was mother
to both of us.

"My infant." The whispered words seemed to come from
her stomach. "More than my life I love you." These words
she uttered in Yiddish. "Look all you want to satisfy your
great thirst. I am yours." Again the last three words were
Yiddish.

I continued to peer, mesmerized, aroused by her eyes
watching me. I put one eye up against the widened opening.
Again I witnessed the original darkness, so to speak. I put
my nostrils between the halves of the speculum and inhaled
deeply the transforming fragrance. Where was it taking me?
Back to my birth in the apartment in Vilna? Back to the tub
of warm water where I bathed Malkele on the Aryan side?
To Inge in Paris after the war? To Inge in the years after she

gave birth to Emmanuel? To Inge that last time we embraced and I found Malkele instead? Perhaps it was an illusion created in Berlin and I was being ushered, finally, into the gas chamber. From one fragrance to another fragrance, and between them one defeat follows another. Enough—that is not what I felt then. *Arbeit macht frei* was not written on the opening to Kristin's body. I must remain objective in my recollection. This is not the time to begin falsifying. Her female fragrance was not a trick. It was not death but life I inhaled that night. If the gas spigots in this room should suddenly function again they could not give Kristin back to me.

I pulled out the instrument and inserted a finger, then a second finger. I felt the silvery wetness. If I had been a Houdini I would have slipped my whole hand in, then my arm, then my shoulder, then my head. I would have climbed in body and soul, but the laws of nature blocked my path. Right now I would be there, within Kristin's vagina, licking the walls, pressing myself further into the depths.

"Yes," she called out to me, in a particular German I had not heard in more than four decades. "Yes, my darling."

I began to fondle her clitoris with two fingers. Through the magnifying glass I watched the red point swell and harden.

"Look into my eyes as you do that." This too she spoke in her German, and I obeyed without noticing it.

Later that night, as she slept beside me, that German repeated itself like a knife in my inner ear, so to speak. Hers was no imitation German. Nor was it Jewish German. It was the efficient and sentimentalized Gestapo German of her childhood. I turned on a small light by the bed in order to clear my mind. Impossible, she insisted as her face reddened, when I told her after she woke up to ask me what was wrong. For years she had struggled to free herself of that German. She had even refused to speak anything but English when

she visited her mother the previous year. Couldn't I have
imagined it? Perhaps I had imagined it, but I stubbornly insisted that I heard what I heard. Kristin was speechless with
regret.

"Please forgive me, Leon," she whispered somewhat formally, careful not to mix any Yiddish into her English. An
obscure regret gripped my heart at that moment. I was grateful that I had failed to react to her German during those mysterious and tender moments earlier that night. To this day I
remain grateful for that small respite from the poisons of
twentieth-century European history.

We looked into each other's eyes as I rubbed the wetness
around her exposed clitoris. I was watching her come to orgasm. She was watching me watch her. Her eyes opened
wider, then wider. "Leybkele," she cried, "Leybkele." I
rubbed her wetness with the palm of my hand, with the heel
of my hand, with the numbers on my forearm, then again
with my fingers—in circles, slowly, confidently. Her forehead
furrowed in intensity. Her nostrils opened and closed. Her
lips, which she had held tightly clenched, parted. Her mouth
was fully opened as she panted. Still she kept her eyes open
wide for me to see into her, pleading with me to see into her.
My eyes were as open as hers, my forehead furrowed, I
panted as she panted. I felt no shame; there was no separa-
tion between us. We had obliterated history for a precious
moment. Her vagina became suddenly warmer and wetter.
Our panting became stronger. She never took her eyes from
mine. Her orgasm lasted longer than I had thought possible.
It was a great gift that she was giving me. She fell back,
spent. I fell with my mouth to her wetness and drank and
drank. Again and again she came to orgasm.

I undid the stirrups and lifted her thighs even higher so I
could kiss the beauty-mark between her cheeks. She sat up,

undid the belt of my purple robe, and took my sex into her hands. She was about to lower herself down and take me with her mouth when I stopped her.

"Now I will get on the table."

"But Doctor," she said playfully. This was not in her script. I shook my head no, to quiet her. I was not ready yet for play.

I felt the marvelous sweat of her body on my buttocks and along my back when I lay down on the desk.

"Yes," I commanded her, "put my feet in the stirrups—I am yours." She hesitated and then obeyed.

The cloth felt damp against my skin. Just as Kristin had earlier, I worked my body down to the end of the table. My knees looked silly in the air above me. My penis had grown timid. I could see Kristin's face from between my legs. I watched her bend forward and take it into her mouth.

"No, my baby, look into my eyes. I am yours."

She lifted her face and looked at me as I held my head up to meet her glance. She was now the most beautiful woman in the world. She put the pillow under my head. With one hand she gripped my hardened penis and began to slowly caress it. With the other hand she cupped my testicles. I was hers. Once again we looked into each other's eyes. My lips puckered as she fondled me. Her lips puckered in response. Our eyes grew larger together. With my heels caught in the stirrups I was wonderfully helpless before this woman I adored.

It was not in Kristin's script for me to be hers so utterly. Tonight I was supposed to dominate her—that was what her heart most craved. Yet she rose to the occasion, as they say. Now she served me by mastering me. Her eyes held my eyes open. My legs dangled above me. Never had I felt so exposed before another. There was no terror, no humiliation, no enslavement, no death. We were exposed to each other—dominated together by a mystery that flowed freely from one to

the other. But why with a German woman? Had Inge and I
never felt so? Images of Inge flickered in my consciousness,
but Kristin held me with her eyes. As long as my eyes remained open I was hers. I longed to close my eyes, to isolate
myself from her as she did this wonderful thing to me. I
longed to find another in my memory, one who was not there
above me holding my sex in her hands, one who was not
German. I longed for Malkele. Had Inge never snatched me
away from Malkele as this German woman was taking me?
Was that possible? Had I simply forgotten Inge's power?
Kristin held me with her eyes, drew me toward her, looked
into me at my naked mind, at my sixty-five-year-old organs,
at the small boy who sat still at the window on Wiwulski
Street, his eyes watching the raindrops pass down the glass
while his mother cooked the Sabbath meal in the next room.

This she saw and more—and she did nothing to hurt me.
Would I be able to transfer to her, finally, all the beings who
lived inside me? Was that truly what she needed from me,
what I needed to give her? Suddenly I knew I was in mortal
danger, but for the moment I abandoned myself even to that.
I would permit her to receive what she could—for the moment Kristin was my eternal companion. Her eyes held
mine.

"Leybkele, bubele," she crooned, "your balls are becoming very tight. Soon you will come but not yet." I was now
simply an extension of her wondrous hands, her amazing
eyes. Every time I was about to come she slowed up just
enough to keep me at the edge. With her hands and her eyes
she conducted my sexual responses slowly, then quickly, then
softly, then more softly. One time she stopped moving her
hands altogether but kept my excitement intense, yet controlled, merely with her eyes. Suddenly, after what may have
been hours or only minutes, her eyes narrowed a drop and I
felt my eyes narrow. Her hand began moving rapidly but

lightly on my penis. Her other hand squeezed my testicles just enough. "Yes," she said, "now you are coming." I never knew an ejaculation could last so long.

"Yes," she said, "yes, Leybkele, bubele, you are coming— it is very beautiful." I wept as I came. A flood came up out of me. I had totally surrendered to Kristin and found it sweet.

She dropped her head between my dangling legs and licked and drank and swallowed. Suddenly my ejaculation was unbearably finished, and even before she lifted her glistening face from my softened organ I felt the indignity of my position on the table. Had she felt the same indignity?

"Please unbuckle the stirrups," I said coldly. Had my soul become so constricted that I could not meet this beautiful woman except for a few moments at a time?

She showed no sign of anger as she unbuckled my legs, and with the towel that she had wet with warm water she wiped off the semen that remained on my groin. I put on my robe and sat down in a chair by the window overlooking the alley that led to 108th Street. Kristin turned out the light and sat on a chair she had pulled over near me. She was naked. My dried semen must still have been on her face. I sat for a long time looking out the window. I could see people pass in the lamplight down on the street. Once two men stopped under the lamp as they passed each other and talked with dramatic gestures. What were they saying to each other, these two displaced Puerto Ricans or Dominicans, that they needed to punctuate their every utterance with such flamboyant movements of their hands? They could easily have been two Jews returning from different synagogues discussing Zionism or socialism in our courtyard on Wiwulski Street. I could have been my mother, mildly curious, awash in despair, the end already dwelling in her like a small silent animal. Kristin could have been me, not knowing how to rescue Mother from her fate. This naked woman will abandon me, just as I abandoned my mother, I thought.

"Leon," she said softly, "come to bed now. It is late. To-morrow you have to go to work."

"Wash your face first," I announced, just as softly.

"It won't change a thing."

"Yes, it will—my semen is not acid. It has not scarred you for life, Kristin."

In bed, my soul softened once again. I kissed her lips tenderly. I called her name three times so I would know whom I was embracing. By some miracle I became hard again. I climbed on top of her and entered her vagina very slowly. In the eye of my mind I could see my penis sliding past her lips and moving in between the pink walls. I could see it reaching almost to the small rosy opening of her womb. I knew Kristin in a way I had never known another.

"I love you, Kristin. You are kinder to me than I deserve." In response she tightened her vagina: I felt held and protected. Slowly I moved down and up. Kristin must have sensed what I needed. She responded in kind, moving slowly, with no hope of transcendence again. Were we saying goodbye?

The following night I banished her.

LIX

I am stopping and starting a lot as I near the end. I am writing on the backs of the sheets of my very first entry more than two days ago. I have stopped to reread it. This terrible air of disintegration has become my natural atmosphere. Soon I will join a distinguished line of forerunners in this room. Why do I continue writing? How have I managed to write so much these past three decades? After all, my life in America has been far from comfortable, to say the least. The answer is simple. It is only when I write that I feel at home. When I am writing I am fully a Jew. Even now I am at home. So long as I keep pen to paper I am a Jew at home. The same question gnaws at my mind—even more urgently than it did two days ago: For whom am I writing this document?

But what have I left out? Should I say? I have written of my darkest secret—my secret life with my sister on the Aryan side and my failure to rescue her. I have discussed my most private habits. I have confessed my greatest humiliations. Yet I have not written, except in passing, of Inge—of our courtship in Paris.

Should I write how each night in those beginning days in my tiny room in Paris, until the early hours of the morning when I had to walk her back to the Luncharsky apartment, I studied Inge's rib cage? Should I write of her breasts which did not begin to mature until after we became lovers? When she lay on her back they suggested two abandoned nestlings, undernourished, anxious, perched in a slight hollow between her fragile ribs. Her scrawny nipples hopelessly scanned the sky. Her breasts were never more compelling. In a matter of months they grew plump and womanly. By then we were married. All of Inge was scrawny those early nights. I could reach my fingers almost around her white thighs. I could grip her two wrists with my thumb and forefinger—and I was no he-man myself. Her buttocks were pointy, like a young boy's. When she tightened her muscles they became concave. Her face was all lips and eyes. The skin on her cheekbones was tightly stretched. Her belly-button stuck up from her abdomen. Her elbows and knees were prominent. Even the black hairs on her mound were sparse. Of course, Inge had surrendered herself to our love every bit as fully as Kristin was to. For such a modest and proud woman as Inge to permit me to

see that half-wasted body of hers was an act of great love on
her part. How could I have forgotten that? She reminded me
then of Malkele.

Once I asked Inge if I could bathe her. I never told her why.
I didn't know why myself. Reluctantly she agreed. It was not
easy. The bath chamber was in the hall. I shared it with two
other men. Fortunately they were both elderly and rose early
to go off to work. They slept soundly. I convinced Inge it
would be safe for us to fill the tub and bathe her—that is
how reckless I was in those days. I would have lost my room
if we had been caught—and perhaps even Inge. When the
tub was full we tiptoed into the bathroom, Inge half-lost in
my robe. When I bathed her I forced myself not to think of
Malkele. I first experienced Inge's lifelong modesty then.
Though we had been lovers for nights now, she would not
permit me to wash either of her openings. I resisted a powerful urge to invent a story about Poopik for her. If Poopikle
had been in my possession then I would probably have left
him on the pillow for Inge to find. By the time I retrieved
Poopikle seven years later I could no longer share him with
her. Inge is now your sister, I told myself then. Her survival
is a miracle. Cherish her.

The night we first made love, the eve of her seventeenth
birthday, in April of 1947, I vowed to devote my life to Inge.
Half the night we fumbled in the dark. Neither of us knew
what to do. To enter a woman required a secret skill I had
not mastered. When I pressed against her opening she jerked
away nervously. When she didn't pull away I grew soft. Over
and over we played Marlene Dietrich on the phonograph to
hide our shame and to keep the magic from dissolving. Finally it was Inge who knew what to do. She held my penis
with her hand and guided it into her body. Yiddish exploded
from my lips. German exploded from her lips. The voice of
Marlene Dietrich taught us to slow down and feel the flesh

of the other one. When she wept, I vowed to devote my life to her. Luckily, she did not become pregnant. Her malnourished body could not yet have nurtured another.

We were married in September of that year, at a simple ceremony. Neither of us had any family left. The Luncharskys invited a few friends from the Institute to their apartment. Four men held up the canopy. Luncharsky and his wife stood with us. The rabbi, a German from Dachau, conducted the marriage in French and Hebrew. We spent a week in a rooming house on the beach near Marseilles. It was the first time I had seen the sea. Inge had spent a number of summers by the Baltic when she was a child. After accepting my marriage proposal three months earlier she had ceased being my lover. She wanted us to wait until our wedding night. Secretly her body was preparing for marriage. Each day that honeymoon week we walked on the beach. When we went into the Mediterranean we held hands. At night we made love with a delicious modesty. I fell in love all over again, as they say, this time with a vision of her emerging fullness, her newly developing womanliness. We would make the transition from death to life, almost. We would succeed in banishing Malkele, almost.

The girl outside my window reminds me less of Malkele— Malkele would never have stepped back into the shadows— than she does of Inge the child-woman, in the early nights, after her seventeenth birthday, when we first made love, to the haunting voice of Marlene Dietrich, in my tiny room in Paris. Is the girl hovering alone in the shadows again? I no longer hear the voices of the others. Should I go and look? Kristin is still in my mind. Have I left something essential unsaid? I could still call her. Is it possible she would abandon me as I abandoned her? Perhaps the shock of my swift banishment has released the anti-Semitism that has lain dormant in her soul for many years. Perhaps she is now a PLO

supporter. Perhaps she is giving herself at this very moment
to Mr. Moses Chikema.

Right now Hirsch and his wife are asleep in their twin
beds in their Brookline condominium. He thinks that I
couldn't call him even if I wanted to. It tickles him that we
have conducted such private business for so many years
without my learning his home address. When he bragged to
me about how much he had gotten for his house and what a
fabulous bargain the duplex was, he was careful not to reveal
his address. Brookline was the only crumb he dropped—only
because he needed this prestigious location to demonstrate
just how great the deal was. Was he offering me a false lead?
Perhaps he lives on Beacon Hill, or far out in the suburbs,
where they sit near a small swimming pool playing poker
with the condo set. None of this matters. I have found a way
of getting his phone number.

Maybe he is sitting right now on the edge of his bed with
chest pains. Indigestion, his wife assures him. Again he
overate. Hirsch is a man who loves his beef—and probably
his pork as well when he and the missus escape from their
Jews for an evening. The Hirsches have their favorite spots,
out-of-the-way and exotic, where she eats like a bird and he
stuffs himself like a pig.

What is there left for me to say to him? His wife would
probably answer. At such a late hour she would think it was
one of her children in trouble. Her voice would contain
panic.

Dawn

LX

"Hello, hello," Mrs. Hirsch called nervously into the mouthpiece. "Hello, is it Jonathan?" I hesitated a moment before replying.

"Let me speak to Hirsch." I enunciated each word from beginning to end, slowly, with no expression, not loud.

"Who is this? What do you want? It is late." Indignation entered her voice.

"Hirsch," I repeated, again with no expression.

"What do you want?" A drop of fear qualified the indignation.

"Hirsch," I said again, stubbornly. I gave her nothing.

"He is not well—call tomorrow." She tried, but she could not defy me.

"Now—I need to speak with Hirsch."

"Howard," I heard her calling, "come to the phone." I heard muffled voices. She had put her hand over the mouthpiece.

"Who is calling?" She was back but her voice was weak.

"A contact." The word made her shiver. Again I heard muffled voices.

"Hello, hello." At last, the frightened voice of Hirsch. I said nothing.

"Speak," he commanded, "or will I hang up?" In his confusion he had turned from command to question. I heard him clearing his throat, attempting to gain composure. I waited a few more seconds before beginning.

"You have a minimum of one hundred and seventy-three documents, Howard, that are the property of the New York Public Library." I said this in my Lewis Schorr accent. I had never called him Howard before—just Hirsch.

"Who is this?" I heard him breathing—rapid, shallow breaths. Hirsch is a man who is very nervous about dying. I stayed with my nasal, clipped, Lewis Schorr inflections.

"A man like you, Howard, with all your dealing and wheeling, is a candidate for a heart attack or even cancer. A cancer could already be growing in your stomach."

"Who is this?" He was terrified. Perhaps his chest hurt. Perhaps he felt too full in his stomach. He didn't hang up because he knew who was talking to him. I kept silent.

"Where are you, Leon?"

I kept silent. Hirsch had never called me Leon. Was he answering me in kind? Perhaps he saw me now in a new light, a more intimate light. Perhaps he was being diplomatic—calm the beast, keep him on the telephone, while Mrs. Hirsch calls the authorities on another line to have the call traced. Impossible. It would have taken them too long, and it was not to Hirsch's advantage to have me arrested again—not in my present state. The Hirsches may have an extension in their duplex, but certainly not another line. For a moment I had him where I wanted him. I felt giddy with authority.

"Leon, what do you want of me?" He had switched to his flawless Yiddish. He lowered his voice in an attempt to sound composed. "If I could help you, I would." He needed to hear my voice. "Leon, are you there?" I could hear his rapid breathing as he tried to outwait me. I remained silent. "I was planning to return your call first thing Monday morning. My secretary told me that you called."

"Whore," I hissed almost silently in Yiddish.

"Who, what?"

"Not Ellen," I shouted back in my Lewis Schorr English.

"Ellen, who is Ellen?" His voice was restrained and frantic. We both waited. I joined my slow breathing to his rapid breathing. We were now a duet. Again I said nothing. I waited for him.

"You mean my secretary?"

"Your former secretary," I said in Yiddish.

"Former?"

"She is no whore."

"Leon, you are making no sense."

"Let me speak to your wife," I demanded again in my Lewis Schorr English.

"My wife? What do you want from my wife?"

"Diseased whore," I hissed in Polish.

"How dare you speak in this way about my wife." Here his English was plaintive. His Yiddish had fled from him. He is not half the man Gellerman is.

"Not your wife." The menace in my voice was plain. Why didn't he hang up the telephone? Hirsch is finally not a decisive man.

"What have you done to yourself, Leon?" He tried to take charge. Again I fell silent.

"It is after three o'clock in the morning, Leon. Call me tomorrow."

"Die before the daylight comes." I could hear him swallowing my words.

"I will hang up." I remained silent. We both waited. I knew I could outlast Hirsch.

"Leon, are you all right?" He spoke first, but I continued to wait. I knew he would speak again.

"Leon," he said again two seconds later, "I know you are there. I can hear you breathing. Are you all right?" Once more he was trying to take me into his confidence with Yiddish. I despise the way he pronounces the word "breathing."

"Please, your wife."

"Leave her out of this."

"Your wife, please—Edna Oppenheimer Hirsch."

"I will hang up if you mention her again."

"No, you won't—not until I release you."

"Where are you?"

I remained silent.

"What do you want from me?"

I remained silent.

"Your troubles are your own doing, Leon."

I remained silent.

"I will have my lawyer charge you with harassment."

I remained silent. He too kept silent.

"Leon, do you hear me?" Again I had outlasted him.

"Let your sons be sterile," I started talking slowly and quietly. "Let your daughter's womb dry up. Let the body of your wife be covered with boils. Let cancer devour your stomach." I was singing now. "Die slowly, you bastard-bitch, you whore. Die tonight of a massive coronary." I hung up before he could, leaving my words to grip his throat through the telephone wires.

Hirsch can no longer sleep. He turns on the light by his bed. Mrs. Hirsch is downstairs in the kitchen staring at the wall. She has just taken two Valiums. The half-empty glass of water sits on the counter. Upstairs Hirsch grips his heart. The pain is intense—perhaps the massive heart attack I wished on him. Mrs. Hirsch starts up the stairs carrying a large bottle of Mylanta.

Hirsch is much too resilient. I am sure he is already fast asleep. He looks like a man who knows how to sleep soundly.

Never in my life have I slept soundly. I have survived by not sleeping. Hirsch survives by sleeping the sleep of the innocent, as they say. He will last longer. There is no way I could kill him over the telephone, thank God. Enough of Hirsch. Enough of Hirsch. Let him live and prosper and enjoy his grandchildren. There are worse men in the world who will outlive me.

Are you wondering how I got Hirsch's number? I called Ellen Meyers and she gave it to me. Her number I simply got from Information. "E. Meyers," I told the operator. "Cambridge." I had guessed correctly. Though it was past two in the morning I called her: it is now Saturday, she can sleep late.

"Don't try to trace this call—I am in a booth." Why did I start like that? Why was I frightening the girl?

"How can I help you, Mr. Solomon?"

"Give me Hirsch's number. Do you have it at home?"

"Yes, right here." She sounded more asleep than alarmed. Was I disappointed?

"You do? Why do you have it at home?"

"It's in my address book."

"In your private address book?"

"Why are you grilling me?" I had succeeded in waking her up.

"Why do you have his number in your private book? Does Mrs. Hirsch know?"

"Stop that. Stop that."

"I am sorry. Forgive me. I am not myself. Please listen to me for a minute." I told her about Inge and Emmanuel. I gave her their address. I asked her to write to Emmanuel. She promised me that she would.

"Could I come to you on the shuttle?" I asked this so urgently I shocked myself.

"When?" She spoke with no hesitation.

"As soon as the next one leaves—at dawn."

"Yes, I'll meet you at the airport."

"How will you know me?"

"I've seen a picture of you in your Institute's newsletter."
Immediately I wondered if she thought me handsome.

"Listen, Ellen, I was only teasing."

"But I want you to come." I had to stop her before she
persuaded me.

"I have no more change."

"Give me your number and I'll call you back."

"Then you will report the number to the authorities."

"No, I promise to respect your privacy."

"No matter what?"

"Yes, no matter what." I gave her the number and waited
until it rang three times before I lifted the receiver.

"Mr. Solomon, Mr. Solomon, I am so worried about you."
Again I had to keep her from softening my resolve.

"If I thought, Ellen, that you were about to do something
as foolish as face your destiny, I would report you immediately. I would lie and deceive to save you."

"Why do you torture me so?" She started to cry.

"I'm so sorry. Don't cry. I am not myself tonight." I added
the word tonight to let her think that there would be other
nights for me.

"Is this your first job since college?"

"Yes, it is."

"I thought so. What will you do next?"

"Perhaps I will go back to school to study writing."

"That is a good idea."

"We will never meet, will we, Mr. Solomon?"

"I don't know. Ellen, perhaps we will meet." I said this so
gently that I knew I needed to get off the phone before I too
started to cry. "Can you give me the number now?"

I thanked her and promised to call her again.

LXI

It was a mistake to call Fulani again. From a telephone booth it is just not the same. The main reason not to call, however, was Kristin.

I have thought often of the breathtaking outrage that for an instant crossed Kristin's face when she looked into mine after she let herself into the apartment the fourth night. The next day I changed the cylinder, since she neglected to leave my key when she departed. A demure white dress coolly covered that long body that had kept my own seething with lust for four days and three nights now. How had she read me so instantaneously and so accurately? Was my face already ashen with this new loss? Just a second passed, then she smiled warmly and called out my name. Her shoes were also white. The spiked heels made her taller than her six feet. When this woman in white stepped over and planted herself next to my chair, she towered over me, as they say.

"Leybkele," she called out to me a second time. Immediately I thirsted to unzipper the front of her white dress.

I resisted the urge by closing my eyes. If it hadn't seemed too foolish—an admission of weakness—I would also have put my hands over my ears. To thoroughly eliminate her I would also have had to pinch my nose: she was faintly scented with Joie de Patou. She misunderstood the squeak I emitted involuntarily when I tightened my lips to keep from speaking—or perhaps she knew that squeak better than I did. She grasped my head and buried my face just beneath her breasts. I could feel her heart pounding against my eyelids.

"Tonight I am going to bathe you and shave you, you pretty boy." The last three words she cooed in Yiddish.

I tore my head from her grasp and stood up. With those

spiked shoes on her feet Kristin was almost a head taller than I was. She ignored my roughness and half unzipped the bodice of her dress. I lusted to see her with nothing on but those shoes. Never had I seen a woman so, except in magazines.

"I am sick of your naked body." I said this in English, quietly.

Kristin smiled at me as though we were playing a new game, and pulled open the zipper to where it ended just below her navel. She reached downward to the hem of her dress and pulled it up over her head.

"Stop that! Stop that!" My German sounded like a dog barking. I roughly yanked her dress back down and pulled at her zipper. The momentary sight of her nakedness had so unraveled me I almost fell to my knees before the delicate twist of blonde curls between her legs. She would have had me again that night. In her pocket. And if she had prevailed then, she would have prevailed the following night, and the night beyond that one.

With this Gestapo daughter the keeper of my body and my soul, my pilferings would have been just that. I would have been just another petty thief. But alone, my thefts of documents had dignity and historical necessity.

Ben Schwartz would never have permitted Kristin to lure him as she lured me. His dignity was always greater than his needs—except when he "stole" Inge from me. Why do I say "stole"? Is this not slander? Didn't Inge need to be rescued from me? Ben delayed as long as he could, and then he did what was proper and dignified. The two women I have loved most in my life Ben also loved. The only bedroom in my life he had no access to was my mother's. If he had lived to take Kristin from me our unity would be almost complete. Would he not have found a more humane way of dealing with Kristin than throwing her out of his apartment, as though she were a dog, just when she was about to give herself to him a fourth night? How could it be that Kristin Dietrich reminds me so much of both Inge and Malkele?

"This is no good," I said quietly. "Get out, please."

"Please don't throw me out, Leybkele," Kristin begged. "I'll do whatever you want me to—we need each other." Why didn't I simply repeat my command to her to leave? Why did I go on to humiliate her? Perhaps I was simply stalling. The front of her dress was still half unzipped. I could still see the comforting cleft between her breasts. I could still throw myself into her powerful arms. I could once more encounter my cheated youth within her body.

"Will you marry me?" I asked.

"Yes," she replied with no hesitation or sarcasm. "I will marry you tonight if you will have me."

"Even though I am not divorced from Inge?" Underneath my sarcasm I was intrigued, even touched, by her response. Perhaps she sensed that.

"Yes, I will marry you in Mexico, if you like. We can fly there tonight."

"And we can find a rabbi in the Jewish quarter, yes?"

"Oh, yes, Leybkele, there is nothing I would like better than that." She sounded joyous. Why did she continue to ignore my sarcasm? Was she in her right mind?

"How about in Paraguay?" I ignored her frailty.

"Why Paraguay?" She still refused to recognize the poison on my tongue.

"Then we can travel to Freiburg for our honeymoon, yes? We can visit your father in his home, yes?" The shock and sorrow that seized her face at that moment prodded me to continue. Why did I not fall silent?

"Is his friend Pavel still living?"

"His name is not Pavel." Was she prepared to submit to anything?

"Not Pavel? What is it, then? Is it Wolfgang? Is it Johann? Is it Ludwig? Is it Christian, Parsifal, Odin, Siegfried?" I was startled by my harsh, nasal tone. I could have been wearing a black uniform. Was it not somehow pleasurable?

"Stop it," she pleaded.

"What is his name?"

"Herr Schmit. He was called Herr Schmit."

"His Christian name? What was his Christian name? Was it Hermann, by any chance? Or Heinrich? Or Adolf? Or could it have been, perhaps, Josef?"

"Hans. His name was just Hans."

"Oh, is he dead, the poor man?"

"I don't want to talk about him." She cried and smiled at the same time. Was she, too, finding this ugliness pleasurable? The flesh between her breasts looked moist.

"Why not? Did he molest you when you were a girl? Did he push his huge penis into your girlish body? Did he prepare the way for me?" I practically spit in her face I was so close to her. She seemed to have shrunk a number of inches.

"Please, Leybkele, please stop this, stop this."

"Stop it? Why should I stop? Did you enjoy taking his cock into your mouth?"

"Stop it, you fool," she shouted. For some reason the word "fool" silenced me.

Those were the last words Kristin spoke to me that night. Though I encountered her three more times in the next few weeks, the next time I heard her say more than three words was over the air on Fulani's program. Kristin quickly became one of Fulani's most devoted callers. (Was she truly having a nervous breakdown, this beautiful, fearless woman, that she became just another one of Fulani's pathetic late-night callers? Or was she torturing me with her new identity, and laughing about it afterwards with a new lover?)

I stepped back from Kristin and looked down at her spiked white shoes.

"Leave me, Kristin—now. There is no other choice for us. Just leave." I turned away from her and walked into the bathroom she had scrubbed so vigorously two nights before. I shut the door. Half the night I sat there on the toilet. I heard nothing from the other side of the door. Was she simply standing all that time in the same spot? Would she still be there when I emerged? When I did finally emerge, her absence clutched my chest. I had not felt that sort of desperation since my first nights in the apartment, when I could not stop my mind from picturing Inge and Ben and the boy. In these past three days in this hotel room I have fully tasted that sensation again, but not while I write.

How had Kristin exited without making a sound? The door was locked, yet I had not heard the key turn in the cylinder. Had she descended the fire escape in her white dress? The Ukrainian in the alley would have thought he was experiencing a visitation by the Virgin. I found the window gate locked as always. The newly seeded window box looked like a grave in the darkness. Perhaps she had hidden herself, waiting to surprise me, I thought. But with what? With her undying loyalty? With a kitchen knife? With both? I convinced myself that she was hiding in the closet, naked except for her provocative white spiked shoes. Would I throw her out or allow her to make me over into her master? My chest heaved when I opened the door of the closet. A mysterious figure flew out at me. It was my own reflection in a full-length mirror on the inside of the door. Kristin must have brought it up and attached it while I was sitting all day long in my darkened office at the Institute. The apartment was no longer my own. I searched behind my suits and coats before I closed the door, relieved to rid myself of my reflection, but greatly disappointed, I must admit, that I hadn't found Kristin hiding there. The sight of myself in the mirror had filled me with a sudden longing for her embrace. My chest hurt, but I continued searching.

I convinced myself, next, that Kristin had silently slipped into the bathroom right after I emerged. Again I was startled, this time when I looked behind the shower curtain. Kristin's Fulani-style panties and her bra from the previous evening hung on a wooden rack. She must have brought it up from her apartment and placed it in the tub. The same tub where we had so recently soaped each other. I kept myself from opening the refrigerator door or from looking inside the sparkling oven. I would not permit panic to seize me. I did, however, get down on my hands and knees and look for her under the bed, where the sight of the freshly polished floor overcame me—and I began to weep.

I prepared a glass of hot milk and forced myself to sit in my chair. I had not wept so in many years. Kristin's absence surrounded me. Slowly the isolation I felt began spreading throughout my body and I started to calm down. The composure that took me years to achieve, however, had fled with Kristin. More than three months have passed. Except when I am writing I have lived without it since that night. Will I find it again at the very end?

I must confess that before I got into bed I pushed my chair against the door. Still, all night long I kept hearing Kristin. One time I was convinced that she stood on the fire escape looking in at me. The minutes passed, second after second on my clock, and still she did not move. She looked at me. I looked at her. Finally I went to the window to investigate. A bedspread lay draped over the railing. Kristin must have brought it up here for me from her apartment and hung it out to air. How had it bunched up so that it looked like a figure in the dark? There were no strong winds. How come I hadn't noticed it earlier? The apartment was no longer my own. What else had she brought in? What had she removed?

The next morning I was afraid to leave. Kristin had a key. When I emerged from the toilet I saw the white spiked shoes. They were standing exactly where Kristin had stood. How could I have missed seeing them when I searched the apartment the night before? They stood there one next to the other. Why had she left them? Would they be an excuse for her to return? Were they a parting gift? Had she seen the nature of my lust in the minutes before I threw her out? With each thought my heart jumped. I got down on my knees and put my hands into them. My middle fingers stuck through the open toes. The soles felt warm. How could that be? Could a shaft of sunlight have reached them this morning? I lifted them to my face and breathed in the fragrance. I found the inexplicable warmth, the faint scent of her feet quite comforting. It was intermingled with the even fainter scent of the Joie de Patou. I sniffed them like a dog until my eyes watered. I put the shoes down and stood up. I stuck one foot in, then the other. My heels stuck out over the backs and my toes couldn't quite squeeze into the tips. Yet I managed to walk in them, slowly. I crossed the room and opened the closet door. I looked at myself in the mirror, with nothing on but those compelling shoes. I turned from side to side. My calves were shapely, like a woman's. I sucked in my cheeks and smiled sadly.

"Leybkele." I spoke softly, and watched my hands reach out toward me. I watched my penis grow hard and stick out into the air, inconsolable and pathetic.

Instead of going to work I went out and bought a new cylinder. I could no longer permit Kristin access to my apartment. I refused to look at her door when I passed by. Was she watching through the peephole? I felt grateful to be walking in these familiar streets again—as though this were my first morning outside after a month of illness. The locksmith was not yet open for business, so I went into my donut shop for a coffee. The Haitian counterman asked me in French if I was not feeling so well. My euphoria disappeared.

"Why?" I demanded in English, distressed at my lack of poise. I had been chatting with this man in French for more than three years. Now I felt as though I were sitting at his counter with nothing on. "Do I look ill?" I demanded.

"No," he replied, also in English. "Merely you have not come in here for four or five days."

"I was away on vacation," I continued in English so he wouldn't feel encouraged to ask me where I had been. In truth, I was touched that he had noticed my absence, and ashamed of my unfriendly responses. I wondered whether Kristin was a customer. Did he flirt with her in French? Was his black skin as enticing to her as my numbers? I was a steady customer. I am sure I would have noticed her. Soon he will know her, I thought. Now that she knows my comings and goings she will start having coffee here too. I began looking through the glass into the street for a sign of Kristin. She could be in my apartment right now, I thought.

When I returned with the cylinder, I saw immediately that she had returned. The spread covered the bed perfectly. The room looked swept and neat. Was she still there? Again I searched the apartment frantically. Kristin was gone and so were the shoes. I ran to the closet. The mirror was gone. Would this clean apartment be the only reminder of our short affair? This memory would turn to dust very quickly. If I hadn't changed the cylinder would she have continued to come in while I was away, simply to sweep and scrub? Would I have opened my eyes one night to the sight of her standing above me with a hammer in her hand?

She left me another memento. My papers were all intact,

so to speak, even the two priceless specimens that I couldn't resist showing her—without, of course, telling her that I was simply a middleman, transferring them from one powerful institution to another, for a small fee. At least Kristin was not a thief. I ran to the bureau to check one last item. Fulani's panties were just where I had left them, the only unwashed underthing in the apartment. Next to them in the empty drawer sat the white spiked shoes. So that was her gift. Now I would have a choice of fantasy. Perhaps I would combine the two. I could pull the panties over my head and push my face into the shoes—Patchouli and Joie de Patou at the same time. Or I could wear them. If she hadn't removed the mirror, would I grow vain looking at myself with nothing on but the shoes and panties? If I could find a few of Kristin's hairs in the sheets, I could stick them in the lacy crotch. I could get a long cord for the telephone and look at myself this way as I spoke to Fulani in my German accent. I could crow like Emil Jannings with numbers on his forearm. Kristin's hidden camera would record it all for the viewing pleasure of her fast crowd of children of the SS.

This is not the time to begin ranting in self-pity.

But why had Kristin removed the mirror? Was she sparing me the sight of myself alone in this dismal world? Of course, I have two mirrors in this hotel room. I have been spared nothing. Inge never wore such high heels. I wondered whether these shoes would fit her. Probably they would be too large. German Jewesses have more delicate bones than their Teutonic counterparts. Poopikle could sit comfortably in one of these shoes. Where was Poopikle? I searched high and low for him. I turned the apartment upside down, so to speak. So Kristin was a thief, after all. But why Poopikle, of all things? He would be a memento not of her days with me but of my past. Had he too finally fallen into their hands? Little did I know then what she had in mind. I did know that

somehow I had to get him back. Later I almost changed
my mind.

LXII

After I hung up on Hirsch I sat in the phone booth for a
long time. I found the stale odor of the cigarette butts comforting, less hopeless, somehow, than the mixture of sweat
and decay that permeated my room upstairs. I had no reason
to rush back. Perhaps the phone would ring. Perhaps another
guest would come down and tap on the glass. Did the night
clerk notice me? Earlier I had purchased twenty dollars of
change from him for the bargain price of twenty-five dollars.
I was grateful not to pay fifty. How many others have conducted their final transactions with this man? His slicked-
back blond hair was clearly touched up. He had a scar under
his chin and one of his small eyes twitched, giving his fleshy
face a life of its own. It was not cold in the lobby, but a small
electric heater glowed behind his head. If not for the twitch
he would have looked peaceful, almost asleep, as he sat overlooking the entrance to this palace. I could tell, though, that
no one entered without being noted. Perhaps he had the de-
cency not to disturb me at such a time. More likely he didn't
give me a second thought, as they say.

Suddenly there was loud music outside. From the phone
booth, if I leaned out a little, I could see the street. Across
Lexington Avenue stood the pimp. Perhaps he was simply an
assistant pimp. Could the night clerk be the master pimp?
The occupation would fit him. Perhaps he too was simply
an assistant—another functionary in a large network that
reached all over the world, perhaps even to Paraguay, to
Mengele. The man in the street held an immense radio on
his shoulder.

It was only 4 a.m. There was still time to catch Fulani, if I only had that radio. I could even call up. Certainly I had enough change. Without formulating a plan I ran past the night clerk into Lexington Avenue and crossed the street and confronted the man. I was wearing only my purple robe over my underclothes. Luckily I had my cash with me—still more than three hundred dollars. I was suspicious of the management. The night clerk could easily dispatch the porter to my room while I was busy on the telephone. My papers I knew wouldn't interest them. My bourbon—they probably didn't want the trouble a man would cause if he found his whiskey gone. I had put the barbiturates and the cash into the pocket of my robe before I went down to the lobby. These people are expert at finding whatever is hidden. I am sure they will search again, even my remains, before they summon the police. It is all routine with them, as they say.

"Does it play FM?" I shouted above the music into the man's face. For a moment he stared in disbelief.

"You crazy? It plays everything, even short wave."

"Let me hear WBAI—ninety-nine-point-five on the dial."

"You crazy? Get away from here."

"I'll pay you three hundred dollars for this radio."

He was so surprised by my offer he didn't think to simply take the money from me as I waved it in his face. After all, wasn't I simply a demented man in a bathrobe? He could have taken the bathrobe as well, leaving me half-naked, without even my room key, to fend for myself. I could appeal to the young prostitute for help. Or I could simply stand at attention waiting for the officers to inspect us. I would have been selected. They would cart me off to Bellevue—perhaps an easier way to take leave of my present difficulties. Would that not leave a door slightly ajar behind me? Never would I dishonor my profession in this way. Who would seriously consider historical works written by a madman languishing in Bellevue? When I was released I would be right back where I am now, cut off from libraries, on the shelf, so to speak. But when I am dead, the significance of my work will be recognized.

Perhaps he had his hands full with his rebellious girls. Perhaps he thought I was a member of the morals squad in disguise. Perhaps he was simply an honest pimp, giving full value for reasonable overpayment. Was it even his radio? By tomorrow night the desk clerk should have it in his collection. Perhaps he will sell it back to the pimp for twenty-five dollars. Not a bad profit. I told him, though clearly he did not care, that I needed to listen to the Fulani show. Did he ever listen? Was he one of the callers?

Now it is early morning. A heavy rain is falling. When did it start? Is Fulani home, warm and dry in her bed in the heated basement apartment of her father's house in East New York? In his own home, Oscar is not a man to be stingy with heat on a cold night, even in June. The pimp is gone. The girls are alone in their small rooms. Is the timid one crying herself to sleep this gray morning? Has the night clerk been replaced by the day clerk, a fatter man with the face of a bulldog who appeared to sniff me when I checked in three days ago? The pigeons have flown off into the wet streets. The rain is washing their droppings from the windowsills. The streets will remain deserted on this rainy Saturday. I should not have listened to the show. I should not have called her up. Have I cheapened these grave final hours by using Fulani to help me orchestrate them? I convinced her to locate Ravel's "Pavane for a Dead Princess." She ended her program by playing a medley of pieces, beginning with the "Pavane," in a piano version no less, and ending as we started more than a year ago, with Stevie Wonder. In between she played "Goodbye, Mr. Porkpie Hat." Was she saying goodbye to me? Was this her way of giving me courage? Perhaps she was thinking of someone else. I'll never know.

A few years ago, when I spent that weekend by myself in the White Mountains, one evening at dusk I encountered a single deer on a dirt road. It was crossing in the near distance when it sensed my presence. It stopped. I stopped. We gazed at each other for a few seconds, then it continued soundlessly across the road and disappeared among the trees. Something in my body, softer, smaller, more sorrowful than Leon Solomon, trembled in recognition, and I was left feeling weak and sweetened. Could I have been as wondrous in its eyes as it was in mine? What had we recognized? Was it simply that the other existed and that neither could do anything for the other? I thought back to my long nights in Auschwitz, to those rare occasions when my prowling eyes met the eyes of another, and we paused a moment and gazed, two speechless men, two Jews who were at that moment two aliens whose paths crossed for a moment in the endless darkness. Fulani makes me think of that deer. A few times our ears have been alert to each other's voice. Yet she remains, and will eternally remain, alas, an alien creature in whose eyes I see my own isolation.

Twice when I passed Kristin's door during the week after I threw her out, she opened it a crack. Other times I stopped before her locked door but did nothing. Was she in there? Was she alone? The first time she watched me passing I didn't stop. I was unable, however, to prevent my eyes from looking over at her. She was dressed in a black dress and black shoes. She wore a black kerchief. She looked like a Bavarian peasant widow. She repeated the same helpless smile that had materialized on her face that abbreviated fourth night.

The second time she so startled me I stopped and looked

into her face. Her blonde hair was now reddish-black, just like Malkele's but a bit longer. Would she have made her blue eyes green if she could? Would she break her nose and have it refashioned for our next encounter? A vertical furrow had appeared on her forehead. Just like the furrow on Malkele's forehead, it divided her face into two sections. Unlike Malkele, who looked like a tragic clown, Kristin looked demented. Had she applied stage makeup to achieve the effect or was she truly crumbling? With what right do I question the authenticity of her response?

For some reason, however, when I thought of Kristin after that, it was not Malkele I saw but Inge. Despite the hair dyed reddish-black, despite her Yiddish words, despite the deep furrow dividing her forehead, despite the tiny scar over her left eye, despite the lack of restraint in her facial expressions, it was Inge I was seeing before me. Does Germany have such a strong grip on its daughters, even its Jewish daughters, that in any German woman you see another?

Let me take leave of her this way, I thought. She lusts to be the Vilna Jewess, Malka Rachel Solomon, murdered in 1941, in Warsaw, by her father's thugs. She made it only partway to her goal. Or so I thought then. She has become a Jewess, but from the city of Freiburg, a Jewess who as a girl lived through her puberty in Bergen-Belsen, barely, and emerged skin and bones, ready to blossom in Paris, in 1947, in my frail arms. Kristin stared at me now with no expression. As I watched she put her fingers to her bosom and tore open her dress and bared her breasts. Then she began to wail—without a sound emerging. With her reddened peasant face so contorted, the furrow looked like a terrible wound. My betrayal of this German woman flew after me like a bird of prey as I rushed from the building, grateful only that she had not also scarred her tender breasts.

"Leyb," she shouted after me. "Leyb," she screamed.

"Leyb! Leyb!" Why was this Marlene Dietrich competing with me for the role of Emil Jannings? Soon she would be crowing for the Bulgarian's entertainment.

The next time I heard Kristin's voice was over the air on Fulani's program the following Friday night. A new addition to Fulani's cast of characters had appeared. She spoke English with a slight but dignified Yiddish accent. She called herself Malka Solomon. She was a survivor of Auschwitz. Her voice kept me from calling for many weeks. But why did I keep listening? Not only did I listen that first Friday. Every Friday since then I've tuned in, more for Kristin than for Fulani. More for Malkele, I must confess. Who needed this caricature of my sister, this German poison? Yet even my last Friday night I craved it, and at four-thirty in the morning, no less.

Kristin condemned the PLO. She took blacks to task for embracing anti-Jewish causes. She supported Israel without reservation. She kept Fulani from simply dismissing her as a right-wing crank by revealing bits and pieces of her two years in Auschwitz. Everything I had told her about Auschwitz those three nights when I unburdened my heart in her ear, I heard now from her lips as she spoke to Fulani. She simply changed the men's barracks into the women's barracks. If Malkele had not been crippled, certainly she could have lived through the events Kristin described. Within a few weeks she and Fulani had become friends, after a fashion. Fulani's voice was always warm when Kristin phoned. She called her not even Malka but Malkele, though she emphasized the second syllable. Didn't she know better? Was it her way of not becoming too cozy with a Jewess?

When I broke my silence tonight did Fulani ask me where I had been, or even how I was? Until the end she remained aloof, even a bit hostile, to Professor Lewis Schorr, though she did fulfill my last request. As always, we sparred with

each other. One time only, almost a year ago, when Schorr
spoke of the death of his Christian wife Inge, had she permitted a momentary intimacy between us. But she and Kristin even laughed together on more than one occasion. They
chatted like two schoolgirls. How could I have continued to
listen to this caricature of my sister?

I must confess that through this German woman Malkele
lived again for me—a little bit. Whenever I heard them
laugh, my heart jumped—with envy, with longing, even with
joy. I was invisible. I could have been a rabbi again, reading
a book in a corner of the parlor, listening to Malkele and
Rivka chatter about nothing. Could Kristin even be sure I
was listening? Did Fulani notice any sudden absence? Not
one caller mentioned Professor Lewis Schorr. Yet my life was
being reenacted for all to hear for a few minutes every Friday
night. How could I not listen?

When I left the apartment for the last time three days ago,
I encountered Kristin one more time. I knew she would open
the door when I passed. She must have been listening for my
footsteps on the stairs and heard me hesitate as I approached. This time she opened the door more than a crack.
She mouthed no words. She simply looked at me mournfully,
even, I thought, with remorse. Did she know this was my
leave-taking? Her hair was still reddish-black, and it no
longer looked dyed. For a split second I wanted to call out
"Malkele" to her. Then I had to resist an urge to slap her
face. She reached into her robe and brought out Poopikle
and held him out to me. I took one step toward her and then
hesitated. Then she simply tossed him at my feet and I bent
over to pick him up.

"Get killed, bastard-bitch." The first two words she whispered fiercely in Yiddish. She shrieked the second two in English, just as my son had done a few weeks before. How could
she have known that? Perhaps I imagined it. Perhaps she

called me simply a bastard or a son of a bitch. "Get killed" I did not imagine. My skin crawled with terror and regret as she closed the door. I heard the lock click. I heard the police bar slide into place.

"Now there is no one." I spoke to the door.

I turned to leave the building. The Bulgarian stood looking at me, smiling broadly. Perhaps she had sworn at him. No matter how many times I've turned over those few seconds in my mind I have not been able to decide. I strode past the stupid man into the street. So came to an end my life on 109th Street off Broadway.

More convincing even than her stories was Kristin's tone on the air. She struck just the right degree of bitterness and suspicion, even when she joked and bantered. Certainly she was more successful as Malkele than I was as Lewis Schorr. So convincing was her tone that Fulani never even suspected. When I tuned in just before dawn on my three-hundred-dollar radio, it was exactly Malkele's tone that met my desperate ears and sounded through this deathly hotel room. She was practically quoting from an article I wrote in 1950 about the transition from concentration camp to normal life for those who went directly back to their homes.

"Imagine all this coming to an end," she was saying, encouraged, I knew right away, by Fulani's respectful stillness. It wasn't that silence Fulani often employed with me, allowing me enough rope, as they say, but a stillness punctuated with soft exclamations. "The women are going home"— Kristin spoke plaintively—"each one back to her country, her province, her town, her old neighborhood. All over Europe we step from trains, blinded for a moment by the afternoon sun. Our eyes search for a familiar sight, a building behind the train station, a stone wall of the building, a window a little to the side on the wall, the way the late afternoon sun glints on the top left pane of the window. Suddenly we realize—everything is just the same as the day we left from this same train station. But how are we to locate ourselves? The street begins turning before our eyes, making us sick at heart. You must imagine this transformation," she went on, with Fulani's deceitful sighs to encourage her. "From a vast collective human misery, a huge barracks full of hell, into hundreds of lone reunions on hundreds of particular railroad platforms. But where is my father? Where is my mother? Where is my brother?"

I wanted to cry out, "Malkele, Poopikle, Malkele, Poopikle."

"Will I see again my schoolteacher holding the hand of her favorite pupil as she walks her part of the way home?"

She remembered everything, even obscure little stories I had told her about my mother's life. How dared she? I wanted to kill her, but I couldn't stop listening to this German daughter who had stolen my past and turned herself into a monster. My memories of the Solomon family inhabit her, and she punishes me by becoming my sister over the air. I felt as though she were strangling me.

When I finally die I will already be a dead man.

"But somewhere below our feet, beneath the familiar pavements whose every crack we were careful not to step on, mixed in with the unbearably familiar odors of our town, you could still discern the overpowering and even more familiar stench of the Nazis." Then she said something I had not written or told her. "The Nazis all smelled, you know—a peculiar and sickening perfumed sweat." It must have been the smell of her father she remembered, and of his brutish sidekick, Pavel Schmit.

She drove me from my room back to the phone booth with a sentence that she could have plucked right from my brain.

I never said it to her and I never wrote it, yet it was direct from my brain. I had no idea what I would pluck from my brain if I got through to them on the phone.

"It would be," she spoke softly, with exactly the refined Yiddish accent Malkele would have cultivated here in America, "like going to heaven and into hell at the same time."

LXIII

Could Kristin have turned me in? She would rather die—unless she has a split personality. Certainly that is a possibility, perhaps even a likelihood. Did she know enough about my dealings with Hirsch? I was circumspect when I talked about such matters. Kristin looked into every corner of my apartment, rearranged the contents of all my drawers—perhaps even my file cabinet. Could she have discovered the loose floorboards beneath which I kept some papers hidden? How could she not have discovered them? She scoured every inch of my apartment. Why am I allowing this paranoia to grip me? Kristin may have grown to hate me, but she did not turn me in. She begged me not to abandon her. She said that without me she was doomed. But she can find another Jew to torment so. She can find another cause. Perhaps she will embrace the black cause and find a black lover. With Kristin's appetite for extremes she will probably pick the most virulently anti-Semitic black man in New York City. Perhaps she will find him through Fulani's program. There is certainly a wide selection among her callers.

By now I was sitting again in the phone booth, listening to the phone ring in the radio station while Kristin continued her heartrending imitation of my sister. Sometimes you have to let the phone ring for half an hour before Fulani picks it up. If you hang up you lose your place. Suddenly the black prostitute limped into the lobby followed by a huge man. He strutted behind her with a satisfied smirk on his face, as though he had gotten a bargain. She passed right by me with her head down. Then she turned and looked into my eyes. Was she simply startled by Kristin's voice coming over the radio? She glared at me with hatred in her face. I looked over at the man. He looked just like the bully Pavel, on the train from Warsaw to Vilna forty-six years ago. There are many such brutes in the world. I turned the volume up. Kristin was speaking of hatred. She was quoting almost word for word from an article I had written back in 1957. She must have painstakingly translated it by herself. From the mouth of a Jew it sounded like an indictment. To me, knowing that it was the German woman Kristin and not my sister Malkele who spoke, it sounded like a confession. She spoke urgently, with great conviction. Fulani remained entirely silent throughout. From her breathing, which was audible, I knew that the silence was respectful. If Schorr had uttered these words, Fulani would have interrupted more than once.

"Why do they hate us so? Certainly they hate us when we have what they have not. But even when they have everything and we have nothing they hate us. Why? When they plunder our possessions, murder our loved ones, strip us naked, radically naked, even the hair on our heads and bodies, even our names, we still have one thing that they need and simply can never get, especially by force. We have our Jewishness. They hate us because they are not Jews and can never be Jews—blinded as they are by their envy, their arrogance, their hatred. How could they so desperately crave what they have labeled so inferior?—subhuman was the concept they used. Their deepest secret makes them madmen. Every Nazi wanted to be a Jew, to have a Jewish mother and a Jewish father and a Jewish sister—to have Jewish love."

She paused, not merely to catch her breath but to compose

herself. You could tell from her voice that she had started to sob. Never for a moment had she dropped her Yiddish accent. The sobs themselves sounded Yiddish, somehow. It was a masterful performance. This sobbing, though, was also entirely authentic. To me it was triply chilling. She sobbed as my sister, Malka Solomon, brutally cheated of her doomed life, on the edge of the Warsaw Ghetto, in 1941, when she was only nineteen years of age. She sobbed also as Leon Solomon, who wrote those words thirty-five years ago, when he had not yet washed the Nazi stench from his body. And she sobbed as Kristin Dietrich, stricken daughter of a Nazi murderer. It was her own shame, her own yearnings she was confessing. None of the listeners could know that. Did Kristin know that I was listening? In previous weeks she might have crept up the stairs and listened at my door for the radio. Tonight she would have been met by silence. As far as she knew, she was sending the deepest message embedded in her speech into an emptiness. I am this woman's only witness, and I am about to depart. Let these words be my parting gift to Kristin Dietrich.

"Ressentiment, the French have labeled this phenomenon, speaking of the consuming plebeian hatred of patricians in ancient Rome." Again, her voice struck just the right degree of bitterness. "When it comes to the life of the emotions, we Jews are the aristocrats of Europe. Since they could never become us, they set out to destroy us. The Nazis perfected a machine, not to conquer Europe, but to rid themselves of their Jewish Problem."

Fulani didn't even draw a parallel, as she would have if I had spoken so. She permitted her Malkele to speak for both of them. The night clerk caught my eye with his narrow eyes and signaled to me to turn off the radio. I held up my last twenty and gestured for him to come and take it. I knew he wouldn't be able to resist. When he emerged from behind the desk, I saw that he was much shorter than I had imagined. He looked older and scrawnier and walked with a limp. How many decades had he worked here, in this decay? His thin arm reached out and plucked the bill from my outstretched hand. Two of his fingers were missing. He smiled with satisfaction when he saw how shiny and large the radio was.

Kristin left nothing alone this time. She even started to speak of a brother named Leyb.

"What is that in English?" That was the first time Fulani had interrupted her.

"Leon."

"I thought so. Leon Solomon?"

"Yes," Kristin said without hesitating.

"Does he live in New York?"

"No, no, Leyb was beaten to death by the Nazis in Warsaw, in 1941. I watched him slowly die in the public square. There was nothing I could do." Her demented voice was so convincing that I gasped. I couldn't find it in myself to hate her for so violating me. In her own desperate way was she not honoring the memory of my sister? Was I not, in fact, hearing her honor the memory of Leon Solomon?

Where I had mainly failed, Kristin had succeeded. Slowly Fulani was starting to concede some humanity to Jews. Two liars, one a pathological creator of smoke screens, and the other the demented daughter of a Gestapo officer, were getting through, as they say, not only to Fulani but even to her hate-poisoned audience.

By the time Fulani answered my call, Kristin was no longer on the air. We are not destined to talk again—though I could go down even now and call her. I still have a few quarters left.

My last conversation with Fulani was almost satisfying. Perhaps she was glad to hear my voice after so many weeks. Perhaps she was still under the influence of Kristin's voice. Perhaps she simply felt superior to me even in a Jewish way now that one of her best friends was an authentic *Ostjude*. I had expected her to have had enough of Jews for one night, but her voice was friendly. Suddenly I wanted to ask her how Oscar was and what was the latest news from the Jewish History Institute.

I began by telling her I found the words of Malkele very informative. I pronounced my sister's name the way Fulani did, by emphasizing the second syllable. Then I began paraphrasing from the same article.

"European civilization is made of two types of people, Fulani—Jews and those who hate Jews. There is no other way of being a true European."

"That sounds like bragging to me, Professor."

"What is true is true."

"What of blacks and those who hate blacks?"

"Not blacks, blacks have never been considered a part of Europe, but contempt for blacks—yes, that too is a test for membership in the Greater European Community, as they say. But that is a secondary phenomenon, inasmuch as it flows from the older European obsession with Jews." Lewis Schorr's pomposity embarrassed me a little as I spoke, but mainly it was a relief not to be myself, especially tonight. "Listen, my dear Fulani, today in Warsaw, the same Warsaw where your one other Jewish caller, Malkele, claimed her brother was beaten to death at the edge of the ghetto by the Gestapo, there is only an Aryan side. There are no Jews left. Yet the hatred of Jews continues without stop. In Germany, where there's but a handful of Jews, Nazi groups are sprouting. Without this, European civilization would devour itself."

"So you come in first in suffering?"

"I am not speaking of who suffers more. Who can measure that? I speak simply of European civilization. When it comes to being hated, Jews have been the role model, to borrow a term from my son's Holocaust advisor."

"I didn't know you had a son." She couldn't resist baiting me over my mental slip.

"Did I say 'son'? Not exactly a son. I am speaking of the son of a woman of my acquaintance, a dear woman whose son I have helped in certain ways from time to time." I felt proud of my quick thinking.

"Do you mind if I take another call?" She sounded tired, perhaps, but not unfriendly.

"Do you want me to hang up?" I spoke calmly though I felt suddenly desperate.

"No, not at all. I just want to add a call. 'Most everyone has given up trying to reach me at this late hour, but one caller has been ringing nonstop since we started talking." I knew it was Kristin. Could I permit her to demean me at this juncture?

"I know who it is." I spoke without thinking.

"Let's find out if you are right." Again she sounded tired.

"Wait! Let us make a wager."

"What's with you, Professor? Why are you so nervous?"

"I'll bet you an hour of my life against an hour of yours that it is the Jewish woman again, the one who calls herself Malka Solomon." Why did I need to speak my sister's name just then? She knew who I meant without my saying Malkele's name out loud. Surely I was crumbling, but I went on. "The one who has called every Friday for six weeks now."

"I know who you mean, Professor."

"Well, is it a bet?"

"What kind of crazy bet is that? How can you pay off an hour?"

"If you win, I will serve you in any way you want for one hour. If I win, you must go to the Jewish History Institute on

East Eighteenth Street and you must read every word and look at every picture in an exhibition they have mounted titled 'Jewish Resistance in Vilna.' If you are diligent, it should take you an hour."

"Does that include my traveling time, Professor?"

"I will not dignify that with an answer."

"Don't get so high and mighty, Professor. It is much too late for that."

"There is even an Indian luncheonette around the corner on Lexington where you could stop for lunch."

"I know the place, Professor. My father works there."

"Is he one of the scholars?"

"No, he is in charge of protocol."

"Well, have you looked at the exhibition yet?"

"Not particularly." Before I could go on with this spiteful exchange she picked up the phone.

"Well, I do dig that Jewish woman Mal-kell, but I am most definitely not her." I recognized the voice of the suicidal young black. He sounded almost cheerful. Could he have worried about me those six weeks I had not called? "You lose, Professor, what you going to do for Fulani for a whole hour?"

"Whatever she wants me to."

"We didn't bet, Professor. But if you insist, you can come on down to the station and do volunteer work for an hour every week."

"Is that all you want from him, Fulani?" Just the week before, this young man had been at the end of his rope. Now he was happily teasing us. Perhaps he was relieved I was still alive. Perhaps he could hear in my voice that I was at the end of my rope. I thought of Emmanuel.

"Yes, have you not a more urgent request?" The anger in my voice surprised me. Was I so deeply upset that Kristin hadn't called back? Had she even continued listening? Was she cleaning the apartment of her new lover? Was she naked

on her hands and knees upstairs in the apartment next to
mine with Mr. Moses Chikema? Has she already become a
Jewish woman who rejects her background and gives herself
to the long-suffering blacks? But why would she continue to
call and imitate my sister? How could she resist the deep
voice and seductive pronunciation of Moses Chikema?
Could Fulani know she has three listeners from one building? Soon she will have but two. Kristin will reject him when
she discovers more drastic men—men Chikema referred to
as heartless thugs one night on the Fulani show. I know it
was him. I lowered my radio and I put a glass to the wall
separating our bedrooms and heard him speaking to Fulani.

"What do you mean by more 'urgent'? Be more direct,
Professor." There was a new edge in her voice.

"Is a Jew not good enough to touch you?"

"Oh, man," the young black interrupted, "that's not the
point."

"Oh, isn't it? And this Mal-kell that you 'dig,' wouldn't you
like to possess her?"

"Oh, man—lighten up. She's old enough to be my
mother."

"Well, I can give you her address, but you are probably too
late. Another listener, one just like you, has already gotten
her tonight." I couldn't stop myself.

"Cut that out. I said I liked the woman. I didn't say I
wanted her." Remarkably, Fulani remained silent.

"Is she not good enough for you? She might save your life,
even if she is Jewish."

"Don't talk to me that way, man."

"She is not even Jewish, and her name is not 'Mal-kell,' as
you say it. And she is not old enough to be your mother. She
is young. And beautiful. Very sexy. And why shouldn't I talk
to you that way? Someone has to. Every week you call and
threaten to kill yourself—when all you need is love. Find

someone to love. It does not matter whether she be black or Jewish—or even a German. Listen to me. Without love you really will crumble. The fantasy will become real." I spoke now without thinking.

"Mr. Schorr," Fulani interrupted and I fell into silence. "It may be impossible for you and me, but it is not impossible for a black woman and a Jewish man to connect, even intimately." She referred to me as "Mister" rather than "Professor." Was she talking to me, to me? Was she on the verge of saying "Mister Solomon"? Even "Leon"? Even "Leybkele"? Even "Leyb"? For Fulani I could be always a "Leyb."

"And one more thing, Professor. Never again will I permit you to harangue a young black brother on these airwaves."

"Forgive me, Fulani. Forgive me, young man—though I meant what I finally said. I am not myself tonight."

"It's time to go now."

"Wait, Fulani, you can find me a few blocks away, not far from the Institute where your father works, at the Hotel America on Lexington Avenue. In Room 512. Do you hear me, Kristin? Malkele? Poopikle? The Hotel America, Room 512." But she had already hung up on me. She remembered my request. A piano was playing the "Pavane for a Dead Princess." Maurice Ravel. I turned up the volume.

The night clerk was staring at me. My shouting irritated him, but my twenty dollars still kept him quiet. I sat in the booth and listened to the music. After Malkele's piece, which I had never heard anyone but her play before, I heard Stevie Wonder singing "You Are the Sunshine of My Life." She ended with jazz, Charlie Mingus playing "Goodbye, Mr. Porkpie Hat." When it was all over, I walked over to the desk clerk and placed the radio before him.

"This is for you." He smirked at me with his chalk face and took the radio without a question.

Late Morning

LXIV

I was soaked through to the skin when I returned from my errand. My shoes were waterlogged. It was impossible to avoid the deep puddles. I was shivering. There will not be time enough to catch cold, of course. I could postpone the event on account of illness, the way they postpone an execution if the victim is indisposed. I removed my jacket and hung it, still dripping, on a hanger in the closet. Then I removed my shoes and leaned them against the door, heels up. Why, I don't know. Was it a way of sealing the door? My socks I spread on the floor in front of the shoes. I removed my shirt and hung it over one of the black iron bedposts. My trousers I hung over the other bedpost. Then I stripped the wet underclothes from my body and spread them down on the floor, on either side of the shoes. If the two gas spigots still functioned, I could roll up the wet underclothes and socks and squeeze them into the crack under the door. I stood by the sink and held my forearms in the basin filled with warm water until I stopped shivering. With my teeth I plucked the string before my eyes and lit the bulb over the medicine chest. For the second time in two days I began studying my face in the mirror. No longer did it look like stone. No longer was it filled with scorn. Why was my face filled with confidence now? Why was it so debonair, even sweet, at this juncture?

My feet were a different matter. When had the toenails become so gray? When had my ankles become so white? Had Kristin noticed? I lifted a foot and placed it into the sink and washed it with warm water and a small bar of soap. I washed the other foot in the same way. For years I had not lifted my feet so high. Had a sense of abandon made my body more limber? Slowly, carefully, with soap and warm water, I started to wash myself. Part by part, I was taking leave of my body. The moist warm cloth felt soothing against my armpits. How many times have I washed them just this way? When Malkele was a child she always giggled when I washed her tiny armpits.

"When will I have hair under my arms, Leybkele, just like you?" Now that I had grown a few hairs under my arms, she would ask me this every time I washed her. Later, in Warsaw, when I started bathing her again, she playfully resumed asking me that question. By then she had wiry black hairs that I loved to kiss. Never, she told me, would she shave there, and she never did. Even when Samuel had courted her. I could never convince Inge not to shave her armpits, though I asked her many times. Only in Paris, at the beginning, when her body was emaciated and her eyes enormous, did she have underarm hair—as dark as Malkele's, but softer and sparer. She squirmed with embarrassment when I tugged on these hairs with my lips. When I blew noisily into her armpit, goose bumps immediately covered her shoulders and arms. Kristin's, on the other hand, were as silky as the hair on her mound. She uses the most fragrant shampoo and rinse in all three places, just as she works it into her long, golden tresses. She was the only woman to kiss my armpits.

The warm cloth felt just as soothing on my shoulders and

chest. How alive my body is, I thought. Yet I did not feel self-pity. I felt prepared for the end and separated from my flesh as I observed its pleasures. In a way I felt proud of my body at that moment, for it was still well disposed to continue living. I was determined to wash every part, even my back. For the last time I rolled up the warm soapy cloth and dangled one end behind my neck. With my other hand I deftly gripped the lower end and started pulling the cloth up and down on my back. How many times have I performed this simple solitary act? How many times have I neglected to? My wet back tingled in the chilly air of the room. Before I got to my hair I carefully washed the crack between my cheeks. The coroner will have nothing to smirk at when he examines the corpse. Inge will have nothing to be ashamed of when they call her in to make a positive identification.

Washing my hair for the last time was more than a poignant act. I experienced a moment of excruciating anguish. As I worked the shampoo into my wet hair I started to crumble. I struggled to keep from weeping. "What beautiful black curls you have, and bedroom eyes." I have been told this more than once. Even my mother and sister said it to me. I thought of the time Mother and Malkele washed my hair, curl by curl, in the apartment, in Vilna. It was my mother who said what beautiful curls I had. It was Malkele who added that I had bedroom eyes. Where had she heard such a provocative expression? Had she and Rivka discussed my bedroom eyes? I blushed that she spoke so before our mother. Mother didn't blush. She girlishly added that I must already have made a few women happy. Malkele pinched my bare shoulder. Had Mother forgotten how young her daughter was?

It was raining outside that morning also. I have often thought of my mother, sitting by her window in Vilna, when it rains in the streets of New York. In honor of her memory I will die on a rainy Saturday morning. If I had her courage I would walk through this rain to the harbor. On the ferry to Staten Island, I would study the black water below me, the way I imagine Mother did. And then, like her, I would throw myself into its icy embrace. I am not a vain man, but secretly I have been proud that, unlike so many of my colleagues, my head of hair has remained full and still practically black. I succeeded in composing myself as I worked the fragrant shampoo, from a bottle Kristin had left me, deeper into my scalp. Was I preparing for my wedding? Three times I submerged my head in fresh warm water to rinse the shampoo from my hair. This primitive style of bathing at the sink felt as luxurious, and as otherworldly, as my first shower, in water that didn't spurt ice-cold from a hose, after the Liberation.

While the growth on my cheeks and chin was still soft and moist, I shaved for the last time. Since I separated from Inge more than seven years ago, I have not shaved before a mirror large enough to show me my whole face. With each stroke of the razor I grew younger before my eyes. When I finished, my face had the pale complexion of a young scholar. I was prepared to go out and meet Inge all over again, and hold her safely in my arms night after night, while her beautiful malnourished body started to fill out.

I realized that I had neglected to wash my crotch. I was surprised how much my penis had shrunk, even though I had just thought about Inge in Paris. Had my forthcoming death already gripped me so firmly? It had grown as small as it had been in Auschwitz, when there was barely enough there to urinate from. I gripped it with two fingers and tried to imagine Inge holding it so. Instead, the young Vilna whore on the train held center-stage in my brain, with the scarred face of Zbigniew behind her, urging her to arouse me—and now the small worm, as he called it, began to swell. I forced myself to think of Inge, of her breasts filled with milk, of her flimsy cream-colored nightgown, and even of Schwartz possessing her while I watched. But my penis shrank again in shame. How could my body remain so responsive to my thoughts and my thoughts so perverse, at this time? Is that how small it will be when they discover the remains? Does this happen to all men at the end? The undertaker will have a good laugh. If I hanged myself, it would, they say, grow hard.

I crossed the room and stood before the larger mirror that hung over the bureau. A naked sixty-six-year-old Jew, holding his disappearing penis. I was determined to stimulate myself. Perhaps I needed to fully feel my body one last time. After all, the phenobarbital will remove my body from my consciousness before it removes my consciousness from the world. I wanted to think not of Kristin, not of Fulani, not even of Malkele, but of Inge, my wife, with whom I had a son. Inge—without Schwartz ravishing her. My penis resisted my brain and my brain continued to resist my desire to reunite with my life's companion. The Vilna prostitute who looked like a countess in her lemon-colored blouse and pin of black opal flew into my mind again and took me over, and I watched my penis swell between my fingers—which were also her fingers. In the mirror I saw my aging body sway, as though in prayer, as I caressed my sex. In my mind it was the whore who caressed my sex as the Nazi Zbigniew directed her slightest movements. Again his hand held her breast toward my lips. Pavel's brutish hand was not needed to hold my head in place. I thirsted for the girl and for her master. Desperately I needed another memory to seize me.

But why shouldn't another humiliation be the prelude to my death?

How could I have imagined that humiliations were no longer in store for me? Inge, I begged in my brain, please help me. I welcomed the pain that started in my heart. But still my brain would not let go of the girl, would not let go of the Nazi who tortured us both. Through all this my face in the mirror reflected what looked like simple pleasure. Inge, I begged again.

"Inge, Inge, Inge, Inge, Inge." I chanted her name as though it were the sacred tongue. Even the girl alone, without Zbigniew behind her, would be redemption at this point. But my brain would not loosen her from his grip, that poor child who undoubtedly perished a few years later at the edge of the Vilna ghetto. Just as my sister perished at the edge of the Warsaw ghetto. How could my brain be so grotesque as to excite my body this way, with visions of a Nazi humiliating two young Jews? Why didn't I simply stop caressing myself? I needed to go on, no matter what. The cravings of my flesh were overpowering. Then, just as one slide replaces the one before it when the carousel clicks, Inge appeared in my brain, exactly as she was when we first made love in Paris after the war. I saw again her scrawny back when she removed her clothing in the semi-darkness. I tasted again my thirst for her tiny breasts: they looked like fledglings hiding within the hollow of her rib cage as she lay on her back in my small bed. I felt again the nervous trembling of her narrow thighs as she parted her legs slightly to let me touch the moist opening to her body. Even our fumbling, even the simple task of entry into her vagina which eluded us half the night—these filled my heart to bursting as I caressed myself before the mirror. Before I started to come I closed my eyes to keep Inge the child-woman enclosed forever in my mind. How could I have forgotten for so many years how this Inge, whom I adored as no other but Malkele, with whom she shared a middle name, this Inge who had menstruated but the one time, and miraculously, in Bergen-Belsen, this fragile girl who then gave herself to me so fully in Paris— how she lives on in Inge my estranged wife, mother of my son, just as the boy I was in Vilna lives on in my consciousness and will die when I die, forever. Even with Ben Schwartz embracing her there was still the same child-bride Inge Rachel Solomon.

The ejaculation was tender, not dramatic.

Afterwards I realized how much my chest hurt all along. The warm semen that had spurted into the cup of my hand became quickly cold. I crossed the room again and washed my hands in the sink. Before I washed my penis I carefully squeezed it until the remaining drops of semen glistened on the head. Then I washed it and the hairs that surrounded it with warm water. There would be no dried semen on the remains for Detective Sawyer to smirk over. Clean and drained of desire, I lay down naked on top of the bed to allow my chest to stop hurting before I commenced.

LXV

I am sitting in the phone booth as I write this on a fresh pad. I bought it when I went out in the rain earlier to mail Poopikle back to Kristin, giving him to her care as once I had given him to the janitor's daughter in Warsaw. I put a note between his jaws. On it I had written in Yiddish: For Malka Rachel Solomon.

You can't believe that I am sitting in the phone booth again? I came down to call Inge. I got only her answering machine. I called her answering machine seven times, not only to hear her voice repeatedly tell me that she was not available, but also because I had some vital things to tell her. I would have continued to call, for my messages seemed endless, but I ran out of coins. By the time she receives these seven messages I shall be gone.

I have a plastic glass filled with bourbon. I am sipping it slowly. Will I be simply another drunk who expired in a telephone booth—a routine D.O.A., as they call them? Will I be the first in this particular booth? The rain outside has become a downpour. If I topple sideways against this door that folds in, they will not find it so easy to get to me. The clerk will have to call the police without going through my pockets. My chest still hurts. Perhaps I will die a natural death after all. Even then these phenobarbitals will not be a waste. If they are not killing me, they are making it easier for me to bear the pain. And face the future. The same clerk is still there. Does he work twenty-four-hour shifts? He looks as white as a ghost behind his sunglasses. When was the last time he was out in the sun? He is listening to the radio I presented to him, to a constant drone of bad news and worse weather predictions. Has he no curiosity about me? He acts as though I've rented this phone booth. Perhaps I have, with the radio and the twenty dollars I handed him last night. What if someone comes to make a call? They will have to go elsewhere. I am not about to relinquish this spot. I can see water rushing along the curb across Lexington Avenue.

Right after I swallowed the first twelve capsules, a little while ago, I knew that I could no longer stay in my hotel room. The mirrors had become lusterless, a dull deathly gray. The loud gurgling of the pigeons huddling from the rain on the windowsill was too painful to bear. Their sounds scraped against my eardrum, stirring memories. It was an old terror that pervaded my heart. At this grave time I wanted more than the men dying in my barracks, the men who lie on shelves, one next to the other, stored in the back of my brain, unnamed, uncatalogued. I moved the wet shoes, the socks, and the underclothes to one side and fled the room. I was afraid to walk down, so I waited for the elevator.

I encountered the young prostitute when I entered; she didn't recognize me from last night, but she was impressed with my Parisian suit and looked right at me, what did she want from me? This elevator was as slow as the one in the Institute. I had nothing but seven quarters in my pocket. Would I fail the last woman who will ever encounter me? She was a tall girl, about my height. I carefully removed my double-breasted jacket and handed it to her just as the elevator shuddered into place.

"Please, my dear, accept this as a gift from me. I have no more need of it and it is now so stylish for beautiful young women to wear such jackets. Besides, it is pouring out in the street and this is large enough for you to wear over your delicate silver windbreaker." She was wearing one of those short jackets woven of metal threads. She was bolder now that the elevator door had opened.

"That sure is sweet of you, honey." She smiled at me. Her teeth were still very white. Her voice startled me. The deep and confident voice of a worldly woman emerged from the mouth of this youngster. Unlike Fulani's deep voice, for example, it held no resonance. It sounded practiced. Her natural voice must be an octave higher. I was touched by her valiant effort to hold her own in a world of predators. Did she take me for a customer? I had nothing else to give her except my trousers and my seven quarters. I didn't even have a wedding ring to offer her. Still I could go with her, I thought. By the time we were finished, payment would be the furthest thing from her mind. But how could I steal a final comfort from an embrace that would end in pure terror for the girl? Better to expire in a phone booth.

"Think nothing of it, my dear child." She blushed. I expressed more feeling than I had intended to. I spoke the word "child" with a low, tender voice. Before she could reply I bowed and turned on my heel like a Polish aristocrat, and walked away from her. I regret that I had no more to give her than my Parisian jacket, which she has probably tossed in a garbage can by now. I have just swallowed six more phenobarbitals. I have six left in my pocket. The bourbon is making my stomach hurt and my eyes squint. I'll sip it slowly. I am still clearheaded. I will stop writing before I lose perspective. I have no intention of ending in gibberish. My obligations as an historian do not carry me that far. Another historian can re-create the final minutes. But he must have sufficient historical evidence for his account. One voyeur of my life is enough. Outside, the downpour has grown worse.

LXVI

I have thought often about my mother in recent months. Had I already expected this final trouble—in my subconscious mind? That afternoon in her room when she spoke to me of Father she was just thirty-five years old. If by some miracle she had lived she would now be eighty-five. She would have had to survive not only the abuse of her father, the timidity of her husband, the indifference of her doomed daughter, the lack of commitment in her son, but the Nazis as well, and then—perhaps the most difficult of all for a woman of her passionate and private nature—decades in a foreign land where she would be perceived as quaint. She would still be nineteen years older than I. But then she was thirty-five, a woman given to weeping spells and melancholy. She was a full twenty years younger than Inge is now and less than a decade beyond Kristin. There is not a single snapshot remaining of her, but she was a striking woman. Her rich brown eyes were given greater dignity by the delicate crow's-feet around them.

Had she been able to see from then to now, could she still have loved me? She would have seen a bitter man almost her father's age—a failure, an unworthy wretch who has treated his son no better than her father had treated her, an apostate of sorts who has cavorted with the daughters of the enemy of our people, and worst of all, a traitor to the dream of a just world. Yet I have, as she demanded of me, "become something entirely": an historian. I have devoted more than forty years to the historical enterprise, as they say, more than forty years to bring life again—posthumously—to our slaughtered people. Is this not worthy of the impossible standards my mother took intact to her cold black death? Old enough to be her father: soon I will know what she knew in her final moments in Smargon. I have never stopped grieving for her.

And my father? Could he look at me now and still believe that the Jewish people will live forever? If I reach out I can almost take the hand of my father again, as we walked, through the streets of downtown Vilna, holding hands, one Saturday morning, when I was a boy.

"Leybl," he called to me in his flattering man-to-man voice, "your mother has not been well and today is her birthday. We need to decide what gift to buy her."

"We should get her a bottle of perfume," I said, sounding as decisive as I could.

We went into a large department store on Phohunlank Street.

"Let my son decide," Father said to the beautiful salesgirl.

The salesgirl dabbed my wrist with one perfume, then another. Then she dabbed the crook of one elbow, then the other. Was her touch very hot or very cold? Still I could not choose. Then she dabbed the top of her own hand and reached it toward me. I held her hand as though I were about to kiss it, like a gentleman. I breathed in and I knew.

"This one. This is the one for our dear mother." I spoke formally in Polish.

"Are you absolutely sure, my son?" Father spoke just as

formally but in Yiddish, failing, of course, to honor the illusion of self-importance. Perhaps he was teaching me a
lesson.

"Absolutely," I assured him stubbornly in Polish. Father
bought it, though it was very expensive, even then.

"You have exquisite taste, my young man," he said in Polish and spoiled it by winking at the salesgirl.

Mother accepted it almost graciously. She allowed me to
dab a drop on the back of her hand. Father put his lips to her
hand. She put the small bottle on her bureau and never used
it again.

Years later I discovered the same perfume again, when I
met Inge at the Luncharsky apartment.

I have just swallowed the remaining six capsules. My heart
no longer hurts. I feel drowsy but still my head is clear.

Seven times I called Inge's answering machine and still I
haven't run out of messages to leave her. I have no more
quarters. Will the clerk give me a few? Will he give me even
one? Just last night I gave him a twenty-dollar bill, as well
as a three-hundred-dollar SONY radio with stereo speakers.
More likely he will throw me out into the rain. I still need to
tell her that I have kept her name on my safe deposit box,
and that she should immediately open it and remove two
bankbooks, one held in trust for herself and the other for
Emmanuel. I also wanted to remind her of one afternoon
and one night and one morning early in our marriage. Some
things will not get said. I am sure Inge will know what to do
without my instructions.

I did manage to leave thirty-second messages seven times.
Can I still recall them? It will be a test of my clarity. The first
time I spoke to her machine I said that I had mailed her a
package with five legal-size yellow pads covered with writing.
I asked her to read these pads. Before I was cut off I told her
there was a sixth pad that should soon find its way into her

hands. The second time I spoke into the machine I asked
her to speak to the Director of the Institute and apologize for
my recent behavior. Tell her, I continued, that it was not for
money I did these things. I wanted Inge to know that too.
The third time I spoke into the machine I told her that I was
deeply sorry I had not been a good father. I was proud, I said
to the machine, that Emmanuel had joined a children-of-
survivors group. Please convince him, I asked her, that I love
him. I may have been cut off before I spoke the last three
words. The fourth time I spoke into the machine I gave her
Ellen Meyers' phone number and address. I told her that the
girl would make a wonderful mate for Emmanuel. I added
that I thought she was a graduate of Bennington College and
that she was a lover of fine literature. I knew that would
heighten Inge's interest in the project. The fifth time I spoke
into the machine I asked Inge to forgive me for forgetting
how much I loved her. Those last three words, "I love you,"
left me so speechless that I let the last fifteen seconds go to
waste. Will Inge notice that absence and for a few seconds
remember us as we once were? The sixth time I spoke into
the machine I told her that no matter how much I tortured
myself into forgetfulness I have never stopped desiring her.
Will she believe me? I begged her not to feel disgusted by
certain things she learns about me when she reads the yellow
pads. The seventh time I spoke into the machine I had to
speak very quickly. My last quarter was gone. I asked her to
please continue lighting a memorial candle each year for
Malkele, not only in my name but in Ben's name as well. Was
I wrong to bring up his name? Then I quickly added some
words in German that I knew she would remember. "I Am
Ready for Love from Head to Foot." These words were her
equivalent of Malkele's "To what are Chopin's Preludes preludes." One night in the second year of our marriage I refused to respond to this Dietrich invitation. "Stop speaking

German in my ear," I snapped. She never uttered the words
to me again. I don't think this part of my message will reach
her in her machine. I spoke it too late. Was I attempting to
torture Inge with these messages, or to comfort her? Perhaps
both at the same time.

It is too late to undo what I have done.

The glass of this booth is so steamed over that I had to
wipe a small circle just now with my hand in order to see out.
It is raining even harder. The desk clerk's head is drooping.
Is he sleeping? His sunglasses make it hard to tell. Should I
have brought my sunglasses down? Will he inherit those as
well? I should walk out into the rain and make my way down
to the Battery. In the water is where my life should end. I
could look down into the water and cease thinking about my
life. Perhaps I could know what my mother knew forty-six
years and seven months ago less four days. Could I find her
resolve and throw myself into the icy blackness? But my way
is different. I will remove my shoes and socks and trousers
and shirt and leave them folded neatly by the railing before I
dive in. I am a strong swimmer. I will begin swimming toward the open sea. And after a time I will slowly fall asleep.
I am starting to fall asleep now. I will sink below the surface.
Will I find my mother there? Will I find my father? Will I see
the faces again of the men staring from their shelves, men
whose beings my soul has carried for more than forty years?
How will I find Malkele, my Poopikle, again in the afterlife?
Have I not become a Jewish historian because I know that
none of us will find one another again? Because I know there
is no redemption in death? Because I know that Malkele will
have been cheated for all eternity? Because, the Jewish
people will live forever?

I am not yet ready to sleep.

Why am I so theatrical?

I could simply make my way outside and lie down with my

face in a puddle and expire like a drunkard. I could simply sit here and let the steaminess of my own dying breath entomb me.

I should stop writing. Let me end as I have lived, with no heroic resolution.

The eighth message would have been about the few days we spent at the seashore on our honeymoon. Can I still remember what I wanted to tell her? Was it not on the second day, in the late afternoon, that we climbed among the rocks, in a secluded spot, beyond the public beach? We saw thousands of newborn fish. They were caught by the ebbing tide in small pools just out of the reach of the waves. They were like streaks of light as they darted in unison to and fro in the afternoon sun. Suddenly seagulls swept down from all sides. I was mesmerized. The smell of the sea. The waves. The shrieking birds. Their wings flapped, grotesquely long wings, as they attacked. Their beaks tore and devoured the helpless creatures. "They can't be more than a few minutes old," I whispered to Inge, but she had already started climbing down the slippery rocks to rescue the infant fish.

"Don't," I called out to her. "Come back!" I shouted over the roar. I was afraid she would slip into the water and be swept off before my eyes. Inge swung her arms through the air. She shouted and twisted her body. Did the seagulls fly up a few feet? They continued flapping and screeching in rage. Inge calmly squatted down and with her hands, over and over, she scooped up the tiny fish and with one motion flung them into the waves. Most were dashed back against the rocks. Did the enraged birds fly lower and lower?

Inge was not yet ninety pounds.

Was I afraid they would beat her to death with their wings? Was I afraid they would rip her to pieces with their beaks? Was I afraid they would pluck out her eyes?

She turned and waved to me to join her. I held back. Was

I not poised to rescue her? When she climbed back she was pale and sullen. Her body stiffened when I hugged her.

Later we fought for the first time. Didn't I claim that nature must be allowed to take its course? "Liar," she screamed at me. I slapped her face. She wept. She would not let me touch her that night. The second night of our honeymoon. Why had we flared up like that? Could I have been so contemptuous of her sentimentality about the tiny fish? Was it my own passivity, even before my bride, that so filled me with contempt?

Now why did I want to remind Inge of this quarrel when I had no money left to talk to her machine?

It was the morning.

I can taste the morning clearly.

In the early morning, before the light was more than a glow from the sea, she kissed me and kissed me and climbed on top of me and took my still sleeping flesh into her own childish body and promised in my ears that she would always protect me. I promised that I would always protect her. I told her that I loved her more than my life. She told me that she loved me more than her life. I promised that I would die before I let anyone hurt her. She promised she too would die first. I promised her that I would never abandon her. As I had abandoned my sister. Then she simply spoke my sister's name: "Malkele," she said. She put her lips down on mine. We touched our tongues together and held them that way for a long time with my flesh within her body that almost made no movements at all—until we heard the first bathers of the morning screaming like birds in the waves. I can hear the voices of the young prostitutes chatting in the lobby. They are up early. I hope one doesn't need the telephone. I can see nothing.

That was the sweetest morning of my life.

ACKNOWLEDGMENTS

I am grateful to William Smart and the staff of the Virginia Center for the Creative Arts and to Harriet Barlow and the staff of the Blue Mountain Center for their generous support, and to my agent, Harvey Klinger, and my editor, Corona Machemer, for their wise counsel. I would also like to thank a number of friends for their kind encouragement: Jeriann Hilderley, Nancy Willard, Eric Lindbloom, Danny Silverman, Susan Matheson, Frank Bergon, Holly St. John, Catherine Murphy, Harry Roseman, Fred Kaplan, Richard Pommer, Linda Nochlin, Deborah Dash Moore, Tony Phillips, Judy Raphael Gordon, Sheba Sharrow, Sarah Shankman, Kelly Cherry, Tzvi Avni, Paul Russell, Susan Bergholz, Beverly Coyle, James Day, Roz Don, Victor Perera, Dorien Grunbaum, Esther Cohen, Ed Geffner, Paul Hecht, Konstantinos Lardas, Tom Beller, Josie Foo, and most particularly Gail Kinn.

A NOTE ABOUT THE AUTHOR

Jerome A. Badanes was born in Brooklyn, New York, in 1937, and educated at Brooklyn College and the University of Michigan, where he won the coveted Avery Hopwood award in poetry. In the mid-1960s, he founded and edited the radical literary journal *CAW!*, and later he cofounded the Burning City Theatre, a street-theatre group with which he wrote scripts and performed throughout the United States. In 1978 he began writing and conducting the interviews for *Image Before My Eyes,* an award-winning documentary about Jewish life in Poland before the Holocaust, which was released in 1981. Formerly a lecturer in literature, religion, and American culture at the State University of New York College at Purchase, at Vassar College, and in the urban studies program at Vassar, he now teaches in the creative writing program at Sarah Lawrence College. He received the Edward Lewis Wallant award for *The Final Opus of Leon Solomon.* He writes, and lives in New York City.

A NOTE ON THE TYPE

This book was set in a typeface called Walbaum. The original cutting of this face was made by Justus Erich Walbaum (1768–1839) in Weimar in 1810. The type was revived by the Monotype Corporation in 1934. Young Walbaum began his artistic career as an apprentice to a maker of cookie molds. How he managed to leave this field and become a successful punch cutter remains a mystery. Although the type that bears his name may be classified as modern, numerous slight irregularities in its cut give this face its humane manner.